PRAISE FOR
SYMPATHY
FOR THE DEVIL

"Hard to put down...the story line succeeds in large part because of the gritty and stylish narrative, the virtually nonstop action...those looking for some top-shelf adrenaline-fueled escapism will be rewarded.

—*Publishers Weekly*

"Merges the brilliant old school spycraft of Charles Cumming and John le Carré with the technology and contemporary feel of Alex Berenson. The action is fast and furious in this hard-as nails thriller but what sets it apart is McCauley's grasp of how modern spy technology finds and tracks its targets.

—*Library* Journal

"(A) fast-paced spy thriller...tautly written, tightly plotted...delivers action and suspense aplenty."

—*Booklist*

"A fast-moving noir spy thriller...a fun read for fans of classic espionage."

—*Kirkus Reviews*

D0104979

"A fascinating, fast-paced spy thriller for the modern age, equal parts techno-wizardry and old-school tradecraft, and featuring a terrorist plot that reads like it's been ripped from the headlines, SYMPATHY FOR THE DEVIL is an exciting first entry in what's already a gripping intelligence saga."

—Owen Laukkanen, *New York Times* bestselling author of THE PROFESSIONALS

"Fans of Jack Bauer rejoice, your new hero just rode into town. SYMPATHY FOR THE DEVIL by Terrence McCauley has enough gadgets to satisfy tech junkies and enough character to bring humanity to a story that is all too terrifying in its plausibility."

—Criminal Element

"Intense to the very end, SYMPATHY FOR THE DEVIL is a 'must-read' for connoisseurs of the genre."

—*Midwest Book Review*

"Terrence McCauley takes the grand old style of the classic masters of the genre, spits in its eye, then artfully polishes a sharp sheen onto his words with a modern sensibility. But the key to what he does so blisteringly well, is that he never loses respect for what makes the classic style great—all the while doing so in a way that makes it wholly his own."

—Todd Robinson, Anthony Award-nominated author of THE HARD BOUNCE

A MURDER
OF CROWS

A MURDER OF CROWS

TERRENCE McCAULEY

The following is a work of fiction. Names, characters, places, events and incidents are either the product of the author's imagination or used in an entirely fictitious manner. Any resemblance to actual persons, living or dead, is entirely coincidental.

Copyright © 2016 by Terrence McCauley

Cover and jacket design by 2Faced Design

Interior designed and formatted by

E.M. Tippetts Book Designs

ISBN 978-1-943818-01-3

eISBN: 978-1-943818-11-2

Library of Congress Control Number: 2016937526

First trade paperback edition July 2016 by Polis Books, LLC
1201 Hudson Street
Hoboken, NJ 07030

POLIS BOOKS

ALSO BY
TERRENCE McCAULEY
FROM POLIS BOOKS

Prohibition

Slow Burn

James Hicks series

Sympathy for the Devil

TO RITA
FOR EVERYTHING

CHAPTER 1

New York City
10:00 AM

HICKS KNEW HE was being watched.

The question is why?

There was no reason why anyone should have been paying attention to him. He had put a lot of effort into looking anonymous. He had intentionally let his hair grow shaggy in the two weeks since the bio-attack on New York. He hadn't touched a razor in days and his face bore a healthy amount of graying stubble. His jacket and hooded sweatshirt were from the discount rack at a sporting goods store and both were in dire need of washing. His sneakers were five years out of style and looked it. The cheap nylon backpack over his left shoulder was scuffed and filthy.

Hicks looked like a bike messenger down on his luck or an actor who had been fired from his gig waiting tables. He looked

1

like he may have been homeless or awfully close to it. He looked like the type of man you didn't want to look at for long because he might ask you for something.

That was the point.

Blending in had always been easy for him, but it had never been more important until now. Capturing the terrorist known as The Moroccan had changed everything for Hicks and for his organization, The University.

As soon as he crossed Lexington, Hicks continued walking east, checking the street for obvious signs of surveillance. He looked for someone trailing him on foot or eyeing him from a doorway. He was mindful of people sitting in parked cars or posing as a tourists taking pictures of him as he moved.

But no one paid attention to him and no one seemed to act out of the ordinary. If anything, people were going out of their way to avoid looking at him, exactly as he had planned.

But he still couldn't shake the sense of someone tracking him. It wasn't paranoia. He had spent half of his life in the field in various parts of the world. Over the years, he had developed a finely attuned sixth sense of when he was being watched. He knew someone was watching him now.

It wasn't surveillance in the modern sense where most people are captured by security cameras simply by walking down the street. Such passive observation was like background noise to him as constant and unavoidable as car horns and sirens in Manhattan.

But there was nothing passive about this feeling of being surveilled. It vibed intentional. Focused.

But where? Who? How?

Hicks crossed Third Avenue and decided to walk uptown.

He decided to stop mid-block, step off the curb and hail a cab. Unpredictable movements often caused surveillance teams to make mistakes. He glanced around to see if someone had stopped short or suddenly walked across the street, but the rhythm of the Midtown street hadn't changed. Deliverymen kept making deliveries while office workers pushed their way through the revolving doors of office buildings and pedestrians kept walking to wherever they were supposed to be.

No one seemed to give a damn about James Hicks, but he still couldn't shake the feeling he was being observed. Maybe it instinct. Maybe it was one of the only reasons why he was still alive after so many years in the Game.

He didn't have to see someone tailing him to know they were there. He knew.

A cab broke out of the flow of traffic and stopped in front of him at the curb. Hicks climbed in the back seat and told the driver to take him to Eightieth Street and Third Avenue.

Hicks had no reason to go to Eightieth Street and Third Avenue. He had no intention of going that far, either, but he had to tell the driver to take him somewhere. A random street corner on the Upper East Side seemed as good a destination as any. The back seat of a cab allowed him to blend in for a while until he figured out what—if anything—was going on.

He spotted the sign pasted to the plastic divider between the passenger and the driver:

SMILE! YOU'RE ON CAMERA RIGHT NOW!

After a recent rash of robberies throughout the city, many cab owners had installed cameras in their cabs to photograph attackers. Hicks saw a small wireless camera had been installed next to the rearview mirror. He happened to be familiar with that particular model and knew a red light should be on if the camera was active. The red light was off. He bet the damned thing had never been set up properly. A half-hearted attempt to satisfy the cab owner's nervous insurance agency.

Hicks pulled out his University-designated handheld device and entered his access code. If the driver had bothered to look back at him, he would have assumed his passenger was merely another phone drone checking his email or posting something on Facebook.

Nothing could have been further from the truth.

After entering his access code, Hicks tapped a benign-looking icon on the home screen which activated the phone's camera. The camera scanned his facial features while the screen read his thumbprint and biometrics.

In nanoseconds, Hicks' identity was confirmed and a bland screen appeared asking for his secure twelve-digit identification number. After entering it, Hicks was granted access to one of the most advanced computer networks in the world: the Optimized Mechanical and Network Integration protocol (OMNI). The name was a relic of the University's past and had been around almost since the beginning of the University itself. But like most institutional phrases, it had a habit of hanging on even though the system had outgrown its name.

The driver edged the cab back into the sluggish flow of northbound traffic, but got stuck at a red light at the corner. Hicks decided to put the delay to good use. He tapped through a series of OMNI's prompts until he gained access to the satellite the University had parked in permanent orbit in space high above Manhattan.

Tapping a few more prompts allowed him to direct the

University's satellite to identify all secure signals in his general vicinity. If anyone was tracking him remotely or communicating via a secure signal, OMNI could identify and track it.

Hicks' narrowed the scope of the scan to filter out standard cell phone traffic and emergency responder frequencies, including his cab's radio network. He focused the search on identifying secure networks used by a select few law enforcement agencies and other, more covert groups. If someone was watching him, it was most likely someone from one of those sectors.

OMNI's results appeared as icons dotting a real time map. He was surprised to see the number of federal frequencies in range of his current position. Some were easy to explain. Both United States Senators from New York had offices in the building across the street from his cab's location. Secret Service agents guarded each senator's district office, hence the secure federal signals. That had nothing to do with him.

OMNI also detected a few stray FBI signals, but they were moving west from his position. They didn't appear to have anything to do with him, either. More good news. Although he could dodge FBI surveillance, it would take a lot of caution and time, which could be spent on more important efforts like breaking The Moroccan.

But he grew concerned when a third icon on the handheld's map began blinking red. Hicks tapped on the screen and saw OMNI had identified it as another secure signal being emitted on street level.

Right outside his cab.

Hicks looked out the cab's window at the spot where OMNI had located the signal. All he saw was the usual endless parade of Midtown foot traffic streaming in both directions. No one was standing still. No one was watching his cab. There weren't even any homeless people panhandling in front of the ATM at the corner.

Hicks checked his handheld again and verified the location of the secure federal signal. The source was stationary. Even from thousands of miles above the earth, OMNI's global positioning system was accurate to an area the size of a dime. If OMNI said the signal was off to his right, it must be there.

Hicks took a second look outside the cab and saw there was only one place where the signal could be coming from.

The security camera on the ATM.

Hicks looked back at his handheld and tapped the icon to identify the nature of the signal. A new window opened beneath the icon, identifying the signal as part of a secure bandwidth the federal government had used various times in the past. The ATM camera only faced the street, so whoever had hacked such a complex security system clearly didn't care about the bank. They cared about him.

Any number of government agencies could have hacked the camera feed for any number of reasons. He decided to find out who and why.

He typed in a five-digit code on his handheld and waited for one of the Operators at the University's Varsity desk to answer.

A male Operator answered on the second ring. "Switchboard. How may I help you?"

Despite the security of the University's closed network, a strict standard protocol was observed whenever a field agent contacted the main switchboard.

Hicks followed University protocol and gave the pre-assigned safe phrase. "This is Professor Warren. I seem to be having some trouble with my service."

This told the operator he was James Hicks and he was safe, but was not in a location where he could speak freely. Hicks didn't need to bother with details. The moment the call had connected, the Operator could see Hicks' handheld's screen on his own monitor. He knew where Hicks was and what he was trying to do.

The Operator stayed within protocol. "We're so sorry to hear that, professor. I believe I see the nature of the problem. Would you like me to investigate it further?"

"Thank you. It would be a big help."

He heard a blur of clicks from the other end as the Operator's fingers flew across his terminal's keyboard. Hicks knew he was directing OMNI to run a trace on the source of the signal, something Hicks could not do from his handheld device.

A moment later, the Operator came back on the line. "I believe we have tracked the source of the problem sir, but the situation has grown worse in the past few seconds."

Despite the coolness of the early spring morning, sweat broke out on Hicks' back. Operators were trained to be bland. They didn't exaggerate. "How bad is it?"

"The problem has spread to your immediate location, sir. To be more specific, the camera inside your cab."

Hicks froze. He had been deceiving people for more than half his life, so he knew how to keep his facial expression from changing. He casually glanced at the camera next to the rearview mirror.

A small red light now glowed next to the lens. That light hadn't been on when he'd gotten into the cab. The driver's hands hadn't moved from the steering wheel, so he knew the driver hadn't turned it on. Someone must have turned it on remotely.

This wasn't a random hack of an ATM camera by a government agency.

This was focused on him.

Hicks looked out the cab's window as if he had been given some mildly annoying news. He knew the camera didn't have audio, but they could always hack the cabbie's cell phone if they wanted to listen in. "I see. Is there anything you can do?"

"We can try, sir. Hold on for a moment." Another blur of sound as fingers once again flew across a keyboard. "We seem to have located the exact source of the problem. You should be free and clear in a couple of minutes, professor. We'll email you a full report of the incident shortly, and we apologize for any inconvenience."

The line went dead as the traffic light finally turned green. Hicks didn't know what the Operator had done. He only hoped it stopped the surveillance on him. Fast.

He eyed his handheld's screen as the cab began to roll. The icon for his cab was now blinking red on the map, showing the federal hack on the passenger camera was still active. The red icon of the ATM camera disappeared from the map, only to be replaced by another red icon flashing over his position. He tapped on this icon and saw the feds had hacked into one of the traffic cameras installed above the traffic light.

Whoever was watching him was both capable and determined. Hacking two separate, complex camera systems at once took a technical capacity few entities had. Entities like the University.

Hicks watched the icon representing his cab fade from the map, followed by the red icon symbolizing the hacked traffic camera. The Operator had successfully spiked the hacks on all devices in the area. He eyed the handheld screen as the cab moved with traffic, waiting for another red icon to symbolize a new hack. But the map remained blank. No more red icons.

It was time to move. *Now.*

"Looks like traffic's a mess." Hicks dug a ten-dollar bill out of his pocket and handed it to the cab driver through the plastic partition. "Pull over wherever you can. I'll take the subway instead."

Traffic wasn't a mess, but at ten dollars for a three-dollar trip, the cabbie didn't argue.

Hicks got out of the cab and walked back toward the Lexington Avenue subway. Since several train lines stopped there, he would take one at random in an effort to confuse whoever was tracking him. Later, he'd switch trains at a station without a functioning security camera and head back into Manhattan.

He walked quickly, but was careful not to run. He moved with foot traffic, blending in so as not to draw attention.

Hicks kept glancing down at his handheld as he walked, the way many of the people around him looked down at their smartphones. But while they were tapping out text messages or playing another round of Candy Crush, Hicks was watching for another red icon to appear on his map.

He kept his mind blank as he waited for any new red icons to appear on his screen. He didn't allow himself to dwell on who was tracking him or why. He didn't allow himself to worry that they had hacked the camera inside the cab and now had a clear image of his face. An image they could now use to identify him through any airport in the world.

He didn't allow himself to ask who 'they' might be because he didn't have enough information yet. Pondering the unknown might throw him in a panic, which could only get him killed. He remained focused on what little he could control. He remembered his training: *Blend in. Disappear. Resurface when safe. Get back to work. The Moroccan is close to breaking. He's all that matters now.*

He looked down at the handheld when it buzzed in his hand. The pattern of the vibration indicated he had received a secure text message from the Operator who had spiked the surveillance signal.

The terse message followed the University's protocols for field communications:

SIGNAL TRACED BACK TO THE BARNYARD. FULL REPORT TO FOLLOW VIA EMAIL.

Hicks stopped walking.

He hadn't decided to stop. His legs had simply refused to keep moving.

Two words had been enough to stop him cold.

THE BARNYARD.

Stopping suddenly in the middle of a busy street was a mortal sin to New Yorkers who were always hurrying to or from someplace. A few people cursed him for blocking their path without warning. One gave him the finger and called him an asshole.

But Hicks didn't apologize or respond. Instead, he read the text several more time to make sure he hadn't made a mistake. He hadn't. The two words didn't change: THE BARNYARD.

Other intelligence organizations always referred to The Barnyard by different names, like The Firm or The Farm or, simply, The Agency. But the Dean of the University had always resented the arrogance and inefficiency of this organization, which was why he insisted upon its official University designation being The Barnyard.

Hicks knew calling something a different name didn't change what it was. The Barnyard was The Central Intelligence Agency (CIA).

The CIA had been tracking him through Manhattan all morning.

Hicks also knew the CIA was forbidden from operating within the continental United States. Domestic surveillance fell under the jurisdiction of the National Security Agency (NSA) and similar agencies. The CIA and the NSA enjoyed a healthy sibling rivalry, but usually cooperated with each other on matters of domestic surveillance.

If the CIA was tracking Hicks unilaterally, there had to be a reason.

The reason could have been their investigation into the location of The Moroccan. The reason also could have been James Hicks.

But technically, James Hicks did not exist. And neither did The University. That's what bothered him.

His training kicked in once more. *Get moving.*

Hicks put the handheld away and resumed walking toward the subway, trying to ignore the questions flooding his mind. *How did they find me? Why were they looking for me? The CIA. Fuck me.*

He forced his mind clear as he walked down the stairs to the subway. He couldn't begin to get answers until he was sure he was clear of surveillance. He couldn't question The Moroccan until he was sure he wasn't being followed, otherwise he might lead them right to his prisoner.

Fuck Langley. He had a job to do. He had a terrorist to interrogate.

And it wasn't even lunchtime yet.

CHAPTER
2

AFTER TWO HOURS of changing trains to make sure he wasn't
followed, Hicks finally made it to the University's safe house
where they were holding The Moroccan.

At some point in the 1970s—for reasons lost to history—
the University had acquired a dilapidated three-story walk up
in Alphabet City. None of Hicks' predecessors had ever used
it for anything more than a temporary hideout for Assets and
Faculty Members in need of a place to lie low for a couple of
days.

But when Hicks had become head of the University's New
York office, he decided to put the building to use. The Dean of
the University, who had always resisted having actual facilities
or campuses of any kind, surprised him by agreeing to fund it.
Hicks' secure facility at Twenty-Third Street was the only other

University facility in Manhattan.

The building had long been deemed an eyesore in the community and for good reason. Layers of graffiti marred the building's masonry; the doors and windows had been boarded up for years. It had served as a squatters den for the homeless, a shooting gallery for junkies, a flop house for runaways, and a den where crack whores brought their johns.

Hicks had decided to put the building to good use the day he took over. Knowing any activity in front of the building would only bring unwanted attention, he had purchased the old tenement building behind it and had University contractors enter through a common basement both buildings shared. This way, work could go on inside the original dilapidated building without drawing unwanted neighborhood attention. The University had always emphasized secrecy at all costs.

Secure contractors had worked around the clock to secretly reinforce the decrepit building's interior. Steel plating was installed behind the wooden boards. All other access points had been sealed, save for an old door at the back of the building which could only be accessed through a dim, grimy service entrance. Here, a state-of-the-art security portal was welded to the newly-re-enforced infrastructure.

Security cameras and motion detectors were subtly installed at the perimeter to make sure no one tried to gain access. No one could get in or out without biometric permission.

Except for extensive rewiring and a few improvements to transform part of the safe house into a holding area, the Dean's funding ended there. Few of the old apartments had been gutted and much of the abandoned furniture had remained as the junkies and vagrants had left them.

Periodically, neighborhood activists still called for the building to be revitalized or turned into a homeless shelter or school. Hicks saw to it they were subtly—but effectively—convinced to turn their attention elsewhere. Over the years, several developers had tried to buy the property but were told the owner had no intention of selling. Few had taken "no" for an answer. Hicks hadn't been as gentle in changing their minds.

Junkies and drug dealers and homeless still tried to gain entrance to the building. They were dealt with in a far more permanent manner.

After arriving at the safe house, Hicks spent the next several hours alone in one of the building's former kitchens as he scrolled through Roger Cobb's latest interrogation reports of the prisoner they had dubbed 'The Moroccan.' The only light in the kitchen came from his tablet and a graying florescent bulb high above in the ceiling.

Roger's report made for somber reading. Two weeks before, The Moroccan and his followers had carried out the first biological attack on the continental United States. The operation was as simple as it was evil: inject thirty immigrant men, women, and children with a weaponized amalgamation of the MERS, SARS and Ebola viruses, then send them throughout the metropolitan area to spread death simply by breathing.

The infected had all been Islamic refugees The Moroccan had smuggled into the country from Sierra Leon, Mogadishu, and Somalia. They were desperate, faithful people looking to secure a better place in the afterlife. The Moroccan had called them 'Allah's Faithful.' Each one of them had endured countless hours in a cargo container at sea simply for the opportunity to die a martyr.

The Moroccan had planned to send the infected children to schools to spread the disease among other children and their teachers. He planned to send the men and women into the subway system at rush hour to infect as many riders as possible. He had ordered them to go to fast food restaurants, train stations, bus terminals, and airports to spread the disease as far and wide as possible before the virus ultimately wore them down and killed them.

The Moroccan's plan did not end there. As they were brought to emergency rooms and hospitals throughout the city, their infected corpses would spread the disease to the first responders and hospital staff who treated them. They would unknowingly bring the virus home to their families at the end of their shift, spreading the disease even farther and wider.

The Moroccan had hoped his genetically-engineered plague would grow exponentially, infecting thousands before doctors might recognize it as something more than the flu. Thousands more would be dead or dying before a treatment protocol could be implemented.

But The Moroccan hadn't counted on his monster being too perfect. The scientists he had paid to create the strain had done too good a job. The virus burned through the hosts' immune systems too fast for them to be effective carriers. Many were incapacitated before they could leave the house where The Moroccan's men had been allowing them to live before they carried out their mission.

Hicks had seen some of the victims when he had led the Varsity raid on the house. He had seen the contortions of the dead and the dying. He had also seen the crime scene photos of the would-be martyrs who had coughed themselves to death as the virus ravaged their bodies as the fever drove them mad. He saw the corpses of mothers clutching the bodies of their dead children.

The face of one of the victims haunted Hicks most of all, a little girl whose dead eyes looked up at her mother's corpse as if to ask '*Why, Mommy? Why?*'

Death was as much a part of Hicks as his own life. He had seen hundreds of dead bodies in his career, men and women and children caught up in conflicts and wars around the world. Death was nothing new to him, but that particular little girl visited him in his nightmares each night. She wasn't looking up at her mother. She was looking at him. 'Help me.'

The University had captured The Moroccan and helped thwart a greater attack, but didn't have the resources to perform autopsies on all of the bodies. Instead, OMNI tracked the CDC autopsy reports. None of the bodies bore signs of struggle or confinement. Each of the infected appeared to have taken the injection willingly.

That was what scared Hicks the most. Each of these people had willingly come to this country to kill him and any other American they encountered. He should have hated each of them, but he didn't. That scared him, too.

The Dean had passed along the information on the virus to the CDC via backchannels, which helped hospitals take the necessary emergency procedures to limit the spread of the infection. But some of Allah's Faithful had managed to live long enough to infect others. Twenty nurses, emergency room doctors, EMTs, and police officers throughout the city had died after coming in contact with the infected before hospitals could be alerted to take precautions.

He knew the number would have been much higher if it hadn't been for the intelligence Hicks and his people had gathered. The number was a mere percentage point of the how many the Moroccan had planned to kill, but still too high for Hicks to tolerate.

The Dean had also exerted enough influence to get the Federal government to quash news reports of the event as being nothing more than a horrible strain of Legionnaires Disease.

It was an easier ruse than Hicks though it would be. The media ate what had been fed to them with few questions. The whole incident was forgotten within a week.

The families of the dead first responders had been told their loved ones had died doing the jobs they loved. The Dean had worked with federal agencies to quietly arrange a foundation dedicated to offering healthy settlement packages in exchange for their silence under the guise of national security.

None of The Moroccan's followers had family in the country. There was no one to make public appeals for answers on the six o'clock news. They were the anonymous dead and Hicks knew the outbreak would soon be forgotten. The public didn't like to be reminded of the fragility of their existence. The news cycle had since focused on covering celebrity deaths and pregnancies and political scandals. The world had moved on. The world had forgotten.

But Hicks didn't have the luxury of forgetting. Neither did the University.

After raiding the house, Hicks had been able to track The Moroccan and his accomplice to a motel in Philadelphia. He brought both of them into custody following a bloody gun battle in the motel's parking lot. Data he had been able to retrieve from

The Moroccan's cell phone and computer led Hicks to discover plans to infect people in D.C., Atlanta, and Miami.

Despite successfully hiding the attack as an outbreak of Legionnaires Disease, Hicks knew the scientist who The Moroccan had hired to engineer the virus had figured out their mistake. And if they were clever enough to create it, they were clever enough to perfect it. He had to stop it before that happened.

Which was why he had assigned Roger Cobb to get The Moroccan to tell him what it was. No one could lie to Roger. Not for long.

Roger liked to employ a variety of established and new methods—a delicate mix of sleep deprivation, water boarding, time confusion, mild electrocution and narcotic injection all designed to break the prisoner's will and make him talk.

Another of Roger's favorite tactics was time distortion. The Moroccan may have only been in custody for two weeks, but thanks to Roger's tactics, the prisoner was convinced he had been jailed for over two years.

Roger's methods had caused The Moroccan to yield some results about the scientists who had engineered the virus, but Hicks needed more. He had to know about the Moroccan's superiors, his network, and where they were located. He needed to know the nature and timing and location of any other attacks they were planning to launch before they struck again. And Hicks never doubted they would strike again and soon. The University estimated the bio-weapon operation had cost millions to engineer. No one spent so much money to leave an objective unachieved.

On the previous day, Roger reported The Moroccan was

finally close to breaking. He was ready for Hicks to enter the interrogation process and close the deal.

Such news would have been the highlight of his day if it hadn't been for the surveillance of the CIA.

As the words and charts of Roger's interrogation reports began to blur, Hicks flipped the tablet shut and tossed it on the table. A dull headache began to build behind his eyes as the enormity of it all began to settle on him.

As if stopping one bio-attack and trying to stop the next one wasn't enough, now the CIA was hunting him. Hicks had been in the Game for over twenty years, but learning he was in the CIA's crosshairs still gave him pause.

His mind drifted to why the CIA was suddenly interested in him. There had to be a reason, but why? The only other people outside the University who knew Hicks had The Moroccan were Agent Tali Saddon and her handlers in the Mossad. The two agencies had worked closely over the years, with the Mossad often using the University's information as a secondary source to their connections with intelligence agencies throughout the world.

From media reports and intelligence she had gathered on the dead men left behind in the shootout, Tali had deduced Hicks had been part of the shootout in Philadelphia. She had heard the dead men had been guarding someone important, someone Hicks must have taken with him. He confirmed it had been The Moroccan, but Tali and her handlers in Tel Aviv had agreed to remain silent in exchange for daily interrogation reports on the prisoner. They also wanted The Moroccan transferred to them whenever Hicks was done with him.

He doubted Tali or the Mossad had turned him into the

CIA. Tali had always been loyal to Hicks. Bringing the CIA into the mix only would have complicated her intention to bring The Moroccan into custody.

Still, the questions about the CIA rattled around in his mind. Why me? Why now?

Hicks snapped out of it when he heard his handheld begin to buzz on the table. He was scheduled to interrogate The Moroccan in fifteen minutes. He planned on allowing the call to go to voicemail.

But when he saw who was calling, he took the call.

One didn't allow a call from the Dean of the University go to voicemail.

HAVE YOU TOLD Roger about your run-in with the Barnyard today?" the Dean asked.

Hicks responded with the formality the Dean demanded. Details were to be conveyed clearly—without opinion or conjecture—in a concise manner. Speculation should only be offered if specifically requested. Orders were never to be questioned, though reasonable objections could be presented in a certain way at the proper time if they were followed by a viable, alternative suggestion. The Dean subscribed to the theory of complaint without solution was whining. He hated whining. "Not yet, sir. I've been reviewing Roger's latest interrogation reports on The Moroccan in preparation for my interrogation of him in fifteen minutes."

"Have it your way, but I advise you to inform him of what happened immediately after your session with The Moroccan. I have been able to uncover some information about why you were being watched this morning. I am afraid what happened to you this morning may involve Roger before long."

Hicks was glad he was sitting down. Like the Operators, the Dean usually didn't exaggerate, especially when it came to bad news. "That doesn't sound promising, sir."

"All of the hacked systems this morning were done from Langley servers," the Dean explained, "but the surveillance was part of a greater effort. You are being hunted by the Defense Intelligence Agency, who is working in conjunction with the CIA and the NSA."

Given what the Operator had told him about the hacks, Hicks had assumed the NSA and the CIA were working together, but the DIA was a new wrinkle. "What would the DIA want with me?"

"Not you, James. The Moroccan."

Hicks closed his eyes. Uh oh. "I checked the watch lists myself, sir. The prisoner wasn't being watched by any agency."

"Not officially," the Dean allowed, "but he seems to have been something of a pet project for the DIA for quite some time. They have had him under passive surveillance since his days aiding rebels in Kabul. They we unaware The Moroccan was even in the country until your Rambo imitation down in Philadelphia caught their attention. By tracing the associates of the dead men you left in your wake, they have determined The Moroccan is not only in this country, but is in the custody of some unknown entity. That entity is us, of course, but the DIA does not know that yet."

Hicks grew still. He'd gone down to Philadelphia and grabbed The Moroccan on his own, without proper tactical coverage. It was still a sore point between him and the Dean.

"How, sir?"

"You left a parking lot full of dead hostiles, James. Dead hostiles who were, in fact, on several watch lists throughout the world."

"But it doesn't explain how they found me, sir."

"Because the DIA got hold of some security footage from the motel. Upon further analysis, they were able to identify both you and our prisoner."

Hicks checked his temper as it spiked. The Dean hated outbursts as much as he hated informality. "Impossible, sir. Our Operators went back and scrubbed every image off any camera feed in the area. They even scanned any cell phone footage of the incident shot by civilians. There's no way they tracked me that way."

"Our Operators did their usual commendable job, but there was a camera we missed. It appears the hotel manager—one Mr. Edward Zimmerman—had installed a small security camera of his own in the motel stairwell. He told the authorities he had installed it in order to spot vandals trying to gain access to the motel via the parking lot door. He eventually confessed to installing it so he could film his illicit liaisons with various prostitutes who frequented the motel. The owners had installed a security camera in the office that was controlled remotely, so the night manager conducted his assignations in the obscurity of the stairwell."

Hicks pounded the table and dropped his head in his hands. That's how they found him. And now they knew what he looked like.

The Dean continued. "For obvious reasons, the camera was not tied into the main computer system of the motel and, instead, went wirelessly into Mr. Zimmerman's personal laptop. In their haste to cover your involvement, our Operators missed it."

Hicks knew apologizing once again for his actions wouldn't get him anywhere with the Dean, so he didn't even try.

The Dean went on. "If we had been given the opportunity to plan the operation properly, we would have detected the presence of the camera and handled it. Alas, you were in too much of a hurry to 'get your man.' Someday, I may be able to enjoy the irony of one of my best Faculty Members being undone by the illicit hunger of a grubby little man in a hot sheet motel, but today is not that day, James."

Hicks knew the Dean hated excuses, so he offered an explanation instead. "We didn't have the time or the resources to plan a proper operation, sir. Grabbing The Moroccan was worth the risk, so if nabbing him put me on the DIA's radar screen, I can live with it."

"I have no doubt you can live with it, but can the rest of us? Can the University?"

Hicks knew it was one of the Dean's rhetorical questions. He wasn't looking for an answer, and Hicks wouldn't try to offer one.

"Your carelessness aside," the Dean continued, "we do have a shred of good news. My source at the Barnyard told me the man spearheading the hunt for you is a DIA agent named Mark Stephens. Stephens is not his real name of course, but who uses their real names in this business? I will send you his file when we are done here. You will see he is a most capable man. In fact, many believe he is one of the best Beekeepers in the DIA. He used to run abduction and rendition operations against hostile enemy targets for the Air Force. Now, he has been assigned to a black bag outfit they are calling G-One for some reason." The Dean laughed. "G-One. The bureaucrats love their codenames."

But Hicks didn't laugh. He had worked with Beekeepers before and knew they weren't only interrogators. They didn't grab high value targets off the street and beat confessions out of them. They carefully chose their targets and played them for the long haul—pumping them for information with methods specifically crafted for the target's psychological profile. They nurtured a prisoner and got them as comfortable or as uncomfortable as it took to extract information from them, the same way a beekeeper gets honey.

Stephens wasn't some cowboy hacking off jihadi limbs in the desert or beating some poor bastard with a phone book. Beekeeping was a tough, tedious job only a certain kind of person could do.

People like Roger Cobb and James Hicks.

Hicks chose his next question carefully. "Were you able to determine if Stephens knows anything about my identity, sir? Or of the University?"

"All they seem to have for the moment is your image, which they were able to trace back to New York City by using traffic cameras and other media. It took considerable effort, but as much as I despise them, I do not question their abilities or resources. They have confirmed your presence in New York. As they do not know who you are or who you work for, you should expect them to try to apprehend you. Their interest in you will only be heightened by our success in spiking their surveillance of you. For obvious reasons, we cannot allow them to succeed."

"I know, sir." He closed his eyes and steeled himself for the standard lecture he knew was coming.

"So I assume you also know The Barnyard and their ilk have been trying to get a toehold in our institution for years. Throughout our existence, we have managed to avoid a direct confrontation with them by posing as helpful amateurs who pass along information as we get it. They have taken us at our word because we have never stood in their way. Now, we have something they want. The Moroccan. Unfortunately, we cannot give him to them without tipping our hand and proving our existence." Another long silence. "Do you appreciate the difficulty your rash actions have caused for both our current mission and the broader mission of the University, James?"

Hicks had been the target of the Dean's anger several times in his career. There was only one way to respond to such a question. "What do you want me to do, sir?"

"The wolves may not be at the door yet, James, but we can certainly hear them baying in the forest. I will attempt to delay them as much as possible, but they have your scent now. This is why it is essential for you to break The Moroccan and break him quickly. Employ all methods at your disposal and hold nothing back."

"I will, but I can't go too far, sir. Our agreement with the Mossad in exchange for their silence…"

"Our agreement with our Israeli friends is secondary. Find out what the prisoner knows and report back to me immediately. The information he provides may be enough to stave off our enemies before Stephens and his ilk find you. Time has suddenly become a luxury we no longer have."

The Dean killed the connection.

Hicks tried to stall his growing headache by squeezing the

bridge of his nose. His hand began to shake, but he willed it to stop. He read between the lines of what the Dean had told him.

Stephens wasn't hunting the University. 'He is hunting you.'

He remembered his training. Stay focused. Work on what's in front of you. Break the Moroccan.

Hicks looked up when he heard a gentle knock at the kitchen doorway. It was one of Roger Cobb's new men—a trainee whose name escaped him.

"Sorry to bother you, sir, but Roger says the subject is ready for you now."

Hicks blinked his eyes clear. "Tell him I'll be up in a minute."

CHAPTER 3

Hicks had ordered The Moroccan to be held on the top floor of the safe house in an area which had once been a one-bedroom apartment. The space now housed one of Roger's latest inventions—a plastic containment module he had dubbed 'The Cube.'

It had been constructed on a raised platform of soundproof material to prevent the prisoner from hearing sounds or sensing vibrations from the outside world. The exterior of The Cube had been encased in one-way glass from floor to ceiling. Inside, the prisoner could only see his own reflection no matter where he looked. Cameras had been mounted on the other side of the glass to provide unobstructed three-hundred-and-sixty degree surveillance of the prisoner's movements. Various kinds of tiny sensors placed throughout the cell constantly monitored his vital signs, body temperature, and brain waves. Those same sensors also served as a lie detector to determine how truthful the prisoner was being during an interrogation.

Once inside The Cube, the prisoner had no contact with the outside world. Lighting, temperature and sound were all controlled electronically by Roger and his technicians who could adjust them to encourage a desired effect. Roger could blare Megadeath to jar the prisoner or crickets to soothe him or radio static grate on his nerves.

Hicks knew Roger preferred to keep The Cube silent for undetermined periods of time. Absolute silence broke a prisoner's will most of all. Meals were slid through a slot in the door, depriving a prisoner of any human contact for as long as Roger saw fit.

Other than a small air conditioning vent beneath the cot, the toilet was the only thing connected to the outside world. It led to the building's main sewer line, but first went through a tank lined to block all sound and vibration. A steel table and two chairs were bolted to the floor and used for interrogation purposes only. Even eating at the table was a privilege he had to earn through cooperation. The Moroccan had not earned such a privilege yet.

A cot against the far wall served as The Moroccan's only comfort.

If he disobeyed any of the rules Roger decided to enforce on any given day, the punishment would be severe.

Roger had decided constant sleep deprivation would disturb the Moroccan's circadian rhythm. A lack of access to natural sunlight only enhanced his distress. In the course of his interrogation, Roger had discovered The Moroccan was also claustrophobic. When the prisoner was belligerent or uncooperative, the lights were shut off and all sound quelled. Roger often allowed him to shriek himself hoarse in the darkness of the mirrored room until he was ready for his next session.

Hicks knew The Cube was as medieval as it was high tech. And whenever he began to have sympathy for The Moroccan, he remembered the dead little girl of his dream. Help me.

Hicks found Roger sitting alone at The Cube's control console, making notes in a cheap spiral notebook. The cell's environment could easily be controlled from his tablet, but Roger was a bit old fashioned and preferred making his notes on paper. Hicks supposed even torturers could have a sentimental side.

The monitors of the workstation showed a green-hued image of the Moroccan shrieking in the darkness of his cell. Numbers at the bottom of the screen calculated the prisoner's heart rate, brain waves, and other vital statistics. The sound had been switched off, but the image of the prisoner's muted agony was clear.

Hicks was not happy. "He can't talk to me if he screams himself hoarse."

Roger looked up from his notebook and smiled, the way an old professor might greet a favorite student, though Roger and Hicks were roughly the same age. "There you are." He looked at the monitor and froze the image. "Don't worry. This feed isn't live. I was killing time waiting for you by listening to one of our prisoner's greatest hits. I'm glad you're finally here. I was beginning to worry about you." His eyes narrowed as he looked at Hicks more closely. "What's wrong? You've the look of a Russian opera about you, maudlin and overdrawn."

"Bad morning. I'll tell you all about it later." He looked at the monitor. "Give me a live shot of the prisoner."

Roger toggled to a live view inside The Cube. The Moroccan was sitting in the dark on his cot, holding a filthy towel up to the left corner of his face. The quality of the night vision cameras was excellent, and it was clear the entire left side of the prisoner's face was sagging.

"What the hell happened to him?"

"Oh, that." Roger winced. "Let's call it an unintended consequence. He had a stroke during one of our sessions late last night."

A bad day had gotten worse. "A stroke? Jesus, Roger …"

"He's fine." Roger handed him his tablet. "It's all documented right here. His vitals were reading perfectly normal at the time of the interrogation. We were hitting him with a steady flow of electricity when he suddenly seized up."

Hicks shoved the tablet back at him. If The Moroccan died, they didn't only lose a valuable source of information or violate their agreement with the Mossad. They lost their leverage with Stephens and the Barnyard. "I warned you to take it easy with that shit."

"There was no reason to expect he'd stroke out. We've given him a hell of a lot more current in the past. Electricity is the only thing that's ever gotten the bastard to talk, not that he has told us anything."

"I'm not happy, Roger."

"Oh, don't be so dramatic. These things happen in the interrogation process."

Hicks knew he couldn't win an argument with Roger, so he didn't even try. "The son of a bitch is no good to me if he's a fucking vegetable."

"Forgive me if I don't shed a tear for the poor bio-weapon terrorist. He's perfectly fine now. Most of the sensation has returned to his extremities and he's able to speak." He brought up a new screen on his tablet and showed it to Hicks. "These are live scans of his brain waves and they show he's got full mental capacity. The only obvious residual effect is the palsy on the left side of his face, which will physically impact his speech. I've got him on Prednisone, which should clear up his condition within the next day or so, assuming we keep him alive that long."

Hicks pointed at the monitor. "His left leg looks limp."

"So? It's not like you're going to take him golfing, are you? We've given him a mild dose of stimulants. Not much, but enough to make him ready for your interrogation." He brightened. "And, like I said in my report, he might be ready to crack." He flipped to yet another new screen on his tablet. "Take a look at his sleep patterns. Even when we do let him rest, his nightmares have become more frequent and severe. He's been crying out in his sleep for the past few days. Our scans of his REM activity are off the charts as his nightmares seem to be getting progressively worse. He was showing mental strain even before the stroke, which is good news. I believe he's finally primed to fall if you're ready to push him."

"That the same belief that told you he wouldn't stroke?"

Roger set his tablet on the table. "You're not a nice man."

"I know. Lucky for me, this isn't a nice line of work. I want you watching his vitals the entire time I'm in there to make sure we don't lose him. We need him alive until he gives us some hard Intel we can use."

Roger wasn't smiling anymore. "I know. I would have

skinned the bastard by now if that wasn't the case."

He knew where Roger was concerned; the notion of skinning him alive wasn't necessarily a figure of speech. And it was as close to an apology as he would get. "Turn on the lights. I'm going in."

Roger tapped his tablet screen. The images on the monitors went from green to full color as the lights came on in the cell. The prisoner squinted and shielded his eyes.

Hicks picked up his own tablet and walked toward the cell door. "The next time something like this happens, I expect you to tell me immediately. You know I don't like secrets."

Roger laughed as he took his seat at the monitors. "Then you're in the wrong line of work, aren't you?"

CHAPTER 4

THE MOROCCAN DIDN'T move when Hicks entered the cell through the revolving door. He didn't even adjust the towel he was using to prop up the left side of his face. He simply sat quietly on his cot and watched this strange new man enter his world.

Hicks could tell prisoner didn't recognize him at first. How could he? Hicks' hair and beard had grown in since they'd last seen each other. He looked entirely different. In the prisoner's mind, it had been so long since they'd met. A lifetime ago. The Moroccan wasn't the same man who'd been captured in Philadelphia. That man was dead and there was no bringing him back.

Hicks saw the prisoner watching him as Hicks sat at the table in the center of The Cube, the same table he was forbidden to use, save for when he was being tormented. Hicks felt the man's black eyes hang on him as Hicks popped out the kickstand of his tablet and set it on the table so the screen faced the prisoner.

Hicks noticed the prisoner had acquired the same hollowed out look most of Roger's patients eventually acquired. Knowing his hair and his beard had great religious significance to him, Roger made sure The Moroccan was restrained and shaved each morning, including his scalp. He had looked painfully thin with a full head of hair and a beard when Hicks brought him to the safe house. Now that he was bald and clean-shaven, he looked skeletal and haunted.

His skin once had a rich tan, but now was much paler. His cheeks were fallow and his dark eyes had sunken deeper into his skull, giving him an almost feral look.

Hicks knew Roger had worked hard to make The Moroccan look this way. Any sleep the prisoner had enjoyed since his capture had been chemically induced and regularly interrupted as part of the standard University interrogation regimen. Disorientation and discomfort were the cornerstones of Roger's tactics. They had yielded impressive results with many other patients over the years and stopped dozens of attacks throughout the world. The patients never lived long after he was through, but at that point, they usually didn't want to.

Despite the silence, Hicks could almost see The Moroccan's mind working; trying to piece things together. There was something familiar about this stranger, but he couldn't tell what it was. Maybe he had interrogated him years ago. Maybe not. So much had happened since.

Hicks saw a glimmer of change in the prisoner's eyes; something close to awareness. The Moroccan was beginning to put things together as his broken mind drifted back through all the perceived years of pain and anguish and loneliness and blood. The sight of Hicks had triggered his mind to force itself to go back to the time before all of this began. To a time when he had been someone else. To when he had been someone at all.

His eyes flared as the pieces of memory finally fell into place. This man in his cell was the man who had delivered him to the hands of his infidel tormentors all those years ago. This man had brought him to this hell he now called home.

Hicks saw a glimpse of the man who the prisoner had once been. It was the one innate part of The Moroccan's psyche which all of the drugs and the pain and the torment hadn't dulled. It was the one thing that had turned him radical in the first place, an element as critical to his being as oxygen.

Hate.

Hicks saw hate was the only thing keeping this man alive.

And hate would be the hammer Hicks used to break him.

Hicks returned prisoner's stare. "Hi. Remember me?"

The prisoner didn't say a word, but his eyes screamed HATE.

Hicks gestured at the left side of his face. "Sorry about your face. It was a mistake on our part."

"Are you sorry because it happened?" The Moroccan's British accent was subtle and tempered by Islamic inflections. "Or sorry because it was a mistake?"

"Because it was a mistake."

The prisoner's right eye blinked as fluid from his sagging left eye overflowed his eyelid and into the towel at his cheek. "You are a barbarian, but at least you are honest."

"Of course I'm honest. I've never lied to you, have I?"

The look again. Hate.

36

Hicks went on. "When I caught you over two years ago, I told you what would happen if you didn't cooperate. I also promised you a quick and painless death if you worked with us. Do you remember what you did? You spat at me."

The good part of The Moroccan's face smiled at the memory.

Hicks looked at the wet towel The Moroccan held against his cheek. "Now you're sitting in a cell drooling on yourself. If anyone knows I'm a man of my word, it's you."

The Moroccan adjusted his grip on the towel and propped up his sagging face. "Yours is a harsh truth."

"The truth is rarely gentle. Comforting, at times, but never gentle." He decided to begin increasing the pressure. "I also promised you'd crack eventually. It's taken a couple of years, but you finally have. You've turned into a hell of a chatterbox lately."

"Lies." The prisoner jammed the towel tighter against his face. "I have told you nothing. You have taken all that I have. You have left me with nothing and nothing is what I have given you."

"Don't be so modest. You've been a big help to us. And I'm not talking about the bottom feeders you tossed us at the beginning. You've told us important details about you and your work."

"And who exactly is this 'we' you and your torturer refer to? CIA? NSA? None of your people have ever properly identified themselves."

Hicks looked at the prisoner's sagging face and limp leg. "What difference does it make?"

"It makes all the difference in the world, for under the Geneva Convention, I have a right to be told who my captors are."

Hicks laughed. "Geneva's a long way from here, Ace, and whatever convention they held doesn't mean shit to us. You're not part of an army, and neither are we. You're not even important to anyone, I'm sorry to say."

He began to turn the knife. "Do you know no one has ever come looking for you? Your name has never been mentioned on any of the chatter we've intercepted from your known associates. You weren't mourned or missed or even prayed for by anyone. No one took hostages demanding your release. After all your hard work to strike at the heart of the infidels, your own people simply forgot about you and moved on. Guess they don't like failure."

"As is our way." The Moroccan used the towel to prop up the dead side of his face as he leaned forward on his cot. "We both know if you have not gotten me to talk by now, you will not be able to do so. I have grown too weak to withstand any of your torments and tactics, so you might as well kill me now and save us all a lot of time and bother."

"There you go again being modest. I already told you how helpful you've been." He folded his hands on the steel table, like a bank manager turning down an applicant for a loan. "For example, you already told us your name is Mehdi Bajjah and you're thirty-six years old," adding two years to the prisoner's current age.

Bajjah's eyes widened. "There is no way I told you this. I never told you my name. Never. I...I know I didn't."

He may have said the words, but his eyes weren't so sure. Bajjah had, in fact, never given them his real name. The other man Hicks had apprehended with Bajjah at the Philadelphia motel had given them Bajjah's alias which had been enough to lead them to discover Bajjah's true identity. Once they had a name, OMNI began to spit out all accessible details about the Moroccan's background in nanoseconds.

Hicks stayed on message. "After all this time and all the drugs and all of our methods, how can you be sure of anything? You told us you were born in Morocco, but your family moved to England when he you were an infant. Mom and Dad moved because they wanted to give you and your sister a better way of life. You were a great student, educated at Eton and later Trinity College. After graduate school, you came to the United States and found work as a software engineer."

Bajjah drew his good leg closer to him. "How do you know all of this? I never told you any of this. I know I didn't." He began babbling to himself. "I know I didn't."

"How else would we have known? You burned off your fingerprints. All of the identification we found on you was false. How else would we know so much about you unless you told us?"

Bajjah turned toward the mirrored wall of his cell, his own ruined face staring back at him.

Hicks kept reciting the results of OMNI's search. "My biggest question is why you're doing all of this. You've already admitted you weren't particularly religious growing up. Hell, you didn't even marry within your own faith. You married an Irish Catholic girl soon after you moved back to London. Guess outcasts attract. Mom and Dad didn't even mind she wasn't Muslim. You also told us you had two kids together. Well, one and a half, I guess. You didn't stick around long enough to see your second child come into the world, did you?"

Although Bajjah wasn't looking at him, Hicks tapped the

tablet and the screen came alive with a picture of a pretty woman with dark brown hair and pale skin rolling around in a pile of leaves with a little girl around seven years of age.

Bajjah may not have turned to look directly at the screen, but Hicks saw him watching the tablet via the reflection in the mirrored wall.

Hicks tapped the screen again and showed a picture of the same woman and girl, but with a little boy about five years of age. Hicks hadn't needed to alter the images. Bajjah had abandoned his family years before he'd been apprehended. He knew for a fact Bajjah hadn't had any contact with his family since the day he'd left.

From his cot, Bajjah finally turned to look at the screen.

This was the first time he was seeing his son.

Hicks decided to rub salt in the wound. "Cute kid, isn't he? Too bad you abandoned him for the jihad before he was born. Did you even know it was a boy? I bet it must sting. I know sons are a big deal to you bastards."

The Moroccan slowly pushed his legs off the edge of his cot. His dead left leg flopped down; his foot smacked on the floor, but he barely noticed. His eyes remained fixed on the image of the son he had never seen. The son he had abandoned for his war against the West.

When he spoke, it was barely above a whisper. "Don't."

Hicks folded his hands again. "Don't what?"

"I know how men like you operate. Don't threaten them or hurt them in any way. If you do, it will say more about you than about anything I have done."

Hicks waived it off. "You've been with us long enough to know we don't make threats here, Mehdi. We make promises.

Back in the hotel room in Philly all those years ago, I told you I'd bring you and your friend back here alive and I did. When I dumped you in this cell, I promised you'd know more pain than you ever believed possible. You have. I promised you would eventually talk and you have. Today I've told you this will go on for years and, believe me, it will. I don't threaten people. I don't have to. I break them and throw them away."

Hicks motioned back to the picture of the children and their mother on his tablet. "Besides, you're the guys who kill women and children. Remember all the people you infected in Queens two years ago? Your followers of Allah? Well, the good news is they all grew too sick to infect anyone before I had them brought into isolation. The only people you killed were your own. No one else got hurt," he lied. "All those men, women, and children who believed in your cause died horrible deaths for nothing. All of your planning and expense wasted on a few dozen peasants no one gave a shit about anyway."

"Americans love their statistics." Bajjah used the towel to wipe the drool and tears from the left side of his face and propped it up again. "My movement is more than one man. More than a million men. Next time, there will be many more."

"More innocents," Hicks motioned to the image on the tablet, "like your wife and daughter and son. Your wife named him Alan, by the way."

Despite the paralysis in the left side of his face, the Moroccan managed to sneer. "Before he was born, his mother and I agreed his name would be Ali, not Alan. How typical of an American to Anglicize names."

"Guess she must've changed her mind after you left her high and dry. She called him Alan when she had him baptized in the Catholic Church." The fact gave Hicks the desired response and he kept going. "That's right, Ace. Your son is going to be raised Catholic by your wife. Or should I say ex-wife, since she had you declared legally dead years ago. I forgot to mention it earlier. She's moved on. Got herself a new husband, too."

Hicks tapped the screen and a new image appeared: Bajjah's ex-wife in a white dress standing next to portly man a bit taller than her. Bajjah's daughter clung to her mother's leg. The groom held Bajjah's infant son. Hicks hadn't needed to alter that image, either.

The Moroccan's good eye flashed. *HATE!*

Hicks kept going. "The new husband's a bit of a simpleton, but a nice guy. Systems Engineer from Dublin. Guess she's got a thing for computer geeks. Hope she has better luck with this one than she did with you. Your kids love him, by the way."

Bajjah looked away. "If she took another, it is only because Allah willed it so. I never expected her to remain celibate the rest of her life. I knew what I was giving up when I left to take up a cause far greater than myself."

"A lost cause which cost you your job, your family and, pretty soon, your life." Hicks tapped on the screen and cycling through a couple of more pictures of the family at birthday parties and school plays in the years since Bajjah had abandoned.

Hicks saved the best picture for last. The family's most recent Christmas card, showing a large, pale man with his arms around Bajjah's ex-wife and the two little ones hugging either side of him.

Hicks saw the look on Bajjah's face and twisted the knife. "What's it like to know another man has taken your place and is enjoying the fruits of your labor? Another man is raising your children. Your children, my friend, who will never know their father ever existed and all for a lost cause."

Bajjah tried to lunge at him from the cot, but his limp leg wasn't strong enough to hold his weight. Hicks watched him collapse; his head smacked off the hard plastic floor of The Cube.

Hicks didn't try to help him up. He simply craned his neck to look over the table and watch Bajjah struggle to get to his feet. The slick surface made it difficult to get traction with two good legs. With one paralyzed leg, it was nearly impossible. Still, Bajjah managed to flop over onto his left side and use his right foot to push himself into something of a seated position against the wall.

In his years with the University, Hicks had interrogated dozens of men like Bajjah. He knew abandoning their family for the Cause was easier if they cut off all ties and buried themselves in their mission. The memory of the family they'd left behind stayed frozen in time. Rarely were they confronted by the reality of their choices.

In only a few minutes, Hicks had shown Bajjah what his zealotry had cost him. The sudden palpability of it was all too stark and real. Even extremists had egos and Bajjah's was taking a hell of a beating.

Hicks made a show of ignoring the prisoner's struggle by examining his own fingernails. "You know, that's the first glimmer of emotion you've shown since we brought you here, Mehdi. I could be forgiven for congratulating myself for hitting a nerve right now."

The prisoner picked his towel off the floor and held it to his left cheek, still panting from the effort of sitting up straight.

"You and your cheap parlor tricks. Do you believe you can make me talk by showing me pictures of my family? Do you think a few snapshots will weaken my faith and my resolve? I won't beg you to keep your filth away from them. I won't beg for their lives, either and I despise you for trying to make me do so." He tried to spit at Hicks, but his sagging mouth turned it into a feeble dribble. "Allah will protect them if it pleases Him. He will allow you to harm them if He chooses. Either way, they are in His hands and beyond your feeble grasp. Sentimentality is a Western emotion."

"Baptism makes them Catholics, Mehdi," Hicks reminded him. "Muddies the religious waters a bit, doesn't it? But I already told you I'm not threatening your family. Hell, as far as they're concerned, you've been dead for years. Your daughter is too young to remember you, and your son doesn't even know you existed. Your ex-wife told them you died in a car crash on your way home from work one night. She doesn't even have a single picture of you in the house anymore," he lied. During a search of her home, the University's Varsity squad had found their wedding photo in the copy of the Koran he'd given her on their wedding day.

Hicks stood up and sat on the edge of the table. It closed the distance between him and the man on the floor. The gesture showed he didn't view Bajjah as a threat, striking another blow to the prisoner's already damaged ego. "Your own children know less about you than they do about Santa Claus or the Easter Bunny. You mean nothing to your own flesh and blood. And if you want it to stay that way, you're going to tell me what I want to know about your network. And you're going to do it right now."

"Never!" he screamed into the towel. "I will never tell you anything!"

Hicks spoke over his muted screams. He was closer to breaking now than ever before. Hicks couldn't let up now. "You've already told us a lot, and now you're going to tell us the rest of it." He reminded himself to speak in the past tense. "You're going to tell us the names of the men you worked for and the men who served under you. You're going to tell us where they lived and what they were planning."

"Anything I tell you will be years old!" Bajjah's voice was hoarse from screaming. "I would not tell you even if I knew."

Hicks already had an answer ready. "All the more reason for you to tell me. I need to compare your information with more recent intelligence we've uncovered. If you don't, or if I catch you in a lie, I'll know. I'll show your family your file. I'll make sure they know about your attempt to spark a disease epidemic. I'll show them the pictures of the bodies of all your followers who you ordered to be injected with disease. The women and the children. And I'm going to tell them you let those poor people die."

Hicks tapped the screen to activate a slide show. Crime scene pictures of dead women and children; bug-eyed from suffocating to death. Their corpses soaked in sweat. Crime scene videos of men writhing on cots, covered in sores. He had intentionally kept the image of the dead young girl out of the mix. He didn't need to see her again. She was always with him. She was with him now as Hicks pushed the man who had killed her. *Help me.*

Bajjah looked away, but Hicks didn't stop. "Those images will leave a mark, especially on your daughter." Hicks thumbed the tablet screen so a new image appeared of an Arab woman and two small children outside a marketplace. "And I'll tell your old family about your new family in Karachi."

Bajjah banged the back of his head into the wall and buried his face even further into his towel. Hicks had seen this reaction from prisoners before. Everything they had once cherished was now being used as a weapon against them.

Hicks talked over Bajjah's sorrow the way a parent talks over a toddler throwing a fit. "I'll go to Karachi and tell your new family and all the people of your village how you have become an informant for the West. I'll show them proof you died a sniveling coward right here in this cell, all too willing to betray your cause for the sake of a few hours of peace. I don't have to tell you what will happen to your family in Karachi after that. You'll be remembered by anyone who ever loved you as a fanatic and a coward and a traitor. Your own flesh and blood in both the west and the east will curse your memory for the rest of their lives because they'll know their misery meant nothing to you."

Bajjah's screams turned to retching before becoming quiet sobbing. The death throes of impotent rage.

Hicks folded his hands again. "Is this what you want, Mehdi? To be remembered as a coward and a traitor? Do you want to have your soul cursed by your own children?"

Bajjah crammed his face into the towel. His body shook with silent sobs.

Hicks thumbed the screen to the final image: a split-screen of his old family and his new. He watched Bajjah's torment ebb into nothing.

Hicks didn't offer him solace. He made no attempt to console him. Because what was happening right there—in a mirrored cell in a rundown building in Manhattan's Alphabet City—was the essence of the University's mission: to acquire information on threats to the West through any means necessary.

Breaking the Moroccan's body hadn't yielded them much, but breaking his mind might.

Hicks could practically read his prisoner's mind as he watched The Moroccan lift his face from the soaked towel.

Bajjah had once been the trusted commander of a bold strike against the Great Satan. He had been chosen from many to drive a dagger deep into the heart of the infidels. Now, his mission had failed and he was alone. His followers were dead. His men scattered or captured or dead. He had been forgotten for years. There was no one left to pray for his soul. He was nothing but a crippled prisoner lying in a cell in his own drool and mess. He was more alone now than he ever had been in his life. Whatever God had brought him to this place had long since forsaken him.

Bajjah looked once more at the split image on the tablet screen. Hicks watched him change from the hardened ideologue to a father looking at the children he had never known huddling against the woman who had once been his wife. The woman from whom he had walked away had taken up with another. He looked at his new family. Both sons. Three sons in total. Allah would be pleased.

Hicks watched a single tear run from the Moroccan's right eye and down his cheek. He could almost hear Bajjah's soul crack.

"If I do as you ask," the prisoner whispered, "how do I know you won't tell them about me anyway?"

"Because I promised I wouldn't, and you know I always live up to my promises. Tell me about your organization and what you were planning and I promise none of your children will ever know what happened to their father."

Bajjah wiped at his sagging eye and mouth with his sleeve. "It has been years since I knew these men. Some may have moved elsewhere. Some may already be dead."

"That's my concern, not yours. I still need to know who and where they are."

Bajjah closed his eyes. "I have conditions."

Hicks didn't react. He waited until Bajjah was ready to speak.

"If I tell you what you want to know, I want the torture to stop immediately. I want my food properly prepared according to my beliefs. I want to be taken outside this place one final time so I may pray my morning prayers properly. I want my prayer rug and allowed to pray at sunrise. And then I want to be killed painlessly and quickly."

Hicks had heard many strange requests in dozens of interrogations all over the world. He'd never had a prisoner make their death part of the bargain.

The Moroccan went on. "I ask you to promise me you will live up to each of these conditions now because, as you have said, you have never lied to me."

None of the Moroccan's terms were impossible, but Hicks wouldn't give in so easy. Killing him would complicate his agreement with Tali and the Mossad, but only if Bajjah's information was true.

"I'll consider your requests if the information you give us proves to be accurate. But I'm willing to promise the torture will stop the moment you begin cooperating with us." He looked at his watch. "Your next session with Roger is in fifteen minutes. What's it going to be?"

Bajjah flipped his towel to a drier side and held it up to his face. A dying man's vanity. "Promise me all I have asked for, including my painless death, or there is no deal."

Hicks took a risk. "I promise."

"Good. Tell your effeminate deviant to stay where he is. I wish to begin my session now."

CHAPTER
5

SIX HOURS LATER, in the old kitchen Hicks used as his office, Roger poured three fingers of Bushmills into two reasonably clean glasses. "You were masterful in there today, James. I've never seen you better."

Hicks didn't touch the whiskey. He was too busy typing the ten names Bajjah had given him into the OMNI system. Five men in the continental United States, four spread out through the Middle East and one in London. They could have been ten random names he had pulled out of the air. They could also be working closely together as part of Bajjah's organization. Either way, Hicks had to know. The information was too promising to wait.

Roger sat down in an old kitchen chair next to Hicks. "Take a break for God's sake. Have a drink. You've just put in six hours with that fucking animal in there. You deserve it."

But Hicks kept typing. "No time for breaks. And we have a phone call with the Dean in an hour. We, as in you and me, Roger. I'll need you sober until further notice."

"Shit." Roger took a drink. "Yet another one of Dad's semantic kabuki dances where he never comes right out and tells us what he wants us to do. He never cuts the bullshit and makes himself clear. He always talks around things and expects us to divine his true meaning. He's as inscrutable as a mad Pope and just as infallible."

"Knock it off." Hicks didn't like Roger calling the Dean 'Dad' and he didn't like hearing him criticize the Dean, either, although Roger did have a point. The Dean was a deliberate man, but not an explicit one. He refrained from using contractions and hyperbole and comparisons during briefing calls. He believed a higher form of speech led to a higher level of problem solving. Given the results the University had generated since Hicks had signed on over twenty years before, it was tough for him to argue with his methods.

But after spending six hours inside Bajjah's damaged mind, Hicks could stand a little brevity.

Roger continued. "We cracked one hell of a tough nut today, James. I'd say the prick owes us a bit of thanks."

"He won't give a shit about anything unless we can authenticate the names Bajjah gave us and prove they're connected. This isn't math class. He doesn't care how we arrived at our results. All he cares about is the results themselves."

Roger pouted and went back to sipping his whiskey in silence.

Hicks kept typing.

Hicks was particularly interested in the London operative on Bajjah's list—Shaban Ghasemi. Not because Bajjah had said he was in London, but because Shaban was the first name Bajjah had chosen to give them. In Hicks' experience, the first name a prisoner gave up usually held some kind of importance. Sometimes, a prisoner used it to throw off the interrogator. Sometimes it was a slip of the tongue, but Bajjah didn't misspeak. What was so special about Shaban he deserved top billing?

Hicks typed in the final name and location into OMNI and clicked on the SEARCH button. He sat back watched OMNI go to work.

Within nanoseconds, OMNI began accessing the databases of the world's leading intelligence agencies to determine if the names on Bajjah's list belonged to real people. If they were, the University may have uncovered elements of a new global terror network. The information might give the Dean enough leverage he could use to make Stephens and the Barnyard back off. The Mossad might not be happy about it, but he'd deal with it if and when the time came.

Hicks watched OMNI's search results come in the way a political junkie watches the returns on Election Night. Roger looked on as well.

They knew the search was only the beginning, not the end of anything. If the names came back positive, a more detailed search would need to be conducted into the lives of each man to determine how they were working together.

OMNI may have been the most connected digital network in the world, but it was still only a tool. The Dean often pointed out how hammers and saws don't build houses, humans do. He applied the same logic to technology. He believed a human perspective was needed to wield OMNI's immense power in order for it to be truly effective. If the Dean had a motto, Hicks imagined it would be "Never let the computer do your thinking for you."

The search took less than five minutes, which was an eternity by OMNI standards. One by one, checks began to appear next to each of the ten names Hicks had entered into the system. He didn't react when he saw a green check appear next to the final name on the list.

Every name Bajjah had given them belonged to an actual person.

Roger cheered and slapped him on the back. "Ten out of ten! We broke him wide open!" He finished his drink and eagerly poured himself another. "Looks like Bajjah gets his shot at the forty virgins. Tali and the Mossad won't like it, but I'm sure you and the Dean will handle it."

But Hicks wasn't opening any champagne bottles yet. He had to determine if Bajjah had merely spouted off a list of random names or if he had given up the men who belonged to his own network.

OMNI's initial search showed each man had been flagged as a 'Person of Interest' by at least one intelligence agency somewhere in the world, but it was still the first name Bajjah had given them, Shaban Ghasemi, that caught Hicks' attention. Shaban was living in London and was being passively watched by British Intelligence. Most of the remaining nine names on Bajjah's list were already being tracked by multiple agencies at the same time. It was a good beginning, but now it was up to OMNI to determine if there were any solid connections.

The Dean would want more than a list of confirmed names.

He'd want evidence of collusion. He'd want proof of Bajjah's network. He'd want Hicks to have such proof by the time their conference call began in an hour.

He'd want hard evidence before he agreed to let Hicks kill Bajjah and violate their agreement with the Mossad and Tali.

Hicks opened a tactical search screen. OMNI generated a digital map of the world and quickly populated it with a passport photo or drivers' license photo of each suspect in the state or country where OMNI had tracked them. All of the men were dark complexioned, bearded, and wore glasses. Their ages ranged from thirty to fifty-five, but the thick beards made it difficult to guess how old they were based on their appearance. Hicks knew part of it was for religious purposes but part of it was by design. A common appearance made it more difficult for Westerners to casually identify them.

Fortunately, OMNI didn't do anything casually.

Hicks began typing in the commands directing OMNI to bore deep into the digital lives of each man on Bajjah's list. Phone records would be analyzed, contents of emails and text messages would be scanned, online search histories and social media activity would be scrutinized for anything that might link these ten men together. OMNI would also delve into travel patterns, real estate holdings, and bank account balances to determine if there were any common purchases or payments or expenses. Even the cars they drove would be identified and tracked from now on.

Over the next several hours, OMNI's search would burrow into the lives of each man, revealing more about these individuals than they knew about themselves. Hicks hoped all of this data would help him not only make connections within Bajjah's network, but the network's connections to other terrorist groups throughout the globe.

Hicks finally took his whiskey as he sat back and watched OMNI dig. There was no way the in-depth search would be done before the conference call with the Dean, but it would be underway.

Hicks sipped the whiskey as he watched hints of lines between each subject's photo begin to appear on the map. They represented a vague connection between the men at best. It was to be expected. Since they were all on at least one terror watch list, they'd been on the same extremist email lists or visited the same blogs. Perhaps they'd been in touch with similar people.

But some of the lines became a lighter gray, showing OMNI had found a more solid connection between various men. Soon, each photo became connected to each other as a web of gray lines slowly spread across the digital globe. The lines gradually lighten to white, and yellow, as evidence of the connection between the men on Bajjah's list grew deeper.

He sat forward as he watched the lines on the map suddenly turned red and began to blink.

Roger cheered and almost spilled his drink.

OMNI had found a rock-solid connection between each name Bajjah had given them. The Moroccan had told him the truth. He'd given them his network.

Roger toasted the screen with his glass. "Boom. Got the sons of bitches."

But Hicks set his whiskey on the table. OMNI wasn't done yet. "Wait."

A single gray outline of an image appeared in the upper center of the map's Atlantic Ocean. Hicks had seen this icon before. It was the default location for a suspect OMNI hadn't been able to locate. An equally generic gray outline of a head appeared, the standard graphic for a suspect OMNI hadn't yet identified. The system had found a common connection between the men and an eleventh party. It was working to define it.

The name appearing beneath this icon brought Hicks out of his chair. It wasn't the standard 'Subject Unknown' or an established screen name.

The icon was associated with a profile already in the OMNI system. A profile without a photograph on file, but a profile existed in the database of every major law enforcement and intelligence agency in the world.

It was a profile of the most wanted man alive.

The name beneath the icon: Jabbar.

Roger let out a long whistle as the dark gray line between the ten suspects and the Jabbar icon brightened. "Well, look at that."

Hicks knew not even OMNI could decipher the myths from the facts of the Jabbar profile. No two people who had admitted meeting Jabbar had ever given the same description of the man. No one had any idea about how tall he was, how old he might be, what he looked like or where he had been born.

OMNI's analysis of all descriptions gathered by all of the leading intelligence agencies throughout the world put Jabbar at about sixty, but it was an educated guess at best. No one knew what sect of Islam he followed or if he was even a Muslim at all.

Every intelligence agency in the world wanted Jabbar, but only one had issued a shoot-to-kill order on him.

The Mossad, who were keeping quiet about Bajjah being in

University custody in exchange for interrogating him later.

The Jabbar network was a web within a web spanning the entire planet. And Bajjah had given Hicks a way to track it.

Hicks had never paid much attention to Jabbar before. He'd always figured the Barnyard or another foreign agency would get him one day. Someone would talk or Jabbar might slip up.

But now, Bajjah may have given him a direct link to the most wanted man in the world.

Hicks figured this should be more than enough to give the Dean the leverage he needed to get the Barnyard to back away. And if not, he still had a hell of a problem on his hands.

And so did the University.

"What the hell is the matter with you?" Roger asked. "You've uncovered a network directly tied into Jabbar. A link no one else seems to have. You should be doing back flips right now."

Hicks still hadn't told Roger about his run-in with Stephens and the Barnyard. It had only happened earlier that morning. He could have sworn it had happened a month ago.

Hicks grabbed the whiskey bottle and refilled Roger's glass. Bad news was a lot easier to take with a whiskey chaser.

"Uh oh," said Roger. "If you're pouring, this must be serious."

Hicks filled his glass. "You have no idea."

CHAPTER
6

"**G**IVE ME ALL of the details on the prisoner interrogation," the Dean said. "Assume I do not know anything."

Hicks told him about the ten names Bajjah had given them and the results of both OMNI scans. But he made sure he followed the Dean's rigid format while he did it.

Roger usually watched porn on his tablet and made vulgar gestures to distract Hicks during these conference calls. But that evening, Roger was quietly attentive—like a boy on the first day of school. He hadn't even touched the whiskey Hicks had poured for him earlier. Hicks understood why. Finding out you're a target of the CIA tended to have a sobering effect.

It took Hicks fifteen minutes to summarize the results of the Bajjah interrogation and the link to Jabbar. He told the Dean about the deal he had made to kill Bajjah if he had cooperated.

He also reminded the Dean that Tali Shaddon of the Mossad was scheduled to interrogate Bajjah at the end of the week. Hicks made sure to not suggest the Jabbar information should be enough to get the Barnyard to back away. The Dean liked to arrive at his own conclusions in his own time, lest he felt like he was being led to make a decision.

The Dean was quiet for a time after Hicks finished his report before saying, "I watched your entire interrogation on OMNI as it happened, James. Exemplary work. Roger, my compliments to you and your staff on an effective rendition. I believe this is the closest anyone has come to confirming the existence of the elusive Jabbar."

Hicks saw Roger looking at him. He knew Roger wanted him to ask the Dean about using Bajjah's list as leverage to get the Barnyard to back off. But Hicks knew the Dean didn't like interruptions. Hicks would have to wait for the right time to raise the question.

The Dean went on. "Are you certain Bajjah's followers are not planning another attack?"

"I'm fairly confident they're not, sir."

"Fairly confident fails to make me entirely confident, James. Explain."

"Since we've already convinced Bajjah he's been in custody for a couple of years, we couldn't appear too concerned about plans for attacks that were supposed to be years old. It might've made him suspicious about the length of his incarceration, which could have tainted what he told us about his network."

"I appreciate your concern for the integrity of the incarceration. Why are you 'fairly certain' there will not be further attacks?"

"Bajjah admitted to planning the biological attack alone. He said the east coast outbreak was a trial run. The plan was to hit Europe in force if the attacks here proved successful. Since they were a failure, he said the bio-attack plan was likely scrapped."

"He may be the head of his own network," the Dean said, "but he is not the only member of the network. Others may have risen to take his place. They may be carrying on his work as we speak. Where is his money coming from?"

"He told me his funding comes from 'the network.' I pushed him for information about what 'the network' might be, which was when he gave me the names of the people in the network."

"And did you push him for details? Funding sources? Financial connections? Accounts? Holdings?"

"I did, but Roger's sensors showed I was pushing him too hard. Bajjah's vitals began to spike and I didn't want to push him into another stroke or heart event."

"Yes, I read about the stroke," the Dean said. "You are usually more careful with your subjects. I trust you have already taken measures to ensure it will not happen again."

Roger replied, "Already taken care of." He had never called the Dean 'sir.'

"Given the prisoner's delicate medical condition, I take it that pressing him for further details would be unwise."

"Roger and I agree we've probably pushed him as far as he can go," Hicks admitted. "Neither of us believe he could stand up to further enhanced tactics."

"Pity, though I admit that finding the Jabbar connection to his network fascinating. What details has he provided about the elusive Jabbar?"

"He didn't admit the connection, sir. He didn't have to.

OMNI confirmed a direct correlation between the names he gave us and the Jabbar profile, particularly on the man he called Shaban, who lives in London. The same man he said handled the money for the network."

"And, once again, you are certain the prisoner was being truthful."

Hicks signaled Roger to answer, which he did. "My people were monitoring the prisoner the entire time without his knowledge. His biometric responses indicated he was being truthful."

The Dean didn't sound impressed. "People beat lie detectors all the time, Roger."

"My sensors are better than lie detectors, and they can't be fooled. Bajjah told us the truth."

"Impertinent confidence has always been one of your most admirable qualities. Let us hope for all our sakes you are correct."

Roger gave the laptop the finger.

The Dean went on. "James, I noticed you had promised to kill the prisoner if his information proved valid."

He knew it would come up. "Yes I did, sir."

"And now you have determined the information he provided is true and that he is too weak to interrogate further. Do you intend to keep your promise to kill him?"

"I do, sir."

"Tell me why. And please keep in mind his death will violate our arrangement with the Mossad. We had promised to hand Bajjah over to them after we were finished interrogating him in exchange for their silence. They will disapprove of his execution and Agent Saddon will likely take it as a personal betrayal."

Hicks already knew that, but he couldn't worry about Tali now. "We've already broken Bajjah down as far as we can. His body is clearly beginning to weaken, as evidenced by the stroke he suffered during an interrogation session last night. Since he's too weak for us to work on, I'm concerned he may either shut down or begin giving us false information in retaliation for refusing to kill him. To put it bluntly, sir, keeping him alive simply no longer makes any sense."

"Matters of life and death should be put bluntly, James, but too infrequently are. In killing the prisoner, I assume you are fully prepared to reap the whirlwind of the Mossad's discontentment?"

Hicks had considered that, too. "I am, sir."

"Is fulfilling your promise to a mass murderer worth risking the alienation of an important ally to our cause? Since Bajjah is close to death anyway, why not hand him over to the Mossad to satiate their thirst for revenge?"

Hicks knew Tali would be furious with him. She may even quit and go back to work for the Mossad full time. The risk was enough to make him consider the consequences of killing Bajjah, but not enough to change his mind. "True, but I'm confident once we give them the information we've gathered on Bajjah's network and we inform them of his connection to Jabbar, their rage will be short-lived."

"The Mossad does not have a reputation for simply letting things go, James. Agent Saddon even less so. I have heard she is as deadly as she is alluring. It will take a great amount of effort to mitigate their disappointment."

Hicks understood the point the Dean was making. I'm not saying no. Convince me to say yes.

This was his chance to make his pitch about leverage. "Any mention of Jabbar by Bajjah and the Israelis will move heaven and earth to find him. But, if Bajjah is dead, we can control their response by redacting anything from our report that might spur the Israelis to act unilaterally to take out Jabbar's network. If we control the flow of information, we control the situation."

Hicks had never heard a smile before, but he thought he heard one in the Dean's voice when he said, "Congratulations, James. My thoughts exactly."

Hicks was glad he was pleased because he decided now was an excellent time to bring up the problem of Stephens and the Barnyard. "This way, we can use all of the Bajjah/Jabbar information to barter with Stephens and the Barnyard, maybe use it as leverage to get them to leave us alone and end their investigation of us. We give them what they want, they go away."

"More solid reasoning, James, but I have already decided the University must address the threat posed by the Bajjah/Jabbar network itself. We will topple this organization in-house."

Hicks looked at Roger to see if they had heard the same thing. They must have because Roger looked as confused as Hicks felt.

Hicks decided the Dean must have misspoken without realizing it. During their first meeting two weeks before, the Dean had announced he was suffering from terminal brain cancer. The disease must have finally begun to impact his mind because what he had said was complete nonsense.

Hicks didn't want to embarrass him by correcting him. "Understood, sir. I've already directed OMNI to do a deep dive into the lives of all ten men in Bajjah's network. We should have a detailed packet on each the men and their immediate associates by tomorrow morning at the latest. You can count on being able to pass along our information to the relevant agencies via standard back channels by noontime. It should give us the leverage we need to get the Barnyard to back off."

The Dean's response was immediate. "James, did I stutter?"

"No, sir."

"I already told you we will be handling the Jabbar matter in-house. And by 'we,' of course, I mean you will be handling it. We will not be sharing the Bajjah/Jabbar information with any other agencies. The University will bring down the Bajjah and Jabbar organizations on our own."

The countless hours he had spent overseeing the Bajjah interrogation had finally paid off, leading to solid, actionable intelligence on a known terrorist organization. They had always handed this kind of information to the bigger agencies who were better suited to stop such threats. The Dean was in an excellent position to use the Bajjah information as leverage to stop The Barnyard and the others from encroaching on the University's autonomy.

But the Dean didn't want to do it. He was committing the University to a two-front war. On one side, Bajjah's network which may ultimately lead to Jabbar. On the other side, the combined might of the intelligence community of the United States of America. The University found itself in the middle.

A dull ache began to settle in behind Hicks' eyes. A bad day had suddenly gotten a hell of a lot worse.

CHAPTER
7

"**H**ELLO?" THE DEAN'S voice snapped him out of it. "Are you still there, James?"

Hicks saw Roger silently mouth: What the fuck?

"I'm right here, sir. I'm digesting what you told us. To be clear, you're saying you want us to take down all of the cells in the Bajjah/Jabbar network on our own. Without involving any of the other agencies."

"Precisely."

"And you expect us to do it without help from any of the other agencies?"

"Yes, that is what I said. You seem distressed by this news. I am disappointed."

Hicks knew the Dean's ability to detect the truth beat any sensor Roger had in his arsenal, so he didn't bother lying. "Sir,

Bajjah's network has five cells in the United States, four cells in the Middle East and one of them is Shaban, the supposed money man in Europe."

"You have already told me this, James. You are repeating yourself. One might be forgiven for believing you're the one with brain cancer, not me."

Hicks ignored the jab. "The University doesn't have the resources to hit a multinational terror network while evading the Barnyard at the same time. We don't have the money or the manpower or the firepower to..."

The Dean's voice came through the laptop once again. "Is Roger still in the room? I take it you have informed him of your encounter with the CIA this morning?"

"Yes, sir, as per our earlier discussion."

"Good, because allow me to explain the new reality to both of you at the same time. When you captured Bajjah and uncovered his plans, you caused this institution to stumble into a dangerous part of the intelligence jungle where the larger agencies roam. Think of them as the alpha predators, like lions and tigers. And like their counterparts in the animal kingdom, these agencies do not welcome outsiders. They do not tolerate rivals. In Bajjah, we have something these predators want and they will not stop until they get it."

Hicks saw his chance to reason with him. "All the more reason to hand him over to them now, sir. We can justify why we took him and hand over the information we extracted from him. That should..."

The Dean cut him off. "Sharing the information you obtained from Bajjah will not quell their appetite, James. It will only whet it. They will want to know more about who we are and how we found Bajjah and what methods we used to interrogate him and if we were holding back any information he had given us. I also fear giving the Bajjah information to the Barnyard could risk too many people being aware of it, thereby increasing the likelihood that Jabbar could be alerted. We cannot allow this to happen. We are too close to finding and stopping a monster like Jabbar to allow the Barnyard's bureaucratic bungling to allow him to escape. Capturing Jabbar must be the University's main focus now."

Hicks tried to push through the growing pounding in his head. *He's serious. He's planned this.* "Finding Jabbar will be a hell of a lot harder if we're in the crosshairs of three separate intelligence agencies, sir."

"I know. I am not suggesting open warfare, James. Taking on one of the agencies would be suicide and taking on all three at once would be madness. Which is why we must evade the lion, not fight it. We must use the overgrowth and shadows of the jungle to our advantage while we search for the weapon to slay the lion. Jabbar is such a weapon, James. Not information on his network, but the man himself. Delivering Jabbar in chains will be the only way to quell the appetite of our enemies and give us the bargaining power necessary to get them to leave us alone. Anything less may lead to the destruction of the University."

"I don't mean to argue with you, sir, but..."

The Dean talked over him again. "Stop arguing and devise a way to find Jabbar and end all of this. Your rash actions played a part in causing this, James. Your swift action will be the only way we resolve it. I will expect a full plan of action in my inbox by this time tomorrow. Time is a luxury we can ill afford. And so is failure."

Hicks heard the connection end. And his troubles were only beginning.

CHAPTER 8

H E LET THE silence sit in the kitchen for a full minute, maybe longer, before he finally looked at Roger. "You heard that, too, didn't you? He said what I think he said, didn't he?"

"Complete with jungle analogies," Roger said. "Don't forget those. Lions and tigers and *jihadis*, oh my."

Hicks dropped his head into his hands. "Knock it off."

But Roger didn't knock it off. "No way, man. You Tarzan, me Jane, and that old man is out of his fucking mind. How the hell does he expect us to find Jabbar and fight off the other agencies at the same time? Does he have any idea what we're up against?"

"He knows." Hicks slammed his laptop shut. "That's what makes all of this worse."

"Well, even if he is the Dean, he's out of his mind. We obviously can't do what he wants. We've got to figure out a way to hand this off to the other agencies through back channels."

Hicks didn't dare begin to go down that path. "We can't do that and you know it."

"Why? Because Dad said so? I don't know about you, but I've got no intentions of getting killed by one of my fellow spies because some dying old man got confused."

"He's not confused. He knows exactly what he's asked us to do."

"So how are we supposed to go about giving him what he wants? How exactly are we supposed to evade three of the best intelligence agencies in the world and hunt for Jabbar?"

Hicks' head began to hurt even worse. "I'll figure it out."

"Let's look at it from a pure numbers perspective," Roger said. "How many people are on the University payroll? All totaled, not only the field staff."

Hicks had never been privy to all the facets of the University. He could only make an educated guess. "Maybe around a thousand worldwide. Most of them are part-time analysts, Adjuncts and Assets. Nowhere near enough, but I'll find a way to make it work."

"You don't have to do anything. This isn't feudal Japan. You don't have to fall on your sword simply because some sick old man told you to. We have options, you know."

"We do? Name one."

"We can check with the people above the Dean. See if they'll listen to reason."

In the twenty years Hicks had worked for The University, the only executive he'd ever dealt with was the Dean. Groups like the University didn't exactly have organizational charts. "I don't know if there is anyone else above him. He's mentioned giving reports to the Trustees a couple of times, but I don't know who they are or how to find them. And even if I did, I don't know what kind of authority they have. And I know the Dean would go ballistic if I tried."

The ache in Hicks' head spiked to a full migraine and he began to rub his temples. All of Roger's points had been bouncing around his head while the Dean had given him the directive. He felt like a rat caught in a maze with no way out. Any way he turned only led back to one conclusion: following the Dean's orders exactly as he had laid them out.

"What about leaking the Bajjah information to Stephens anyway?" Roger asked. "Do it through back channels. You already know all the right people to call."

"Not the people at the level we'd need." Hicks dropped his head in his hands again. "Not for something this important. OMNI has lists of field agents and section chiefs, but I couldn't get access to anyone who could do something with the information, not without the Dean finding out. I've seen what he's done to people who cross him, Roger. I've handled plenty of them for him in the past and, believe me, it's not pretty."

Roger had another idea. "We could always make a run for it, you know? Take off on our own and leave all this shit behind. God knows we have enough cash on hand to live like kings."

Hicks lifted his head from his hands. "You mean leave tonight or live and die this way? Who are you? Tracy Chapman?"

Roger didn't laugh. "I was being serious."

"So am I. You know how the University works. Yeah, we've got money, but they know where every penny is and they'd find a way to lock all of our accounts the second we started making substantial withdrawals."

"I suppose it wasn't much of an idea after all." Roger took the whiskey bottle and refilled his glass. "Either way you look at it, we're going to need more people, James. People who know how to handle themselves."

Hicks knew finding qualified, available people in a short amount of time wouldn't be easy. There was no shortage of mercenaries for hire, but mercs could be unreliable and sloppy. Hicks would have to vet them to determine how loyal they were before he even attempted to recruit them. He'd have to match their price and figure out a way to finance them.

Bajjah's ten cells spread throughout the world would require at least ten people per team. One hundred new hires worldwide and it all had to happen quickly.

But the University didn't have the manpower to vet them properly. And he didn't know if the University had enough money on hand to pay them, either. In fact, he didn't have the slightest idea how much money the University's Bursar's office had in its accounts.

The lack of people or money didn't bother Hicks. It was the hurried nature of the entire operation. Speed killed in the intelligence game. Properly vetting new hires was always more of an art than a science, even in the best of times. With the University under Barnyard scrutiny, word of a hiring spree would spread. A single wrong hire in a hundred could jeopardize University secrecy or worse, Jabbar might learn of the mobilization and disappear once more.

It would be best to keep the operation small and contained, instead of a large force. Maybe he could get away with hiring only one person to focus on one man.

Roger looked at him closely. "I know that look. What are

you thinking?"

Hicks opened his laptop and looked at the OMNI search progressing on his laptop. Only one of the men on Bajjah's list wasn't being treated as an actively hostile target by at least one government agency in the world. It also happened to be the first name Bajjah had given up during his interrogation: Shaban Ghasemi in London. The Money Man.

OMNI showed Shaban's emails and phone records were already being passively tracked by British intelligence. He was the only member of the Bajjah/Jabbar network not under close scrutiny. "Nine of the men on Bajjah's list are already being actively watched by other agencies in this country and abroad. We can save time and manpower by having OMNI track the other agencies' surveillance reports while we focus on the one man no one's watching." Hicks tapped Shaban's face on the screen. "Shaban Ghasemi, currently living in London, England."

"There's the answer," Roger said. "Order the London Office to keep an eye on anything Shaban does."

"I wish it was that simple." In fact, the condition of the London Office was one of the reasons for Hicks' headache. The London Office of the University was considered little more than an annex, as the New York Office had been regarded before Hicks took it over. There had never been a reason to make the University's London Office a forward operation. Its Faculty Members and Adjuncts provided critical financial information on Middle Eastern and European groups suspected of acting against the West. It had always been considered a stopover for Faculty Members from more active University offices located in Germany, France, Italy, and Turkey.

OMNI's initial research on Shaban led Hicks to believe

Shaban wasn't a skilled terrorist, but it would still take someone with training to follow him. Bajjah had given Shaban up first for a reason. Hicks needed to know why.

"Peter Tipton is the head of the London Office," Hicks reminded Roger, "but he's a money man. He's lethal with a spreadsheet, but we're going to need someone who knows how to handle themselves in the field for an operation like this. Someone who can shadow Shaban without Shaban knowing it."

"Since you're concentrating on London, I happen to know someone who's available," Roger said. "Someone who also happens to be the best person for this kind of job. Rahul Patel."

"Patel?" Hicks's headache got worse. "Shit, Roger, he's a drunk. We'd have to dry him out for a year before we could use him, and we don't have that kind of time."

"His drunkenness is a temporary condition, I assure you. If there's one thing I know about in this world, it's drunkards and Mr. Patel doesn't qualify. He's hurt and mourning the death of his sister. He's a man looking for a reason to set aside his grief, and I'd wager this is exactly the kind of operation that might snap him out of it."

"I know what happened, Roger. I was the one who found her body and kept him from killing her killers, remember?"

"Yes I do," Roger said. "So does Rahul. He still resents you for it, but I still run into him from time to time. I bet I could talk him into working for us if you want."

Hicks wasn't so sure. Until a year ago, Rahul Patel had been the best counter-intelligence agent in Asia, which was why his enemies murdered his sister in her Manhattan apartment. Patel didn't blame Hicks for his sister's death. He blamed him for preventing him from killing her attackers, who had been involved in an important University operation for years. Hicks had ultimately killed the men responsible, but their deaths hadn't stopped Rahul's downward spiral.

"Find someone else. I need someone in the field, not at a goddamned AA meeting."

Roger surprised him by not giving up. "I'd still like to approach him anyway, even if it's only to cross him off our list. He's right here in New York, working at his cousin's restaurant in Midtown as something of a greeter, but he drinks more than he greets."

Hicks' headache was subsiding, so he decided to not argue with him. He toggled away from OMNI's deep dive into the lives of the Bajjah/Jabbar network and checked his inbox. He was glad to see the Dean had sent him the email about Mark Stephens he'd promised.

"Do what you want, but before you waste your time with Patel, I need you to get up to speed on Mark Stephens. He's the guy the Barnyard has sent after us. I'm forwarding you his file now. This guy is a former Beekeeper, and he's no joke."

Hicks clicked on the email and saw several attachments. It was all the records the federal government had on Mark Stephens, Beekeeper with the Defense Intelligence Agency (DIA). Military record, personal history, DIA activities, and more. Hicks forwarded all of the files to Roger without even opening any of the attachments.

"I'm sure it'll make for some interesting reading," Roger said. A wise man always knows as much about one's enemy as one can. I'll read it over immediately. I'm sure there's something we can use against Mr. Stephens to bend him to our will." Roger grinned. "Their name always cracked me up. 'Beekeeper.' Buzz,

buzz."

Hicks smiled, too, despite himself. Fucking Roger.

Roger checked his watch and wasn't smiling anymore. "It's going to be sunrise in a couple of hours. Tali and her Mossad friends are going to be looking to interrogate Bajjah. Have you decided if you're going to honor your commitment to Tali or Bajjah?"

Another rotten decision leaving him nowhere but fucked either way he went. Hicks closed his eyes and rolled his neck. The image of the dead girl appeared, and she looked at him with the same dead eyes. Help me.

He answered her in his mind. Help me, too, little one. Wherever you are. If you can.

He'd need all the help he could get.

CHAPTER 9

THE SKY HAD begun to brighten as Hicks led Bajjah—shackled and hooded—out onto the graveled rooftop of the safe house. Roger slipped out onto the roof behind them and quietly closed the door. He held his nine-millimeter flat against his leg. Hicks' .454 Ruger was still tucked in the holster under his left arm.

Bajjah's leg irons jingled as Hicks steered him by the back of the neck to a clear spot on the eastern side of the roof. The prisoner's prayer rug, which the Varsity Squad had found during a search of Bajjah's apartment, was tucked under Bajjah's arm. Hicks had already allowed him to perform wudu—the cleaning ritual symbolizing absolution—in his cell before bringing him up to the roof.

Hicks pulled Bajjah to a stop at the spot on the roof where he had a clear view of the eastern horizon and the sunrise over

Queens.

Hicks undid Bajjah's handcuffs and pulled off his hood. He kept the leg irons in place. No sense in risking him running off the roof. A dead body on the pavement would be difficult to explain and nearly impossible to clean up before rush hour. Even the University's abilities had limits.

Hicks took a couple of steps backward as the prisoner automatically laid his carpet atop the gravel and began his morning prayer.

Bajjah buried his face in his hands and chanted quietly before kneeling on the rug. He bowed once and knelt upright, chanting the morning prayers all devout Muslims said each day of their lives. The man hadn't been allowed to pray in weeks, though in his mind, it had been years. His time away from the ritual hadn't changed his practice of it, as he slipped right back into the rhythm of his faith.

Hicks watched Bajjah stop in mid-chant when he opened his eyes in time to see the first glimmer of the sun rising above the eastern horizon.

Even from behind, Hicks could see Bajjah smile. It was the first hint of sunlight he had seen in more than two long years.

Or so he had believed.

Until that moment.

Hicks watched the prisoner's expression slowly evolve into something else, just as it had during his interrogation. This time it wasn't hate. It was something closer to awareness.

The skyline looked familiar. He wasn't being held on an island somewhere. He was in New York City. And the air was cold, as it had been when he'd first been taken. The position of the sun was not so dissimilar to the last morning he had made his morning prayers. Something was wrong. How long…

The little girl flashed in Hicks mind. *Help me.*

Hicks drew his Ruger and fired a single round into the back of Bajjah's head. His body fell face-first into the prayer rug.

The loud crack of the shot echoed throughout the quiet early streets of the Lower East Side, but quickly faded. No lights came on. No dogs barked. No one opened their windows or appeared on their patios to see what had happened. The sound could've been a truck starting up or any number of other things. It was too early in the busy city for people to be curious. Most hadn't had their coffee yet.

The man who had dedicated his life to killing thousands of people in New York City had died alone on a rooftop without notice.

Hicks opened the cylinder of the Ruger and replaced the spent cartridge with a new one. He let the cylinder spin freely before snapping it shut. The clean sound of oiled steel had always given him comfort.

"I'm surprised you gave him so long," Roger said as he tucked his Glock away. "You're getting generous in your old age."

"I promised him the sunrise." Hicks tucked the Ruger back in the shoulder holster under his arm. "Have him tossed in the incinerator downstairs. Dump whatever's left in the lime pit in the cellar."

"Of course," Roger agreed, "though I'd like to keep the prayer rug. As a memento." The torturer smiled. "He was the first subject in The Cube and breaking him was one of the proudest moments of my career. I'd like something to remember it by."

Hicks looked down at Bajjah's body. Blood from the head

wound was soaking the rug and flowing over onto the gravel. "You'll have a hell of a time getting the blood out of it."

"Don't be silly. I wouldn't dream of cleaning it. The blood makes it more personal."

Hicks stepped through the door and headed downstairs. "Blood always does."

CHAPTER 10

I T WAS AFTER eight in the morning when Hicks decided it was time to leave the safe house and head back to his Twenty-Third Street facility. Manipulating the Bajjah intelligence for Tali and the Mossad would be easier on his desktop at the facility than his laptop.

With Stephens and his people hunting him, he knew he should take a cab back to his Twenty-Third Street facility. It would have been safer, even if most cabs had cameras onboard. But, at that point, Hicks didn't care about his own safety. He needed fresh air more, or as fresh as the air in Manhattan ever got. He needed time to himself, away from the University. He craved the anonymity of the New York streets while he got his mind in order.

It was the height of rush hour in Manhattan. If Stephens tried to track him by hacking camera systems, it would be harder for him to get a lock in such crowded conditions. Langley and the NSA may have had the best state-of-the-art facial recognition software at their disposal, but when eight million people were all trying to get to work or school at the same time, even the best systems had a hard time keeping up.

Besides, he'd just killed a man. He believed even the death of a mass murderer like Bajjah deserved pause. Pause prevented him from becoming a murderer himself. At least that's what he told himself as he tried to sleep each night.

It seldom worked, even before the nightly visits from the dead little girl plagued his nightmares. Help me.

He had helped her, at least he'd helped her the only way he knew how. He hoped it would be enough to give her peace. If one of them deserved peace, it was her. He knew he wouldn't have any for quite some time.

As he began walking back to the Twenty-Third Street facility, the memory of the dead little girl began to fade, only to be replaced by the phenomena he called his Carousel of Concerns turning in his mind.

Stephens. The Barnyard. Jabbar. The Dean. The Mossad. Five individual agendas pulling him in different directions. Each one presented a unique threat in their own way.

He knew a drink would ease his headache and calm him down, but one drink would easily turn into three or more. He needed to be sharp now. Too many eyes on him. Too many things could go wrong.

The fucking carousel: Stephens' surveillance. The threat of Jabbar's global network. The Dean's mandate.

He decided against the drink and pulled out a Nat Sherman

cigar from his coat instead.

He was at the corner waiting for the light to change when he clipped off the end of the stick, struck a match, and cupped his hand around the flame as he lit the cigar. He saw the dirty looks he drew from the joggers and hipsters and Millennials also waiting at the corner. He ignored them. He'd just killed a man bent on killing them. He was entitled.

After the light changed and Hicks resumed his walk across town, his mind worked in two directions at once. One part of his brain passively took in the people he passed and what they did, like background music in a shopping mall. He scanned the street for familiar faces, for glances lasting a half second too long and for parked cars with the motor running. He didn't see these things because of Stephens' surveillance. This was something he had done for most of his adult life. The price one paid for being part of the University was a lack of peace.

The other part of his brain actively compartmentalized and prioritized the problems he faced. Two weeks before, the capture and death of a terrorist like Mehdi Bajjah would have been one of the top headlines of his career. Today, it was an afterthought.

He knew the Dean's decision to keep the Jabbar information from the Barnyard was wrong. The University had always excelled at finding important information discreetly before handing it off to various intelligence organizations throughout the world to act upon it. He knew the University thrived on subversion. It had derailed thousands of acts against the West through misinformation or flat out sabotage since before the Second World War.

Effective obscurity had always been the University's greatest asset. It was never supposed to be an active, forward entity. Making the University into the kind of organization with the ability to track down Jabbar while fighting off Stephens and the Barnyard would take time they didn't have. Because now Stephens knew he was on to something. He wouldn't stop until he found he found Bajjah. And, ultimately, Hicks.

He couldn't let that happen.

HICKS WAS ALREADY halfway through his cigar by the time he'd gotten to the corner of Nineteenth Street and Broadway. The crosswalk sign had only just finished blinking red and a small herd of pedestrians ran across the street before traffic rolled. Hicks could've easily made it if he ran, but decided to wait. He had the corner all to himself, which was a rarity at this time of morning in Manhattan.

He decided to enjoy his temporary solitude by taking a deep pull on his cigar and let the smoke escape through his nose. No one was around him to complain. The tobacco and the crisp morning air were helping to kill his headache. The growing strength of the morning sun warmed his back and neck. Knowing it had been the last sunrise Bajjah would ever see made it seem even warmer.

His shadow stretched long and thin into the crosswalk as cars began to roll south on Broadway.

He noticed another long shadow appear next to his before it stopped short and quickly pulled back.

Strange.

New Yorkers never pulled back, especially at a crosswalk during rush hour. Every patch of ground was sacred in a busy city. Armies had surrendered ground easier than a busy New York on their way to work. People only stepped back if they were at the curb and need to avoid getting hit by a bus or taxi. New Yorkers were always jockeying for position, especially at the curb, where they usually stood anxiously, waiting for traffic to thin out or slow down enough for them to cross with or without the light.

But this shadow not only stopped short. It had pulled back, even though Hicks was the only one waiting to cross the street. He had only seen the shadow for a split second, but he could it belonged to a man by the width of it.

A man who had chosen to stay behind him even though no one else was at the corner.

Why?

Hicks' training came to the fore. He decided he wouldn't turn around. If the shadow belonged to one of Stephens' men, looking around only would have made them break off and try again later. The shadow could be from another phone zombie reading an email or sending out one last Tweet while he walked. It could've been someone trying to avoid his cigar smoke. Or maybe it was some guy like him who didn't need to be anywhere in a particular in a hurry.

Or maybe it was someone exactly like him. Maybe it was one of Stephens' men who'd gotten too close and pulled back before he was noticed.

Hicks took another pull on his cigar and let the smoke drift from his nose once more as he pushed the Carousel to the back of his mind and became more actively aware of his surroundings.

Amid the thick southbound traffic, he spotted a white van

with rust spots on the sides make a quick right off Broadway from the center lane. Horns blared and drivers cursed and pedestrians jumped out of the way as the van made the turn. Hicks watched the van duck into a parking spot mid-block on the south side of Nineteenth Street.

The same side of the street Hicks was on.

First Shadow Man, now this.

Maybe it was another coincidence—a hurried delivery man who had lost track of where he was and was forced to make a quick turn before he lost the light.

It also might not be so innocent. Shadow Man and the van could be related. Like the Dean often said, 'You are only paranoid if no one is watching.'

Hicks considered hailing a cab or begin walking in another direction. He could head uptown or downtown to see if anyone followed. If he was wrong, all it would cost him was a few minutes.

But if Stephens' people really were following him, he'd blow their op and lose his chance at identifying them. Changing direction would show them they had made a mistake. People like Stephens never made the same mistake twice. Next time, they'd be a lot more careful and harder to spot.

He decided to stay on Nineteenth Street. The longer this played out, the more likely they would make a mistake. If there was a 'they' at all.

As Broadway traffic slowed to a crawl, Hicks took a final drag on his cigar and dropped the butt down a storm drain grate at the corner. He unzipped his jacket and shook out the sides as if he was getting warm. His Ruger was still tucked in the shoulder holster under his left arm. The padded liner of the jacket kept it out of sight.

The light changed and he joined the crowd of people who began threading their way through the tangle of cars and trucks and buses and taxis blocking the crosswalk. He continued walking west when he got to the other side of the avenue. He kept an eye on the rusting white van that had barreled through traffic and parked next to a fire hydrant outside a vacant storefront. The sliding door was open and the engine was still running. A thin trail of smoke escaped from the exhaust.

He also saw a black man in a brown leather coat holding a cell phone up to his left ear. He looked like anyone else on the street except for one detail: Hicks recognized this man from the file the Dean had emailed him.

The man on the phone was Mark Stephens, Beekeeper—Defense Intelligence Agency.

Hicks recognized the set up. The open door of the idling van. Stephens on the street to his left and Shadow Man behind him. It was the same kind of Snatch-and-Grab operation Hicks had run dozens of times throughout the world. One man buffaloes a target from the back, another hits the target from the side, and both men push the target into a waiting vehicle. The door slides shut and the van pulls away before anyone can do anything about it. It was low-tech. It was old school and effective. If the operatives timed it right, there was no fuss or foul, especially if the target doesn't see it coming.

But Hicks had seen it coming. And it made all the difference.

Stephens flinched as Hicks suddenly stopped short of the storefront entrance.

In one motion, Hicks pulled the Ruger from his holster and brought back his right elbow, slamming it into the throat of

Shadow Man who had rushed to grab him from behind.

Hicks ducked behind the gagging man and wrapped his left arm under his neck, jerking the taller man backward and off-balance. He aimed the Ruger at Stephens, using Shadow Man as cover.

And Stephens was already aiming his nine-millimeter Glock at Hicks.

Pedestrians screamed and scrambled out of the way as Hicks pulled the gagging man back a couple of steps. To Stephens, he said, "You fucked up, Ace. Lay the gun on the deck, climb in the van, and drive away."

But Stephens stayed where he was. "That's not going to happen. Let my man go before you get hurt. All I was told to do was bring you in. No one has to die here today."

"That's not going to happen either." Hicks tightened his grip on his hostage's neck and made the man gag. "You can either go back to your bosses empty handed or you can get shipped back in a rubber bag. Makes no difference to me either way."

The wail of an approaching police siren echoed through the streets. Stephens barely flinched at the sound, but he did flinch.

And Hicks saw it. "I've got nothing to hide from the cops. Do you?"

Stephens tucked the Glock in the back of his pants and moved toward the van, keeping his hands visible as he went. The sirens grew louder. "Okay, mister. You win. Now, let my man go and we'll be on our way."

Hicks struggled to keep the gagging man off balance as he used the Ruger to track Stephens from the store to the van. "Tell me who you work for."

Stephens stepped up into the back of his van; still keeping

his hands visible. "You already know." Stephens looked in the direction of sirens, which had grown louder. "This shit is between professionals, so let's keep it professional. I did what you wanted and stowed my weapon. Now let my man go."

Hicks released his grip on the man's neck and shoved him toward the van with a boot to the ass. He kept the Ruger level as Stephens pulled his stumbling operative into the van and slid the door shut.

As the van tried to pull out into sluggish crosstown traffic, Hicks holstered the Ruger and pulled his handheld device from his pocket. He held it up to the van and thumbed another innocent looking icon on the lock screen. The camera automatically scanned the van for the ID chip placed in most new vehicles. The ping came back positive. It had found the chip before the van pulled out into traffic and headed west. OMNI would now automatically track the van via the University satellite parked high above Manhattan.

Hicks pocketed his handheld as he quickly turned around and began retracing his steps, walking back east along Nineteenth Street. He was careful not to run, but moved quickly through the crowd. No one tried to stop him, but he fought the urge to bolt. Running would have increased his chances of tripping and injuring himself. Running would also bring more attention from more people when he got to the corner. The police sirens were too close to risk it.

He saw a few of the people in the crowd were taking his picture and filming him with their smart phones as he passed. There was nothing he could do about it. He'd have OMNI scan the area and alter the images on their devices later. For now, he needed to get the hell out of there before the cops showed up.

He crossed Broadway again and kept walking at a steady pace until he hit Park Avenue, where he hailed a cab heading uptown. He checked the interior for a passenger camera before he climbed inside, but didn't see one.

He shut the door behind him and told the driver to take him to Grand Central. One or two people had followed him to the corner and were still aiming their smart phones his way. He was sure they didn't work for Stephens. They were regular civilians trying to be helpful, or profit from the footage they would sell to a news agency.

He knew they had taken pictures of the ID number on the outside of the cab, but it didn't matter. He planned on losing himself among the horde of commuters boarding and getting off the trains and subways that ran through the Grand Central Terminal complex. It wasn't a foolproof plan, but it was the best he could come up with given the time.

As the cab began driving north, Hicks activated the secure feature of his phone. For the first time in his career, he tapped the Priority One/Code Red button on the screen.

Tapping that button triggered an immediate, automatic emergency message of his location to the Dean, the Varsity, stating James Hicks was in immediate danger and his cover had been compromised.

An automatic, more general alert immediately went out to all Faculty Members and Adjuncts in the University's New York office, putting them on High Alert status until further notice.

Within a few seconds of pressing the button, his handheld buzzed from an incoming call. He expected it to be the Dean. He was surprised to see it was Jason, the Dean's former right hand man—called a Dutchman—who had since replaced Hicks as the head of the University's New York office.

Hicks and Jason had never been on good terms, but friendship wasn't necessary in their line of work. Hicks gave the all-clear sign by answering, "This is Professor Warren. Thank you for returning my call."

Jason broke protocol by asking a direct question. "Are you hurt?"

"No."

"Good. I have Scott and his men scrambling as we speak," Jason said. "We have your position and also the position of the van you pinged. Where do you want Scott to go?"

Although they were speaking over OMNI's secure network, a direct question under a Code Red was against University protocol. Hicks remained on script. "The other one would be best."

"I'll let him know." A few clicks of the keyboard, followed by, "Do you believe this incident had anything to do with yesterday's tracking incident? Was it Stephens?"

If Jason had been an experienced field agent, he would have known better than to discuss specifics on the phone. OMNI had never been compromised before, but the University had never gone up against the CIA and the NSA before. OMNI would prove difficult to hack, but no system was impossible. Given the circumstances, he answered the question. "It had everything to do with it."

"Did you injure any of them?"

"No. I'll tell you all about it when I'm back in the office on Friday." The term 'Friday' was University code for 'as soon as I'm clear.'

But Jason still didn't get the hint. "I can see you're in a cab.

If I can see that, Stephens and his people might be able to see it, too. Get back to your place the safest, least direct way possible."

Hicks resented the Dean's former office pet telling him how to conduct himself in the field. "That's the idea."

"In the meantime," Jason went on, "I've already got OMNI scanning all the signals in your previous area to disrupt any postings of the images on social media. So far, we've intercepted twenty accounts of the incident and five videos. We'll also alter…"

Hicks cut him off before he gave out more of OMNI's capabilities over a possibly compromised line. "Great. Talk to you later."

Hicks killed the connection. When the phone buzzed twice, he figured it was an indignant text message from Jason about Hicks hanging up on him. The little prick had always been a last word freak. But it wasn't a phone call.

It was a text message from the Dean: **WAS IT STEPHENS?**

Hicks' kept his text reply as brief as if they were having a phone conversation. Text messages were as easy to intercept as calls: **YES.**

The Dean: **DID YOU KILL HIM?**

Hicks' reply: **NO.**

The Dean's reply: **YOU SHOULD HAVE.**

Another message followed seconds later: **YOU WILL HAVE TO KILL HIM EVENTUALLY.**

Hicks put the phone back in his pocket. He looked out the window and watched the city blur as the cab moved up Park Avenue.

He was beginning to believe the Dean might be right.

And that's what worried him most.

CHAPTER 11

FOR THE SECOND day in a row, Hicks spent two hours switching subway trains in the outer boroughs of Manhattan to make sure he wasn't being followed. When he was as confident he wasn't being followed, he ventured back to his Twenty-Third Street facility.

He got off the train at Fifty-Ninth Street and Columbus Circle and took a cab straight to his front door. Security be damned. He had already been away from the facility for too long and needed to get to work.

He checked his handheld the entire cab ride to see if OMNI had picked up any secure signals in his immediate area. Nothing came up. If anyone was following him, they were doing it old school. Eyeballs and shoe leather. No hacked feeds and no secure communications. He had the cab leave him at the corner and he walked the rest of the way to the facility. If anyone was paying attention to him, they were doing a hell of a job of hiding it.

Hicks had always seen the Twenty-Third Street location as simply a University facility. He had never called it home, even though he slept and lived there. He'd never placed any frames of family photos on the desk or personal mementos on his bedside table. There had never been a family to photograph and he'd never had the kind of personality where he collected things. To Hicks, the facility was nothing more than a workspace.

Right after becoming head of the University's New York Office, Hicks had managed to blackmail a young developer into allowing him to build the facility beneath the foundation of three townhouses he was rehabilitating. The University had arranged for secure contractors to work beneath the structures quietly and quickly. Some creative manipulation of the City's Building Department's records had allowed the extra construction to occur without government interference or knowledge.

The garden apartment on street level looked convincingly cozy to any of the thousands of people who walked or drove past it each day. There were curtains on the windows, furniture in the living room, and a bookcase crammed with books. Renters on the upper floors paid market rates for rent, which brought in a nice sum each month to fund the University's Bursar office.

Once inside the garden apartment, Hicks took the stairs to the basement, where a working boiler served the two apartments above. But the basement's principle function was to serve as a stopgap for Hicks' sub-basement facility.

The facility was secured by an ordinary wooden door with a large knob and lock. But there was no key to the lock and the knob didn't turn. The door could only be opened when a scanner in the knob read the biometrics of Hicks' left hand while a camera scanned his facial features. When the two results matched, the door opened inward like an airplane hatch.

The sub-basement facility was a large, steel-reinforced concrete vault constructed beneath the basements of the three town houses above it. The facility slowly bled power off the city's grid and stored it in its three backup generators. It also had its own HVAC unit complete with filters and radiation sensors to detect any poisonous emissions from the outside world.

The facility had been designed to survive, even if the entire building above him was obliterated. Hicks would still be able to operate for weeks before he would have to venture outside. He made sure he always had enough food, weapons, and equipment in the facility for such an eventuality. The Dean had originally called it overkill. But in a post-9/11 world, he had come to see it as a wise investment.

Hicks knew a fixed location was never fully secure, but the Twenty-Third Street facility was as close to secure as anyone could hope to get. He had never brought anyone there, not even Tali, though the idea had crossed his mind once or twice.

Once he finally sat at his desktop, Hicks checked OMNI to learn what he had missed in the two hours since his run in with Stephens.

He saw Jason had already directed OMNI to identify all cellular and Wi-Fi devices located in the immediate area of his altercation with Stephens on Nineteenth and Broadway.

Any image of the incident on any device or any footage uploaded to social media had already been subtly distorted by OMNI to obscure Hicks' identity. Deleting the images would have been easier, but it also would have created suspicion. Poor images meant the media would quickly lose interest. Tonight's film at eleven would be forgotten by lunchtime tomorrow.

Poor images would also make it more difficult for Stephens' people to see where he'd gone after the standoff.

Hicks was more concerned about where Stephens' van had gone after it sped away. He accessed OMNI's tracking display and overlaid the van's path on a street map of Manhattan.

He was impressed the van had managed to speed toward Manhattan's West Side Highway at a decent clip despite the sluggish rush hour traffic. The van had stopped briefly on Thirty-Ninth Street and Eleventh Avenue before it headed into the maze of streets leading to the Lincoln Tunnel. The van was currently parked at an old storage facility on the other side of the Hudson River in Weehawken, New Jersey.

Why the hell did they stop at Thirty-Ninth and Eleventh Avenue?

Hicks clicked on the tactical screen and saw Scott and his Varsity squad was already halfway to the tunnel on their way to Weehawken. University protocol dictated they would report in for further instructions once they were on site.

Next, he checked OMNI to see which Faculty Members and Adjuncts in the tristate area had checked in since Jason had issued the alert two hours before. Of the forty active Adjuncts and Faculty Members working in the city for the University, thirty-nine had checked in, including Tali Saddon.

Only one hadn't checked in. Roger Cobb.

Hicks wasn't worried. Roger would have seen that Jason had issued the alert. Roger had never liked Jason, and Jason had never liked him. Roger was already fed up with the University and its protocols, so his silence could be an act of rebellion. He had done this before.

But a Code Red was a rare event. Rebellion or not, he should have responded.

His silence made Hicks begin to make connections he hoped weren't real.

OMNI showed Stephens' van had stopped on Thirty-Ninth Street and Eleventh Avenue. Roger's club, The Jolly Roger, was on Thirty-Third Street between Eleventh and Twelfth Avenues. The van had stopped close by, but not outside Roger's club.

It was close, but not exact. And Roger hadn't checked in yet.

He had OMNI attempt to locate Roger's handheld device, but the search came up empty.

The University's handhelds had a much stronger signal than normal cell phones, so it should have registered somewhere, even in a subway tunnel, although he doubted Roger had been near a subway in over a decade.

Hicks tapped a coded text message directly to Roger's phone and waited for him to respond.

Sitting and watching the phone to buzz like a teenager waiting for his girlfriend to respond was a waste of time. With a long night behind him and the promise of an even longer day ahead, he decided he needed caffeine. Fast.

He pushed himself away from his desk, went to the kitchen area, and began to make a pot of coffee.

He scooped in the coffee grounds and filled the machine with water. He heard his desktop pinging from all the new messages he was receiving. He hoped one of them was from Roger.

But Hicks didn't allow himself to rush back to his computer.

He forced himself to stay in the kitchenette and watch the coffee brew. He hadn't meditated or performed his yoga routine in days. His mind now felt sluggish at a time when he needed to be sharper than he'd ever been before.

He knew he didn't have time for a yoga routine or a meditation session now, so he used these few quiet minutes to take in the aroma and watched the water slowly fill the pot. He fought to keep his mind blank and the Carousel of Concern from spinning. Brewing coffee was the task he was doing now. He had to remain focused on the task at hand and on all of the other individual tasks at hand in the hours and days to come.

He had already been out of touch from the University for over two hours. A few more minutes wouldn't matter. His mind required quiet balance and the simple act of making coffee was as close to it as he was likely to get.

Balance and planning would give him his best chance of staying ahead of the Barnyard. Balance would give him the clarity to avoid the jumbled confusion which led to mistakes.

The coffee machine began to gurgle. Hicks shut his eyes and slowly rolled his neck to keep himself from getting tense. He paused. He breathed. He remembered his training. Keep focused. Work the problems one by one. Move cautiously. Stay calm.

He waited until the coffee pot was full before pouring a cup. The desktop kept pinging as more messages came in. He brought his coffee with him as sat at his desk. He took a sip and began wading into the responses.

Tali Shaddon had sent him several messages even before Jason's alert went out. **I have not received the daily report on Bajjah's progress today. Has something happened? Please**

advise.

She had sent even more messages after the alert went out. **What happened? Is Bajjah safe? Should we move him to a secure location? We have resources in the area to make this happen. Please advise.**

He wanted to tell her Bajjah was safer now than he'd ever been in his life because the son of a bitch was dead. But the death of the terrorist she had come to view as her co-prisoner wasn't the kind of news delivered via text or an email. He would have to break the news to her when he gave her the redacted report on Bajjah's network. He hoped the personal touch might take some of the sting out of the bad news. For now, Tali's ignorance was bliss for Hicks.

Hicks scanned all of the messages he'd received in the last ten minutes, but none of them were from Roger. He hadn't replied to his text message. Something was wrong.

Stephens' van stopping so close to the Jolly Roger Club looked more ominous as the minutes passed.

He checked OMNI again to get a location on Roger's handheld, but still no luck. Hicks decided to call Roger directly. The phone rang until it went to voicemail. Another red flag. Hicks called him so rarely, he always picked up.

He waited a moment and dialed again. This time, a man answered.

"Hello?" It wasn't Roger's voice.

Hicks killed the connection and, from his desktop, immediately ran a trace on the location of Roger's handheld. The map showed Roger's signal had briefly overlapped with an old storage facility in Weehawken.

The same location of Stephens' white van.

Stephens had Roger.

While out in the field, Hicks needed an Operator to run complicated OMNI procedures he couldn't easily do from his handheld. But at his desktop, Hicks was as good as any Operator, if not better.

His fingers flew across the keyboard, opening an instant message window to Scott, the Dean, and Jason:

PRIORITY ONE ALERT. ROGER COBB IS IN DIA CUSTODY. LOCATION MATCHES SAME WEEHAWKEN FACILITY AS THE WHITE VAN. VARSITY SQUAD TO STAND BY ON SITE FOR FURTHER ORDERS.

Hicks opened Scott's tactical screen on OMNI. He wasn't surprised to see his team had already directed the OMNI satellite to begin a detailed scan of the Weehawken building. Scott and his Varsity boys loved kicking in doors, but they weren't cowboys. They never went through a door without knowing as much about what was on the other side as they could.

If Hicks had only followed their lead in Philly, none of this would be happening now.

He cut the regret short. He forgot about what could have been and worked the current problem instead.

Scott's thermal scan of the building showed it looked like an old warehouse because the readings on the top three floors of the building read black. No thermal signature at all, except from security cameras mounted on the roof to look down at the area below. It was an odd precaution for a building with three abandoned top floors.

Hicks began a frequency scan of the building, directing OMNI to filter out all of the usual noise from cell phones and Wi-Fi networks. He wanted it to focus on encrypted signals instead. The scan uncovered a weak signal pulsing far below all the others.

Hicks had OMNI lock on the signal, amplify and identify it. It was a double-encrypted internal network running throughout the building. It had been mask to read like a domestic network any small business might run. No household Wi-Fi setup was this tough to crack.

In seconds, OMNI identified the network as part of the same elaborate, secure system the NSA had used in other installations. And since OMNI could identify the signal, it could find a way through the firewalls and other measures.

Within minutes, OMNI had gained access to the warehouse network's main hub. He was able to get into the building's computer network infrastructure. He was surprised to find each part of the network had been clearly labeled: email servers, phone servers, and security cameras. It was a typical government operation. Hicks loved bureaucratic predictability.

He ignored the facility's emails and communications servers. He focused on the security cameras. Three floors appeared to be covered by an internal network. He began on the first floor and opened six camera feeds at a time on his monitor. He carefully eyeballed each one. He could have assigned OMNI to automatically identify Roger's face on the feeds, but it would take more load time and analysis than Roger might have.

The first floor cameras covered what appeared to be storage areas and loading bays. Hicks counted seven armed men milling around the loading bays. He counted five vehicles, including the white van from earlier that morning.

No sign of Roger.

Hicks checked the directory again and saw one set of

cameras was listed as L2. He opened those feeds next and saw those were the cameras located in the sub-basement.

The color images showed a dank basement where rows of fluorescent lights had been hung to give the hallways some illumination. A quick check of the camera feeds showed all the hallways were empty.

He switched to the feed labeled COMROOM and saw a room filled with advanced portable communications gear and a bank of desktops. It looked like a dressed down version of NASA's mission control room. Two agents were clicking away at keyboards. One was sipping coffee.

Hicks knew the equipment was too elaborate to have been set up overnight. Stephens and his people had been working out of this building for a while.

He struck gold when he opened the next six camera feeds. The feed from the camera labeled L207 showed Roger Cobb sitting in a steel chair at a steel table in the center of a gray cinderblock room.

A one-way mirror made little effort to hide it was there for observation purposes. Hicks searched the server for a camera in the observation room, but came up empty. All he found was a camera filming Roger through the one-way mirror.

Someone didn't want a record of whatever happened in there. Hicks understood why. He had never allowed cameras in any of his control rooms, either.

He went back to the feed from the camera in the upper corner of the interrogation room and analyzed the scene. Roger's right hand was handcuffed by a long chain cuffed to a thick bar installed along the edge of the table. It was similar to the chain prison guards used while transporting prisoners. The same kind of shackle they'd used to bring Bajjah up to the roof earlier that morning.

Using such a long shackle was a standard interrogation move. It gave the subject the illusion of freedom during an interrogation. It was also Stephens' first mistake. The chain was too long and Roger was ambidextrous. If someone got too close, he could use the chain to break someone's arm or snap someone's neck. Hicks hoped it wouldn't come to that.

Roger didn't look tense or nervous. He looked as passive and unassuming as he always did. He was fair-haired and small. His expression as inscrutable as it was blank. His eyes alert, but unfocused. He was like a blank canvas, but Hicks knew he was storing energy for whatever happened next.

Hicks caught movement at the bottom of the frame. Roger was drumming his fingers on the tabletop. It looked like mindless tapping of a song in his head, but Hicks saw it for what it was.

Morse code.

Morse code might have been a relic from the old days, but Roger had always been a history buff. The code was as effective now as it ever had been, which was why the Dean had insisted all Assets and Faculty members knew how to use it before going in the field.

Hicks zoomed in on his fingers, pulled over a pad and pen and began writing down the letters Roger tapped out on the table with his fingers. He knew Jason, the Dean and Scott also had access to his feed. They were watching this right now and probably doing the same thing. He was sure Scott was following the events as they happened. He wouldn't have been surprised if Jason emailed him to complain about Hicks focusing on Roger's twitchy fingers.

Hicks caught the tap in mid-code, but kept writing until Roger repeated the pattern. When he looked at the letters he'd written down, he saw a clear message:

GRABBED THREE BLOCKS FROM CLUB. BASTARDS WERE WAITING. COVERED MY HEAD IN VAN. THINK AM IN JERSEY. THINK ITS CIA. NOT HURT YET.

Hicks zoomed back out to get a full picture of the room. His desk phone buzzed and he saw it was Jason. "I see what you're looking at but I don't know Morse code. What does it say?"

Hicks told him.

"Good work," Jason said. "I'm glad you were able to decipher it. Let's hope our friends at the CIA don't catch on."

"They were smart enough to know where to grab him, so they're smart enough to see he's tapping in code." Hicks didn't know how they'd known where to grab him, but he'd worry about that later. "Let's hope they're not expecting anyone to hack their system."

Hicks checked OMNI's tactical screen on his other monitor and saw Scott and his team were about ten minutes out from Weehawken. The situation could go hot if Stephens tried hurting Roger. He wanted the Dean's approval before ordering Scott's men to hit the building.

He asked Jason, "Where is the Dean?"

"I haven't heard from him in hours," Jason admitted. "I'm worried. It's not like him to disappear in a crisis."

"He responded to my alert two hours ago. Try locating him on OMNI."

"I already tried," Jason said, "but no luck. Not even a blip anywhere on the system. Given what's happened with you and

Roger, we have to consider he's been compromised in some way."

Hicks couldn't afford to consider that. Losing Roger was bad enough, but if Stephens had the Dean, things would go from worse to the unthinkable.

Hicks shut his eyes and focused on his controlling his breathing, allowing all of the new facts to settle in his mind like snow on the ground.

Speed kills. So does inaction. Find balance. Work the problem. The solution will present itself.

Roger had been captured. The Dean was out of commission. Stephens had tried to grab him on the street. The Beekeeper and his people had been racking up points before Hicks had even known there was a game.

He opened his eyes.

Time to take back some momentum. To Jason, "We're going to do this without the Dean."

"Wait a minute. Let's not do anything rash. We don't have the authority to act on his behalf."

"I've got all the authority I need. One of our people is being held by the best Beekeeper in the DIA, and I've got a Varsity squad approaching five minutes away. I need to stop this thing before people get killed and the only person who can help me is you. If you want to argue about procedures, we can do that later, but for now, we need to act."

Jason surprised him by responding quickly. "Fine. What do you want me to do?"

"I need you to access the Dean's Black Book. Don't tell me you can't because I know goddamned well you can. Call some of his contacts at Langley who have the juice to cut Roger loose.

You were his Dutchman for over two years, so you know who to call better than I do."

"I'll try," Jason said, "but I can't guarantee they'll take the call. They never place a high priority on his calls and..."

"Just figure out a way to get someone on the line. Tell them it's about the Bajjah op they bungled. That ought to get their attention. Get them to pick up the phone and I'll take it from there."

Jason hesitated. "I'll see what I can do, but you've got to keep Scott from barging in there and causing a massacre. If people start shooting, I won't be able to do anything."

Hicks checked Scott's tactical screen again. His team was about five minutes away from the facility. "I'm more worried about Roger."

"Don't be," Jason said. "Stephens is a professional, remember? I doubt he'll hurt Roger so soon in the interrogation process."

"I'm not worried about that. I'm worried about Roger hurting Stephens. Get someone on the line for me. You have five minutes."

CHAPTER
12

O N HIS MONITOR, Hicks watched the door next to the observation mirror open and Mark Stephens walk into the interrogation room. Alone.

Now that they weren't threatening to shoot each other, Hicks got a better look at the DIA's best Beekeeper. He wore a black t-shirt and black cargo pants. His build was slightly more muscular than lean. His smooth head gleamed in the stark light of the interrogation room. He was darker skinned than Hicks had remembered from the street and didn't have a goatee. He didn't need one. Deep-set eyes and angular cheekbones made him look intimidating enough.

Hicks saw the psychological lines Stephens was already drawing as he entered the cell. The holster clipped on the left side of his belt was empty. He could have unclipped it with his gun and left it in the other room, but hadn't. He'd moved it around from the back of his belt to the side so Roger could see it was empty. He wanted Roger to see he could have been armed, but had chosen not to be. Force perceived was force achieved.

Stephens also chose to lean against the wall instead of taking a seat at the table. This implied freedom of movement on his part, and therefore his power over Roger, who was chained to the table.

These were subtleties meant to influence the subject. Stephens clearly didn't know Roger Cobb.

Roger hadn't moved when Stephens entered his cell. Even his fingers had stopped in mid-tap, but his shackled arm remained outstretched on the table. There was plenty of slack to the chain.

"Hello again," Stephens began. "Things were too chaotic back on the street for you and me to have a formal introduction. How about you show some good faith by giving us your name?"

Roger remained still. He didn't even blink. *Good boy*, Hicks thought. *Keep your fucking mouth shut and wait for the cavalry to arrive. Scott is close. Jason is working back channels. Ride this out and we'll all get well in a little while.*

Stephens snapped his fingers near Roger's face. Roger didn't budge or blink.

"Guess you're not talkative today," Stephens said. "Calm, cool, and collected under pressure. Staying quiet and biding your time until your friends figure out a way to spring you loose. Well you're not going anywhere because your friends don't know where you are. No one's kicking in the door or making a phone call or beaming you out of here, little man, because the only one who can get you out of here is the same guy who put you here." He pointed his thumb at his own chest. "Me. And the longer you stall, the more pissed off I'll get. We're being civil now, but unless you talk, it won't stay that way."

Roger didn't move. He sat loose, like an old rag doll waiting to be picked up.

"That's a good strategy," Stephens went on. "Stay quiet for now and get a good rest. You're going to need it because I see through your bullshit, little man. I already know exactly who and what you are."

Hicks cringed when he saw Roger's right eyebrow arch as he finally made eye contact with Stephens. "Is that so?"

Fucking Roger. He could never keep his mouth shut.

"Sure do. I've been doing my homework on you. Still a couple of blanks to fill in, but enough to get started."

"No, you don't." Roger's eyes slowly moved along Stephens' body, head to toe and back again. "You put on a good front— convincingly butch, by the way—but I think you're bluffing. Because if you knew who and what I was, you'd also know I'm more trouble to you than I'm worth. If you knew who I was, you'd be taking these cuffs off me, opening those doors, and calling me a cab back to the city. You'd forget you'd ever seen me and be thankful for the opportunity to do so."

Stephens folded his arms across his chest as he leaned against the wall. "Now why in the world would I want to do that?"

Roger looked at Stephens' folded arms. "Interesting. You've taken a defensive posture meant to convey power and ease in an interrogation. It's supposed to challenge the suspect to be more truthful by implying disbelief. But such a gesture a following a threatening statement from a suspect?" Roger sucked his teeth. "That's a defensive measure. If you'd sat down, it would've appeared to be more like a conversation, like you were holding all the cards. Instead, you crossed your arms and leaned against the wall. Pity. I was under the impression you people were trained better."

The black man looked at him. "You people?"

"Oh, don't get racial on me so quickly. You know what I meant." Roger winked. "Buzz, buzz."

Stephens unfolded his arms. Hicks could see the subtle Beekeeper reference had gotten to him. "You're doing a lot of talking, but you're still not saying much, little man. Let's try this again. Who are you?"

Roger threw up his hands, feigning frustration. "Now you've hit the reset button too soon into the interrogation process. You're supposed to ignore my parry, keep me talking so I slip up and give you the opportunity to catch some small detail. Instead, you backed off and asked me the same question all over again. Poor soul. You're not having a good day, are you? One frustration after another."

Roger's eyes moved over Stephens' face. "Yes, there it is. I can see it now. The unease. The insecurity. You don't hide it well at all. You're insecure about this whole scenario because you're not sure how deep the rabbit hole goes, or if there's even a rabbit hole at all."

He raised his chained hand. "So let's do each other a big favor. Unlock these chains and call me a cab and I'll be on my way. I think we can agree your ego has taken enough of a beating for one day."

Stephens looked like he might be considering it. "Anything else you want?"

"A hand job would be nice, but your hands look a little rough for me, so I'll settle for a cup of coffee while I wait for the cab. Don't want to push my luck."

Hicks watched Stephens laugh, but there was no humor in it. Hicks knew Roger was baiting him, trying to get Stephens to lose his temper. Maybe take a swing at him so he could grab him and use him as a hostage to bargain his way out of there. It was a dangerous play, but the only play Roger believed he had.

Hicks checked Scott's tactical screen again. Three minutes out. He emailed Jason: **ANYTHING YET? HURRY.**

Stephens stopped laughing. "We work on the merit system around here, little man. A prisoner has to earn the privileges we give him. So, you tell me your name, the cuffs come off. You tell me more about you, we get you something to drink. You answer all of my questions, we talk about the possibility of you going home. See how it works?"

Roger looked up at the ceiling. "Sorry, babe, but that doesn't work for me. And soon, you're going to find out it's not going to work for you either."

Hicks tensed as he waited for Stephens to backhand Roger. He checked his other screen for Scott's ETA on the facility. Still three minutes out. He checked to see if Jason had been able to contact anyone in the Dean's Black Book. Nothing yet.

Hicks watched Stephens pull out a small remote control fob from his pocket. He pushed a button and the two-way mirror became a monitor.

Hicks almost gasped when the image of a much younger Roger Cobb appeared on the screen. It was a photo attached to an old passport application dated more than twenty-five years before. Roger's hair was much darker in his youth and parted in the middle. His face was much fuller and kinder. His eyes were softer because they hadn't seen as much of the world yet.

Stephens clicked the remote and an Ohio driver's license appeared on the screen. "That's you, isn't it? Fletcher Geoffrey Schmidt of Toledo, Ohio."

Hicks stared at the image on the screen. Stephens had discovered Roger's real name. His old identity. How the hell did he get that?

Hicks watched Roger glance at the image of the license, his expression as passive as before. "Sorry, brother man. I know all white people look the same to you, but that's not me. I've never been so fucking...plain."

"Sure it is." Stephens tapped the remote again and images of several documents appeared on the screen. College transcripts. A student loan application. And something Hicks had never seen in Roger's file: a divinity degree from The Virginia Theological Seminary.

Hicks looked at Roger to see if watching his long buried past flash across a computer screen had any effect on him. It hadn't. He looked like he was in the waiting room of a doctor's office, thumbing through a travel magazine.

Stephens showed more images. Grammar school and high school year book photos. "The digital age is a hell of a thing, Fletcher. They're easy to search and even easier to manipulate. That's why I'm old school. I love libraries, old books and record rooms filed to the ceiling with files. Every book in every box on every shelf is part of someone's life story and I love a good story. That's how I found out about you, Fletch. I dug, baby. And I came up with you."

Roger demurred. "Now you're being silly. We both know

nothing on that screen could have led you to me. Someone fed you a bunch of old pictures the way they feed fish to a trained seal at the zoo. But where the seal gets a meal, all you got was duped. You're being played for a fool, Mr. Stephens, but you don't seem to mind. So flap your flippers and maybe your master will throw you another fish. Maybe balance a ball on your nose." Roger grinned. "Now that could be fun."

Stephens wasn't as good at hiding surprises as Roger. The DIA man took a step away from the wall. "How did you know my name?"

"Because I already know who you are, little man, and if you're recording this, you might want to stop because I don't know how much of your past you'll want your colleagues in the other room to learn about you. You Beekeepers and your secrets. Buzz, buzz."

Hicks watched Stephens toss the remote on the table as he took another step closer to Roger. "We aren't here to talk about me, Fletcher. We're here to talk about you and your friends."

"Nonsense. Why waste time talking about me when you're far more interesting." Roger folded his hands in front of him on the table. "Last name Stephens; first name Mark. A phony handle, but bland enough to not stick out in one's memory, which is the point. Your real name is Richard Morales and you're thirty-five years old, though the bald head and darker skin makes it tougher for people to gauge your age and Caribbean origin." He winked again. "Obfuscation comes in handy in this line of work, doesn't it, jefe? Mom and Dad back in Oakland were so proud of their baby boy. How you went to Caltech and Air Force ROTC at the same time. First in your family to even graduate high school, much less college."

Roger sighed. "Bet they would've been proud of you if they'd been allowed to know what you did there, but alas, national security supersedes sentimentality, doesn't it, Ricky?"

The long chain on Roger's right wrist rattled as he leaned forward on the steel table, bringing his head closer to Stephens. "Does it ever bother you, Richard? How your parents scrimped and saved all those years and worked all those dead-end jobs to send you to school only to have you lie to them for all these years? I'd imagine it makes the victory of accomplishment seem hollow. Keeping secrets from Dad must be especially difficult. I know his approval has always been so important to you."

Hicks watched Stephens' jaw clench. He didn't move toward Roger, but he was getting close. Which was what Roger wanted, and what Hicks needed to avoid.

Hicks tapped out another message to Jason. **DID YOU FIND ANYONE?**

Jason's response was immediate. **HOLD.**

But Hicks knew Roger would keep taunting Stephens until he made him lose his temper and make a mistake could turn a dangerous situation deadly.

Roger kept pushing. "I can't blame you for keeping it from them. I mean, what would Mama and Papi say if they knew their son tortured people for a living? Anything you'd tell them is mostly classified anyway, right? Tales of scaring the piss out of some poor hajji in Kabul tends to kill the yuletide spirit around the Christmas tree, does it?"

Hicks watched Stephens swallow and clench his fists at his sides. He was taking it, but wouldn't take much more. Hicks typed a new message to Jason: **HURRY UP**

Roger didn't let up. "Shame your parents believe you're a

bachelor working for an energy company in Houston. Mom wishes you'd meet a nice girl and have some kids. She's getting on in years and wants a grandchild to spoil." Roger sucked his teeth. "Why haven't you told them about Marsha and the girls, anyway? Is it because she's white or..."

Hicks watched Stephens step forward as he fired a short left hook at Roger's head. Roger moved his head back enough so that the punch missed.

But Roger used Stephens' own momentum against him by flipping the chain behind the agent's neck and slamming his head down onto the edge of the steel table.

Hicks brought his fist down on his own desk. *Fucking Roger.*

The cell door burst open and two men Hicks hadn't seen before took up position—Glocks aimed in Roger's direction. But Roger had already wrapped the long chain of his handcuffed right wrist around Stephens' neck. He laid his face against Stephens' left cheek, presenting as low a profile as possible in case someone began shooting.

"One more step," Roger said, "and I tighten this chain. You shoot, I'll drop to the floor and snap your buddy's neck."

Hicks watched the camera feed as the two men held back but held their ground. "You hurt him, and there's no way you walk out of here."

Roger grinned from behind his hostage. "Want to bet? Check your phones. See if anyone emailed or called."

Neither of them moved. The one on the right said, "You're not giving the orders here, asshole."

Roger yanked down on the chain hard enough to make Stephens cry out. "Sounds like Agent Stephens begs to differ. Check your fucking phones."

Hicks saw a heavy set man in a button down shirt step out of the observation room holding a phone to his ear. Hicks watched him walk back into the room behind the mirrored glass.

An instant message appeared on Hicks' own screen from Jason: **PICK UP YOUR PHONE WHEN IT RINGS. THIS IS YOUR SHOW NOW. YOU NEED TO UN-FUCK THIS.**

Hicks answered his phone as soon it buzzed. Jason didn't give him a chance to say anything. "I am the only one on this call who knows both parties on this line. For all of our sakes, we should keep specific identities private so we can come to..."

"Fuck private," the other man on the line bellowed. The echo sounded in the surveillance audio and Hicks knew it was the same fat man who was in the interrogation room with Roger. Hicks muted the feed before the fat man heard the feedback and figured out his cameras had been tapped.

The fat man ranted. "This is John Avery of the DIA. Somebody has been back-biting my operation from the beginning. Spiking my surveillance, fucking with my systems, attacking my agents and now this. I'm not promising anyone a goddamned thing until I know who I'm dealing with and what they're up to."

"You already know who you're dealing with," Hicks said. "You're dealing with people who know any move you're going to make before you make it. You're dealing with people you can't define and can't take down. This is the point in the story where a smart man backs off and regroups before he gets his people killed."

"Sounds like you're the one who doesn't know who you're dealing with, asshole. I've got my men sweating somebody right now. Somebody who I'd bet my pension on being one of your people. No one's laid a finger on him yet, but that can change in a heartbeat on my say-so. Unless I get some names to go with voices, I'll treat your boy like he's the enemy and you sure as hell don't want that."

Hicks resisted the urge to tell Avery he was watching Stephens get strangled to death in his own interrogation chamber. They'd cut the feed the second they had any idea it had been compromised.

Besides, Avery's bruised ego was all the leverage Hicks needed. "All you need to know is we've been playing defense until now and we've won each time. If you don't release the man you're holding right now, we go on offense. And, believe me, Ace, you're not going to like that. You're going to like explaining the aftermath to your bosses even less."

Hicks could practically hear Avery redden through the phone. "I don't like being threatened."

An empty comeback. Hicks knew he already had him turned. There was no reason to push the knife in any deeper.

He checked Scott's tactical screen. He and his Varsity squad were now less than two minutes out. "So let's call this off and save ourselves a hell of a lot of trouble and embarrassment. A black SUV will be outside your facility in two minutes. You're going to let your prisoner get into the SUV and drive away. You will not harm him and you will not attempt to follow or track him in any way. If you do, we'll know it and there will be consequences."

"You don't know where we are and there's no way in hell he goes free," Avery said. "I'll put a bullet in his brain before I let him go."

"Don't think of it as letting him go. Think of it as a way of building some good will between your group and mine. You can still cover up all the fuck ups your people made today as long as your prisoner is in my SUV in two minutes."

"And if he's not?"

"Then you're going to be calling a lot of widows tonight. And my next call will be to the media. I bet they'll enjoy seeing a building full of spies scrambling to pull up stakes in Weehawken."

"Weehawken", Avery repeated. "How the hell did you..."

Hicks didn't give him the benefit of an answer. "Some decisions are tough, Ace. This isn't one of them."

He glanced at the tactical screen and saw Scott was two minutes out. "You have two minutes. Now, put my man on the phone."

Hicks looked at the feed from Roger's cell. Roger still had Stephens pinned to the table. Although the feed was still muted, the men appeared to be still yelling at Roger, but hadn't lowered their weapons.

He hoped Avery bought his bluff.

He saw Avery trudge back into the frame. He was holding out his cell phone to Roger.

Roger motioned for him to put the phone on the table and slide it over. The fat man did as he was told. The phone bumped into Stephens' shoulder. Hicks watched Stephens squirm when Roger put weight on the taught chain as he stretched to pick up the phone.

He brought the phone to his ear and gave his confirmed allclear sign. "Hello, mother. This is Norman. How are you doing? You looked a bit drawn the last time I saw you."

Hicks knew the DIA would be recording the call, so he kept

the details to a minimum. "Keep your mouth shut and you're out of there in two minutes. Do what they tell you to do, and don't make anything worse."

"Yes, dear. Do you want to talk to the nice man again?"

He watched Roger flick the phone back to the fat man who trapped it against his chest. He saw Roger smile as he whispered into Stephens' ear before he took the chain off his neck and shoved him off the table. One agent holstered his weapon and helped Stephens off the floor. The other agent kept his gun trained on him.

Hicks watched the fat man bring the phone up to his ear as he walked out of the room. "You satisfied?"

"I'll be satisfied when he's in the car and driving away. Afterwards, I'll be in touch."

Hicks killed the connection and took the feed off mute. He watched both agents help Stephens get up from the floor while Avery unlocked Roger's handcuffs. Hicks goosed the audio and listened in.

Roger rubbed the circulation back into his wrist while the fat man said, "Get your ass upstairs and out of my building before I change my mind. And if I ever see you again, I'm putting a bullet in your brain."

Hicks expected Roger to have some kind of comeback. He was glad Roger kept his mouth shut and simply walked out of the room.

Via the security cameras, Hicks tracked Roger's progress down the hall and up the stairs. The facility's P.A. system kicked on and the fat man's voice echoed over the feed. "This is Avery. The suspect is free to leave. All forces stand down. Do not intercept. Do not follow. Let him go."

Hicks tracked Roger as he called Scott. The Varsity man picked up immediately. "I've been tracking the whole thing on tactical. We're twenty seconds out. We're within sight of the building."

"Get Roger in the car and get the hell out of there. If you see you're being followed, take evasive action and defend yourselves as necessary."

"Got it. And Hicks. I heard the whole thing. That was some cowboy shit you pulled in there. Good job."

Hicks watched the satellite feed and saw the SUV skid to a stop in front of the warehouse. He saw Roger walk outside the warehouse and climb into the back of the SUV and drive away. No one from the building seemed to be following. They were most likely tracking the SUV by satellite, but that was Scott's problem. The Varsity had backup cars in underground parking facilities nearby. He had made a career of beating covert surveillance.

Hicks killed the hack into the facility's system before Avery's people could trace it back to OMNI. There were countermeasures in place to make such traces difficult, but not necessarily impossible, especially for the Barnyard folks. Best not to tempt fate.

He'd already done that enough for one day.

A new window appeared on Hicks' screen. It was an instant message from Jason: **WE NEED TO DEBRIEF AND COME UP WITH AN IMMEDIATE ACTION PLAN. AVERY IS NOT SOMEONE WHO MAKES THREATS LIGHTLY.**

Hicks already had an immediate action plan.

He ran into the bathroom and threw up.

CHAPTER 13

HICKS GARGLED SOME mouthwash and spat it into the sink. It killed some of the taste of the bile, but not all of it. All the mouthwash in the world couldn't do that.

He looked at his reflection in the mirror and didn't like what he saw. It wasn't because of the unkempt hair or the bags forming beneath his blood-shot eyes or the paleness of his skin.

It was because he had just threatened the Barnyard. He had gone toe-to-toe with the American intelligence complex. He had come out ahead, gotten his man out alive, but it felt like a loss.

Men like Avery weren't his enemy. Neither was Stephens. They weren't traitors or spies or greedy men looking to profit from the deaths of others.

Both men were patriots, good men doing their job, working

for the same goals as the University, to keep this country safe. Hicks knew he should be trying to recruit a man like Stephens to the University, not fighting him or threatening him. The country had enough enemies outside its borders. It couldn't afford infighting among the people who were supposed to keep it safe.

Hicks understood the Dean's argument about evading the other agencies until they could use Jabbar as a bargaining chip. He understood it, but didn't agree with it. His strategy was making an already complicated situation even worse. Until now, Stephens and his people had been curious about who had abducted Bajjah. Now Hicks had made them look foolish twice in as many days. A career bureaucrat like Avery would be looking for revenge. And Stephens wouldn't allow Roger's attack to go unanswered.

He gargled another slug of mouthwash and spat it out.

He didn't know how Stephens had found him on the street earlier that morning. Maybe they had gotten lucky by accessing a security camera he'd walked by and had a go team in the vicinity. It had happened before.

But finding Roger was more of a mystery. Roger hadn't been with Hicks when he grabbed Bajjah down in Philadelphia. There was no reason why they should have known who Roger was or what he looked like, much less where to find him.

Something didn't make sense.

He wished the Dean had helped our during this crisis. His expertise would be invaluable right now and help him cut through all of the doubt flooding his mind. Maybe after this incident with Roger, the Dean would change his mind about keeping the Bajjah information within the University, though he doubted it. The Dean never made snap decisions, so changing his mind wasn't easy. Nothing about this life ever was.

He wanted to get over to The Jolly Roger Club as soon as possible to debrief Roger. He knew Avery and Stephens wouldn't hang around for long now their facility had been discovered. Any detail Roger could tell him about the abduction event and the Weehawken facility could be vital.

Hicks kept looking at his reflection in the mirror and knew he had to make a change. Not only in his tactics, but in his general appearance. The Barnyard knew exactly what he looked like. Their facial recognition programs were powerful, but not foolproof. He decided to make their job more difficult.

Since he didn't have any hair dye on hand, he grabbed his trimmer, set it to the second-lowest level, and began to sheer off his hair. The trimmer left a thin layer of stubble on his scalp, which should be enough to throw off any of Stephens' men trying to eyeball him. He also cropped his eyebrows, lathered up and shaved off the stubble on his face. He looked cleaner and squared away, a far cry from the shaggy man Stephens had been hunting. It gave him a more military look than he would have preferred, but given his options, he didn't have much choice. He hoped it would be enough to buy him some time.

He took a quick shower and changed his clothes. Knowing Stephens would be looking for someone in a sweatshirt and jeans, he put on a gray suit and white shirt. He skipped the tie. He took a gray raincoat out of his closet and put it on. He hoped the loose coat might give Stephens' men pause if they tried to grab him again. They would have to consider he might have a shotgun under the coat, which should be enough to give them pause, hopefully enough of a pause to give themselves away again. He popped on a pair of black sunglasses which he knew should be enough to throw off any recognition program scans of his face. He'd still register as a probable match, but it wouldn't be an exact hit. With an angry intelligence complex on his heels, his life might hinge on such margins.

He also pocketed two extra speed loaders for the Ruger, which should make those margins a bit wider.

He opened the hatch and walked through the false basement. He'd always found comfort in the hiss of the hatch automatically locking behind him.

He stopped on the staircase when he heard something he had never heard before.

Someone knocking on the front door of the apartment.

Hicks pulled out his handheld and activated the facility's external camera to see who it was.

His visitor was a man he had known for almost half of his life, but had only met for the first time two weeks before. A black man, about sixty years old and clean-shaven. His brown coat was a bit too big on him now, but looked as if it had fit him well at one time. A brown ski cap sat high on his head, revealing he was bald underneath it. He didn't know if the man had always been bald or if it was the result of the chemotherapy treatments.

Despite knowing this man for over twenty years, Hicks didn't know his real name, where he was from, if he was married or had any children.

In fact, the only thing Hicks knew about this man was the title the University had given him: The Dean.

THE DEAN LOOKED at him for a moment. "You cleaned yourself up. Good. I was going to suggest a change in appearance. I should have known you would have done so on your own."

Hicks shut the door. "We've been worried about you, sir."

But the Dean ignored the question. "I know you must be surprised to see me here, but since I authorized funding for this place, I decided it was time for me to see it with my own two eyes."

Hicks didn't care about where the Dean was now. He cared about where he had been. "Where have you been, sir? A lot has happened today, and it's not safe for you to be walking around by yourself."

"I know. In fact, I know more about what happened today than you do. I have been following everything as it happened on this." He held up a handheld device a bit larger than the standard University model. "I designed this unit myself. It allows me to track the entirety of the OMNI system right from the palm of my hand."

Hicks didn't care about a new handheld device, either. "So why didn't you respond when Jason tried to contact you, sir? We needed you today."

"No, James, you only thought you did. You proved my irrelevance by your own actions. In fact, proving your own abilities to yourself was the point of the entire exercise and the reason why I am here now."

"Exercise? What exercise, sir?"

The Dean lowered himself into an overstuffed chair next to the bookcase. A thin cloud of dust went into the air, which made him cough. "You need to get this place cleaned, James, and soon. I encountered less dust in Afghanistan." He gestured toward one of the dining room chairs. "Please, take a seat."

But Hicks remained standing. "What exercise are you talking about, sir?"

The Dean began pulling off his gloves one finger at a time. "The exercise I had to run in advance of my departure. The exercise that was my final lesson to you."

Hicks didn't like the direction the conversation was taking. "What lesson, sir?"

The Dean finished removing his gloves. "You do remember I informed you I was dying."

"Of course I remember."

"Since our last meeting two weeks ago, I have been a patient at Memorial Sloane Kettering here in Manhattan. Their best physicians conducted every test known to modern medicine and, despite their best efforts, their result matched those of the other doctors I have visited in other parts of the world. My condition is advanced to the point of being terminal."

Hicks had felt compassion when he'd first learned of the man's condition two weeks before. Now, all he felt was the heat spreading through his body. "What exercise are you talking about, sir?"

The Dean held up a hand. "Since chemotherapy would only prolong the inevitable and rob me of whatever dignity I have left, I have decided to end my life on my own terms. Tomorrow, to be precise. My reasons for the quick time frame are my own. And although our organization does not have many customs or ceremonies, it does have one: a new Dean must be in place before my departure or demise. You have inquired about the exercise I mentioned earlier. I needed to be certain my replacement was up to the task of being Dean. A real world exercise would test his mettle in the harshest conditions. Fortunately, for his sake and the sake of the University, my candidate passed with flying colors."

He smiled. "Congratulations, James. I have decided to select you as my replacement as Dean."

Heat continued to spread through his body. He grabbed the top of the dining room chair for support. He didn't care about the promotion or the title or even that his mentor had told him he would be committing suicide tomorrow.

"You were behind all of this from the beginning, weren't you? You're the reason Stephens found me."

"Hardly," the Dean said. "I may be crafty, but I am not evil. Stephens tracked you to New York on his own. But as soon as we used OMNI to thwart the Barnyard's surveillance of you, it alerted Stephens and Avery to the realization they were hunting someone who had not only grabbed their target and killed his cell, but also had technical means at their disposal. This is why they made the independent decision to send Stephens and his team to New York to hunt you down and bring you in for questioning."

Hicks felt the presence of the Ruger beneath his left arm. He became aware of the options it gave him. Options he had never considered until learning of the Dean's betrayal. "And you let them."

"I was in no position to stop them," the Dean admitted. "But after I saw how vehemently you disagreed with my decision to keep the Bajjah/Jabbar information from the Barnyard, I decided you and Roger needed to witness the true nature of the Barnyard for yourselves. So, I tracked you on OMNI, waited until you were both far enough away from the safe house and your respective destinations, and used back channels to tell Stephens where you both could be found. His ability to mobilize so quickly surprised me. He threw it together at the last minute, and it almost paid off."

Hicks felt his left hand ball into a fist. "You told him where we were? You told him where to find us?"

"Yes, I did, and I hope you are not expecting an apology. I had to be sure you were ready to become the Dean, so a real-world demonstration of what is at stake seemed to be appropriate."

But Hicks was still processing the abduction. "You told them about Roger's past."

The Dean waived it off. "Such information was nothing more than the worm on the hook to get Stephens to bite. None of it can lead him to Roger now. Roger had his fingerprints altered long ago and those on file from his youth have also been significantly altered. There is no way Stephens or anyone else can draw a distinction between the Fletcher of yesteryear and the Roger Cobb of today. As I said before, James, I might be crafty, but I am not evil."

Hicks gripped the chair harder to prevent his hand from shaking. "What did you give them on me?"

"Nothing that can lead them to the James Hicks of today, I assure you."

He felt the wood of the dining room chair begin to creak under his weight. "Your assurances don't mean shit anymore." He stopped squeezing the chair and stood on his own. "I'm going to ask this one more time. What did you give them on me?"

The Dean looked down at the gloves he had placed in his lap. "Old files from your youth. Pictures of you and your parents at your father's skydiving school, but nothing more. I did not give him your real name and certainly not your military records. A crafty man like Stephens could have found a way to use them to trace who you are now." He looked up at Hicks. "You have nothing to worry about, James. Your parents were the only family you had and they are long dead anyway. The remainder of your family is either distant or dead. You do not have anyone who can be used as leverage against you. Such circumstances make you ideal for this kind of work. Such qualities are the reasons why you will be the next Dean."

Hicks flipped the dining room chair aside before he realized he'd done it. Dealing with the present was bad enough. Now he had to contend with someone knowing about his past. "You took one hell of a risk with our lives. Someone could've gotten killed. Me or Stephens or one of his men or Roger. They could've begun torturing Roger before I was able to stop them."

"I admit it was a risk, but as you know well, risks come with this kind of work. I took no joy in what I did, but I had to make sure you understood the threat Stephens and his ilk posed to us before I named you as my replacement."

"This was about your fucking legacy?"

"This was about the University, James. Our mission is far too important for me to leave to chance. I am dying and there is nothing I can do to stop it. I needed to be certain I was leaving this institution in the best possible hands. I needed to know you understood the Barnyard and their ilk pose as much of a threat to the University as the KGB did back during the Cold War."

"Bullshit. We've worked with them in the past. You've handled them in the past."

"Yes, but only to a point. You have never been much

of a memo reader, James. Men like you need to experience something firsthand in order to truly appreciate it for what it is. You needed to see for yourself the lengths to which men like Stephens and Avery would go. I can understand why. Trusting in the perceived paranoid ranting of a dying old man never did anyone much good."

The Dean went on. "Your success in breaking Bajjah proves the Jabbar organization is an active global threat the nature of which we are only beginning to grasp. We need time to investigate such a threat before we consider sharing information with the bureaucrats in Washington. We must keep dodging men like Stephens and Avery until we get a clearer picture of the Jabbar operation. You saw how they reacted when they learned where you and Roger were located. They could have approached you another way. They could have attempted to open a dialogue with either or both of you. Instead, they attempted to grab you at gunpoint and interrogate you like common criminals."

The Dean leaned forward in the seat and appeared to grow ten years younger as he did. "You cannot bargain or reason with them, James. Not on this. Not when it comes to Jabbar. Stephens and his people would not go after Jabbar until they knew where our leads came from. It would require them to waste valuable time investigating the University instead of Jabbar. Stephens and Avery and the bureaucrats who pull their strings would not rest until they knew everything about our organization and its abilities. They would not stop until they had brought every byte of information OMNI has ever generated under their control. Or worse, divided our resources among the various agencies."

The Dean pounded the armrest of his chair, sending up another small puff of dust. "The University has proven itself far too important to have it parceled out among bickering bureaucrats like a horde of jackals pulling apart a gazelle. And we cannot allow our mission to be hindered by the staffer of some elected official who happens to be on the Senate Intelligence Oversight Committee in Washington. You know I am right, James. And after today, you have seen the intention of our enemies within our own community."

He had been angry with the Dean in the past. They had disagreed before, even to the point where Hicks was sure there was an excellent chance he might lose his position or maybe even his life. But this was different. This wasn't a disagreement about funding an operation or killing a target. This was deeper and more complex. The Dean had betrayed him. He had betrayed Roger. And he had done it for a reason.

"Does Stephens or Avery know I work for the University?"

"I doubt Stephens even knows the University exists. Avery may have heard whispers and rumors over the years, but not even his superiors—to whom I spoke—know much about us. I think you will find obscurity can be a comfort for you now you are the Dean."

There it was again, yet another event that should have been the highlight of his career lost in the mess of the Barnyard and Jabbar. His elevation to Dean of the University.

Hicks had never spent much time dwelling on his career. He had always been happy as a field man, running operations that generated actionable intelligence. He liked overseeing the corruption of influential people who could become permanent sources of information. He liked ordering Ringmasters and Snake Charmers to seduce those who needed to be corrupted in order to feed the University vital intelligence. He didn't even mind the occasional bit of wet work when necessary.

Field work was the only kind of work Hicks had ever been good at. It was the only life he had ever known or wanted.

Which was why he said, "Get someone else, sir. I don't want the fucking job. I'm busy enough as it is."

"Your reluctance makes you the best person for the job. Duty rarely comes at the time and manner of our choosing, James. There are plenty of people who would want this position. There are some in our organization who have crafted their entire careers in the hopes they might get this position one day. You are not one of those people. You remain focused on the mission, which is something a Dean must do."

He held out his handheld device to him. "When I became Dean, the future of the University was in technology. I helped bring the future to this institution." He looked again at the Ruger in the holster beneath Hicks' left arm. "Now, we need someone to defend the future I helped create. A field man. You."

Hicks looked at the device for a long time. His anger with the Dean had died down. Everything the man had said had been right, even if he didn't like the way he'd made his point.

He may not have given any thought to being Dean before, but as the Dean he could affect some of the changes he'd been thinking about. Changes like sharing the Jabbar information with Stephens in exchange for the Barnyard leaving the University alone.

Hicks took the Dean's handheld. "It's heavier than my handheld."

"Because it has more power and connectivity than any other device in service. Typing is still a challenge, but you will adapt. The connectivity is faster, too. Not as fast as our desktops, but on par with our laptops. You can run scans, compile profiles, access Faculty emails and locations, and almost anything else you need to run the organization. You will also have override authority on any operation in the OMNI system anywhere in the world."

But Hicks barely heard anything the Dean had said. His head was still spinning from learning of the Dean's betrayal. It was still spinning from the realization he was now the man in charge of The University.

"There is something else you will need in addition to that device." The Dean took a yellowed envelope from the inside pocket of his coat and handed it to Hicks. "It may very well be the most important document the University possesses. You should keep it secure in your safe until the time comes for you to select your replacement."

Hicks could see the envelope had been sealed at one time, but now the flap was simply tucked inside it. "What is it?"

"Open it and see for yourself."

Hicks removed the letter from the envelope and unfolded it. If the letterhead at the top of the stationary wasn't enough to give him pause, the signature at the bottom of the paper was. He had to read it twice to make sense of it, then looked up at the Dean. "Is this real?"

"Real, binding and legal, as several Attorneys General can attest to," the Dean said. "You are holding an executive order from President Dwight D. Eisenhower himself, establishing the organization known as the 'University of International Intelligence' as falling under the influence of the National Security Council. The order was deemed classified as soon as it was signed."

Since joining the University years before, Hicks had periodically asked his various superiors about the origins of the organization. He had asked about who started it and why. No one had ever given him a straight answer and he'd never cared enough to push the issue. He knew the organization must have had some kind of formal standing, since he had seen the University extricate its agents from numerous legal situations throughout the world. He had also seen it use its influence to get other intelligence organizations to either cooperate or leave them alone, depending on the need at the time.

The document he now held in his hand explained why. "I never knew."

"You were never been Dean before, so there was no need for you to know until now. President Eisenhower had a healthy distrust of what he referred to as the Military Industrial Complex. He also had reservations about how powerful a centralized intelligence organization may become one day. That is why a few of the founding members of the original Office of Strategic Services convinced him to establish us via executive order. As it was an unfunded mandate, we have never been listed in any budgets and this classified document has mostly been forgotten by history."

Dozens of questions flooded Hicks' mind at once, but he boiled them down to the most important one. "Who else in the Community knows about this?"

"Not many," the Dean admitted. "As secrecy has always been among our greatest assets, we have used it sparingly. There have been times when some Deans have had to produce it to keep other agencies at bay. Some directors have respected it, while others have sought to have it deemed irrelevant. Some directors have decided to ignore it all together. The current director of the Barnyard long ago decided the document had no merit."

"But what about congressional oversight? The intelligence committees…"

The Dean answered him before he could finish the question. "As a self-funding organization, we have been able to avoid wrangling in the muck with the other agencies for funding. And no funding means less interest in oversight, especially when it comes to a document that has been largely forgotten by history."

"Why haven't any of the other agencies tried to use this against us?"

"Because they have benefitted from the intelligence we have gathered for them," the Dean explained. "And shining light on our existence would make their lives much more difficult. I am only sorry I was unable to use that order to force the other agencies to leave us alone in our quest for Jabbar, but like I said, the current director of the Barnyard views that document as a relic."

Hicks folded the letter and put it back in the envelope. He noticed his hand shook a little bit. "Jesus, sir. This is a hell of a lot to digest in one day."

"As Dean, I am afraid you will find there is a hell of a lot to digest every day. That is why you will need to appoint a Dutchman to help you run the operation smoothly, or as smoothly as an operation such as this can hope to run. I know you despise Jason. Believe me, he has no great admiration for you, either."

"Jason's an asshole."

"Perhaps, but a most capable one. What he lacks in personality and field experience, he more than makes up for in his abilities as an administrator. Given all the challenges our organization is facing, it may be wise to have a seamless transition." The man smiled. "But my opinion no longer matters. You are in charge now. You are the Dean. You decide the course the University takes."

The new handheld had a sense of permanence to it, of authority. Like the Ruger under his left arm. Only this weapon was far more powerful than any pistol.

"Do I have to do anything to make this work?"

"I already reassigned my security protocols to you before I came here. Please remember your selection was not simply my idea. You were approved unanimously by the University Trustees. One of them will be making contact with you in a few hours to discuss a few formalities. But you answer to no one but your own good conscience."

"And if I decide to open a dialogue with Stephens anyway?"

"Such is your prerogative. No one can stop you, though the Trustees will hold you accountable for any decision you make. Whatever you decide, I know it will be what you believe is best for the institution. I have made my case for the course of action I have prescribed. I have given you the best evidence I could. The final verdict rests with you now."

Hicks slipped the bulky device into the inside pocket of his coat. "I'll keep it in mind."

"Please do." The Dean grunted as he pushed himself out of the chair. He kicked up another cloud of dust and had to stifle a cough. "However, I do recommend you find someone to come in and dust this place at least once a decade."

Hicks smiled. "I'll get right on it, sir."

The Dean held out a hand to him. "I have foisted a lot of

responsibility on you this afternoon, James, but I know things will become clearer to you in time. In our world, sometimes one can only see the true nature of a thing by watching how the shadows play across it."

Hicks shook his mentor's hand. "I promise to make you proud, sir."

"You already have." The Dean pulled on his gloves as he walked toward the door. Over his shoulder, he said, "And when all else fails, remember a simple axiom which has served me well over the years: do no harm, but take no shit."

Hicks watched his mentor open the door and quietly pull it closed behind him. He'd left Hicks alone in the phony apartment with the responsibility for the institution they had both loved and killed for.

His instinct told him to run after the Dean, to at least offer to walk with him for a while or take him wherever he was going. But the Dean hadn't asked and Hicks didn't offer. The man Hicks had known for so long as the Dean had his own journey to take. He should be allowed to take it his own way. Hicks owed him that much.

Maybe it was the best kind of ending for him after all. In their line of work, any ending of your own choosing was a good one.

Hicks hoped he might be as lucky someday, though with things as they were, he tended to doubt it.

CHAPTER
14

THE JOLLY ROGER Club was known to its wealthy clientele as the most exclusive underground pleasure venue in New York City, which put it in the running for being one of the best in the world. It had become a favored destination for the various types of vice still illegal in many parts of the world, but the Jolly Roger always guaranteed safety and discretion for its customers.

Calling it a nightclub would have been too vague. Calling it a sex club would have been limiting its purpose to the definable. And if there was one thing Roger Cobb had always sought to avoid, it was definition.

Roger's establishment catered to almost any fetish, passion, and proclivity on the Kinsey Scale. Most illegal drugs were allowed, provided the customer didn't get out of line while using them. Roger drew the line at bestiality and pedophilia, preferring to use the latter as test subjects for his more invasive interview techniques.

The men and women who serviced Roger's customers looked like they could have been fashion models or actors. Some even had been. Any service and act they provided was done beneath the watchful eye of cameras strategically placed throughout the building. If and when the time came, the footage would be used as leverage to compel them to serve the needs of the University.

Because of its exclusive customer base, the club had made a lot of money for the University—and Roger and Hicks personally—in the five years since it had opened.

Part of the Jolly Roger Club's popularity was that it never closed. It always had at least a few customers in various stages of intoxication, hedonism, and undress at any time of day. One customer said, 'It's always eight o'clock on a Thursday night at Roger's.' Hicks couldn't remember a time when the door had ever been locked, not even on Christmas Day when Roger held his annual 'Red Gala' ball.

But when he got to the club later that afternoon, he found the front door locked.

Hicks fumbled in his pocket for the keys and let himself in. He took off his sunglasses, knowing Roger always kept the place dimly lit and the music loud. But as he opened the door, he saw all the lights were on and the place was silent. He expected to see one of Roger's bouncers at the door. Roger always had plenty of staff on hand to keep escapades from getting violent.

He was surprised to find only one person in the place. Scott, from the Varsity Squad, sitting alone at the bar drinking a bottle of water. With his blonde crew cut and square jaw, he looked more menacing than normal in the stark light of the club.

He looked up from his handheld as Hicks walked in. "Speak of the devil and he appears. I was about to call you." He looked closer at Hicks. "Glad to see you finally cleaned yourself up. You've been looking like a real piece of shit lately."

The two men had never been enemies or friends. They didn't have to be. They worked together and they worked well together. Hicks saw no reason why it should change now he had become the Dean.

He looked around the place and saw all the couches and booths and tables were empty. "Where the hell is everybody?"

"Don't blame me," Scott said. "Roger threw out all the freaks and told me to keep the place shut tight until he said otherwise. I've never seen him like that. The little bastard was like a dynamo, throwing junkies and perverts out into the parking lot. I'd bet a million bucks that some of those freaks have seen the sun in weeks."

Hicks had seen Roger lose his temper before, but not when it came to business. "Why'd you hang around?"

"I don't like taking orders from him, but after what he went through today, I figured he shouldn't be alone. I was going to call you to let you know what happened when you walked in."

Hicks didn't like the sound of that. The only thing Roger liked better than a good time was making money. Closing the club kept him from doing both. Roger must have been taking his abduction especially hard. "Where is he now?"

Scott looked up at the ceiling. "Up in his chamber or cell or whatever the fuck he calls it."

"He alone?"

"Probably. I don't know and I'm not going up there to find out. I might catch something."

Hicks knew Scott was a capable man, but he never did any more than he had to. Tell him and his people to kick in a door or clean up a crime scene, they did it. But it was nearly impossible to get Scott to do something not mentioned in the initial mission scope. Hicks found him frustrating at times, but at least he was consistent.

"I'd appreciate it if you could hang around for a couple of minutes until I get a read on Roger's condition."

Scott's eyebrows rose as he adjusted himself on the barstool. "Jesus, Hicks. That's the closest you've ever come to saying 'please.'"

Hicks would've said it if he'd had to. Luckily, it didn't come to that.

HICKS FOUND ROGER Cobb alone in his bed chamber. Normally the room was lit by candles, where men and women in various stages of intoxication and undress cavorted in the shadows of the windowless room.

But now, with all the candles extinguished and all the lights on, Hicks saw the room for the gaudy hellhole it was. The velvet wallpaper was stained and torn in several places. So were all the curtains and drapes Roger had hung throughout the room to give the space the illusion of depth and mystery. All of the corners were empty, save for the half-filled glasses and overflowing ashtrays. He spotted a couple of charred bongs and pipes on the floor by the couch, left by clients too stoned to remember to take them. About three to five years' worth of prison time of cocaine residue had been left cut but un-snorted on various tables. Roger hadn't given his customers much warning about last call. Hicks couldn't blame them for hurrying. There had never been a last call at The Jolly Roger Club before.

Even Roger's infamous sex swing hung empty in the center of his bedroom. The entire space smelled of stale sex, spilled wine, and candle wax.

Roger was sitting in an oversized black leather lounge chair. He'd changed out of his clothes and was now wearing a gray t-shirt and faded jeans. He was balancing a glass with three fingers of scotch on his knee. He threw Hicks a boozy smile when he saw him. "Hi, honey. Welcome home. How was your day? And you cut your hair, too. How pretty you look."

Roger sounded like he was already on his third drink, maybe fourth. After the kind of day he'd had, Hicks couldn't blame him for being sloshed.

"I've been better." He walked over to Roger's wet bar and poured three fingers of Johnnie Walker Blue Label into a reasonably clean glass. He decided to skip the ice. "I see you closed the club."

"My, how observant. There's something about being abducted and nearly tortured that killed my mood for tits and Techno right now. Besides, I needed to sweep the place for bugs. Those bastards grabbed me too close to this place. They already knew so much about me, I was afraid they might've made an educated guess and figured I owned this place."

Hicks took his scotch and lowered himself into the leather couch opposite Roger. "Find anything?"

"No. The place was clean. For bugs, anyway. Well, the listening kind. You should've seen what moved when I turned on the main lights. Fucking place has more roaches than a Parisian sewer. An exterminator will cost me a small fortune, but it has to be done. I don't know why they're here, though. We barely have any food. I would've thought a roach would starve to death in here."

"The sugar in the drinks draws them," Hicks said, though he didn't know why. It was something to say because he didn't know what to say to Roger. He added, "I'm sorry about Stephens. I saw how rough it got for you in there."

"Seeing and being there are two different things," Roger said. "On the ride back, Scott told me you'd hacked into their camera feed and saw the whole thing live. I figured you would eventually, hence the Morse code"

Hicks took a swig of Blue Label. The subtle burn felt good at the back of his throat. "Turning on your phone helped. How'd you get access to it?"

"I kept begging them to give it to me. I told them I needed to make a call. I suppose one of the dimwits picked it up and activated it by accident."

Did Scott tell you Stephens tried to grab me before they went after you?"

But Roger didn't look like he had heard him. "Their goddamned van came out of nowhere. Cut off my cab and pulled me out of the back before I even knew what was happening." He grinned. "One of them was in pretty bad shape. Kept holding his throat and had a hard time breathing. I should've recognized your handiwork."

Hicks didn't grin. "It wasn't enough to keep them from grabbing you, though. Maybe the Dean was right. Maybe I should've shot the sons of bitches instead."

"And start a war with our own intelligence agencies? Not smart, my friend. You did the right thing by letting them go.

Speaking of the Dean, I hear congratulations are in order." He raised his glass and toasted him. "Habemus papam."

Hicks lowered his glass. "How did you find out?"

"Dad called me after I got home. We had a nice long chat where I listened while he spoke. He explained all about how he'd given Stephens my location and access to parts of my old file. He explained how it was all part of his final lesson to you and me about the dangers we're facing from the Barnyard. He wanted us to appreciate the true nature of our enemy before he shuffled off this mortal coil." Roger swirled his scotch before he took a good belt. "At least the son of a bitch had the decency to not attempt an apology."

Hicks wasn't surprised. Apologies weren't the Dean's style. "He said he'll be dead by this time tomorrow."

"And good riddance." Roger finished his drink and went to the bar to pour another. "After what that son of a bitch put me through?"

Hicks had seen Roger get worked up like this before. It never ended well. "Take it easy."

"I had every intention of taking it easy today. I had a beautiful day planned until the van came out of nowhere and practically t-boned my fucking cab." He pointed back toward the empty sex swing in his bedroom. "Don't let all the whips and chains and kinky shit you see around this place fool you, James. I don't like being handcuffed and locked in a small room with a goddamned DIA goon threatening my life."

"I know. The Dean told them where to find me, too."

Roger poured himself four fingers of scotch and sat back down. "So he told me, as if we're supposed to forgive him because he admitted betraying us. He's no better than any of the other bastards in his position. Yet another dying old man playing games and moving pieces around the chess board. And after he betrays us, he dumps it all in your lap while he goes off to die alone like some old elephant in the jungle." Roger sneered. "See? There's his jungle analogy again. The fucking coward."

Hicks saw a thin blue vein pulse along Roger's neck up to his temple. "He gave them my file, James. My old file. My old life. Do you have any idea how hard I worked to put all of it behind me? To forget who I was and what they did to me before all of this?"

Hicks didn't know the details of Roger's past, only that much of it had been miserable. He'd never offered details and Hicks had never pried. He could appreciate a man's desire to forget who he was. "It was a rotten thing to do, but it's done. We got you out alive and…"

But Roger didn't hear him. His hand trembled as his fingers whitened around the tumbler of scotch. "Do you know how deep I had to bury that shit to forget it, only to have this punk Stephens throw it in my face? Like it's nothing? And why? Because the Dean wanted to make a fucking point on his way out the door."

The glass shattered in Roger's hand.

Roger didn't flinch. Neither did Hicks. He knew Roger's hands may have looked delicate, but they were much stronger than they looked. He'd seen and heard what those hands could do to a human.

Roger was too focused on his anger to notice the scotch and blood soaking into his jeans. "I don't like being confronted with ghosts, James, least of all my own. And I sure as shit don't like being manhandled by thugs." He looked at Hicks. "The Stephens boy laid hands, James. I cannot allow that to go unanswered."

"It won't." Hicks knew Roger needed a towel, but didn't get one for him. It was his mess. He would tend to it in his own time if he tended to it at all.

Hicks drank his scotch instead. "Now that I'm the Dean, maybe I can broker some kind of deal with Stephens after all."

"It's too late for diplomacy now." Roger seemed to finally notice the glass had shattered in his hand. He began to calmly remove the larger chunks of glass from his lap and set them on the end table. "Stephens knows they're on to something. He'll come at us with everything he's got."

Hicks looked at his drink. "We're going to have to make them stop."

Roger continued removing the shards of glass from his left hand. He didn't flinch or wince. He looked as calm as a child picking paint chips off a wall. "And how do we do that?"

"I've got some ideas. In fact, the Dean gave me an interesting idea before he left."

Roger looked interested. "No shit? What kind of an idea?"

"One I know you're going to like."

He saw Roger's mood brighten, so he quickly added, "Nothing direct and nothing lethal. Shooting Stephens or Avery will make us feel better, but I need you to find a more subtle way to stop them or send them off course."

"Death is far more permanent," Roger warned.

"They're our own people. We're on the same side. They just don't know it yet. And they won't until all of this is over."

He rubbed his face in his hands as the Carousel of Concern began to turn once more in his mind. *Jabbar. Stephens. The University. The Mossad.* Christ, he hadn't even begun to figure out how he'd break the news of Bajjah's death to Tali. Each concern was essential. Each one of them would crush him if he let it. He needed time to quiet his mind and keep everything in order, but time was the one thing he didn't have.

"Speaking of allies," Roger said as he pulled the last piece of glass from his hand, "I contacted Rahul Patel this morning before I left Alphabet City. He's interested in the London job you mentioned. Tailing the Shaban character."

Hicks blinked his eyes clear. "Just because he's interested in the job, doesn't mean we're interested in him doing it. He's a drunk."

"Only if he drinks." Roger went to the bar and began to wrap his hand in a towel. "I've searched OMNI for other operatives who could do the job, but Rahul's still the best one available to work London for us. I was supposed to meet him at six, but I'll never be able to get ready in time to meet him." He held up his wrapped hand. "Not after this nonsense."

He didn't like the idea of using someone on the downswing of his career. But given his abilities, even if Rahul was only half the agent he'd once been, he was good enough to tail Shaban. "Get yourself cleaned up. I'll go. Where are you supposed to meet him?"

"At his cousin's restaurant in Rockefeller Center. I'll give you the address from my phone after I finish dressing my hand. You'll want to be careful, though. He might be a drunk, but he's still a trained assassin. And he hates your guts."

Hicks fought down a yawn. "He's in good company."

CHAPTER
15

"WHERE ARE WE going?" Scott asked when they got outside the Jolly Roger Club.

"I'll tell you in the car." Hicks pulled out his new handheld device and ran an OMNI scan of all frequencies near his position. The speed of the scan was faster than anything he'd seen in a handheld before—almost instantaneous. The scan showed no secured or federal signals in his immediate area.

If Stephens' people were watching him, they were doing it old school. No radios and no Company equipment. They'd be using parked cars and binoculars and cell phones instead. He checked the street and rooftops and windows of the surrounding buildings for anything out of the ordinary. All he saw was the standard decay of Midtown Manhattan's forgotten west side.

Hicks put the handheld away. "I need you to take me to a

meeting I've got up at Rockefeller Center. If it goes well, you'll be taking someone to a private jet in a couple of hours."

They got to the car. Scott got behind the wheel and Hicks rode shot gun.

"And if it doesn't go well?" Scott asked.

"Then you'll be leaving someone on the side of the road. Any problem with that?"

"Makes no difference to me, so long as you remember I'm not your fucking errand boy. I overheard the call Roger got on the way back here, so I know you're the new Dean. Good for you. I want you to remember I'm not your driver, and I'm not going to run all over town doing odd jobs for you because you're suddenly on top of the org chart. I didn't do it for the other guy and I sure as shit won't do it for you. If you've got a problem with that, tell me now and I'll update my resume."

Hicks knew Scott was an alpha type. He needed to be an alpha in order to do the kind of work he did and do it well. Marine Recon vets weren't known for being passive.

But Hicks also knew if he backed down from him now, he'd lose his respect and never get it back.

"You're being well paid to do what you're told, Scott. You're going to keep on doing what you're told if you want to keep on getting well paid. If you want to jump ship and join up with a private firm where you earn half the money babysitting celebrities or sweating your balls off in a jungle for some tin pot dictator, be my guest. For now, you're going to drive me up to Rockefeller Center and wait for further instructions. If you don't like it, tell me now and I'll catch a cab."

Scott laughed more to himself than to Hicks. "Yeah, I get it. Jesus. And you wonder why nobody likes you."

"I couldn't care less. Now let's go."

As Scott drove the SUV up Twelfth Avenue, Hicks pulled up the profile of Rahul Patel on his handheld. He had already read the file months before, back when the Dean had sent him to investigate the apartment of Rahul's sister, but the file still made for impressive reading.

Up until his sister's death, Patel had been one of the most effective counter-terrorism operatives in India's National Investigation Agency. He had not only hunted down the men who had planned the attack on Mumbai in 2008, but he had also thwarted two additional attacks since. He had a reputation within the intelligence community as an agent who was not only good at uncovering intelligence, but acting on it as well. Many had one set of skills, but few had both.

Patel's success also earned him some powerful enemies who had decided to take their revenge by murdering his sister in her Manhattan apartment six months before. Rahul believed he had taken all precautions to protect her identity, but Hicks knew no one in their line of work was ever entirely safe. Loved ones least of all. Heads of state, popes, and presidents had all been assassinated. A pretty doctor living alone on the Upper West Side was an easy target for the kinds of people who Rahul Patel counted as enemies.

Unfortunately, the University had learned of the plot to kill Rahul's sister too late. By the time the Dean had sent Hicks to protect her, she was already dead. Hicks' mission immediately changed from protecting the girl to protecting the killers from Rahul. The people who had ordered her death were essential to several important University operations happening at the time. The arrest or death of these men would have crippled years of expensive and important intelligence work which had helped the University stop several terror plots around the globe.

Nothing ever moved in a straight line in the intelligence game. Not even revenge.

Once Rahul had gotten to his sister's apartment, Hicks ha managed to keep the agent at bay until his superiors from the Indian consulate arrived on the scene. The threat Rahul posed to ongoing University operations may have been stopped, but the death of his only sister had cost a good man his sanity. Rahul had crawled into a bottle since the day of her funeral and refused to come out.

India's NIA had too much respect for his service to the country to ever formally throw him out of the service. Instead, they placed him on indefinite leave and allowed him to wallow in his misery. Now he spent his days with Jack Daniels at his cousin's Indian restaurant in Rockefeller Center.

Hicks knew Rahul could be the ideal man to tail Shaban in London if he could set the bottle down. Hicks had dealt with drunks before. They usually didn't come back so easily.

Hicks sent out a couple of emails and set his plan in motion. If Rahul accepted the job, he'd be on his way to London within the hour.

And if he refused it, the next hour would be his last.

Scott broke Hicks' concentration when he said, "Hey, look over there. Seems like our new friends are on the move."

Hicks looked out the driver's side window and saw a thick column of black smoke billowing into the sky on the New Jersey side of the Hudson River. The wind seemed to be blowing north and east, keeping the smoke on the New Jersey side of the river.

He felt the civilian news apps on his handheld begin to

buzz. 'Breaking News' bulletins appeared on his locked screen. All of them said pretty much the same thing:

Weehawken Storage Facility Burns.

If Hicks still had been holding a glass of Roger's scotch, he would have toasted the scene.

Stephens and Avery were covering their tracks.

Well played, gentlemen. Well played.

IT WAS PAST six o'clock by the time Scott parked the SUV up the street from the Patel family restaurant called Nirvana.

Nirvana was the kind of restaurant that did the Indian theme big, or at least what Americans believed to be an authentic Indian theme. Lots of white furnishings trimmed with gold. Ceramic elephants and monkeys and depictions of Hindu gods positioned throughout the dining room. The hostesses wore saris and glided around the place like royalty, even though there weren't many customers to serve. Attentive waiters wore white shirts and bowed a lot to the ignorant patrons who asked for extra curry.

Hicks spotted Rahul exactly where he'd expected to find him: at the bar nursing a healthy pour of Jack Daniels—neat. He may have only been separated from the NIS for a few months, but the mileage was already beginning to show. He had looked like an Indian version of Cary Grant when Hicks had first met him at his sister's apartment: tall with a thick head of black hair and a natural bronze complexion no amount of time on a tanning bed could buy. Throw in an accent more Cambridge than Mumbai and he could charm almost anyone into doing anything he wanted.

But too much sour mash and too many late nights had given Rahul a drawn, worn look. Thick dark circles had appeared beneath the same brown eyes that had once made women on six continents swoon. His admirable posture and easy charm had given way to a drunkard's slouch. His hair was a touch too long and he was a few days overdue for a shave. He was still a handsome kid, but nowhere near what he had once been. And he was nowhere near what Hicks needed him to be again.

For the second time that day, Hicks hoped he wasn't already too late. He hated jobs like this. He hated not having the resources to go straight for the jugular—to be able to pick up the phone and have someone in London put Shaban under twenty-four hour surveillance. He hated having to move sideways before he could take one step forward. Even if Rahul took the job, there'd be so many variables to consider. Was he too far gone to do the job right? Would he slip while on assignment and drink again? Had his skills been eroded by too much time on a barstool? Could he work for a man he hated?

But Hicks didn't have the luxury of dwelling on a wish list. He had a terrorist in London who needed watching and, for now, Rahul Patel was his best shot at doing it.

Showtime. Hicks got out of the SUV and crossed the street.

RAHUL LOOKED UP from his drink as soon as Hicks pushed through the revolving door and walked past the hostess in the sari. The Rahul of old would never have sat so close to the window or with his back to the street. He would have seen Hicks as soon as he'd crossed the street. The Rahul he had once admired also wouldn't have been drinking in the middle of the day.

Rahul's bloodshot eyes widened as he slid off his stool to face the American. "You."

Hicks tried a smile. "Roger couldn't make it, so you're stuck with me instead. But if you're still interested, we can…"

Rahul telegraphed a straight right hand. Hicks easily dodged it, grabbed Rahul's wrist and flicked an elbow which caught him above the bridge of his nose. The blow wasn't hard enough to hurt him, only knock him off balance enough to take some of the fight out of him.

But in his drunken state, Rahul tumbled backward like he'd been struck with a roundhouse right hand. He knocked over his stool, drawing looks from all the wait staff and the few patrons eating a late lunch. Hicks covered it up by rushing to help Rahul stay on his feet, as if he was helping an old friend who'd stumbled.

"Take it easy, partner," he said loud enough for the benefit of the patrons who were watching. He took Rahul under the arm and helped him to his feet. "Let's grab some air and clear your head."

Rahul was either too drunk or too stunned to fight him. Hicks didn't care which. He was glad he went quietly.

As soon as they went through the revolving doors and on the street, Rahul tried to pull away. "I should kill you right now."

Hicks didn't let go of his grip on his arm. "Kill me? Shit, you couldn't even hit me and I was standing right in front of you."

He decided they should try to blend in with the crowds milling around Rockefeller Center's ice rink and steered Rahul in that direction. The ice rink wasn't scheduled to close down for another month, so there were still plenty of tourists in the area. Since all of the benches of the plaza were occupied by selfie-taking tourists and shopping bags, Hicks led Rahul to the high wall overlooking the rink. It gave him something to lean on without falling over.

Hicks watched the last skater glide off the ice as a maintenance worker fired up the Zamboni machine that would roll onto the rink to smooth the surface. "You're doing a hell of a job of wasting yourself, my friend, and if there's one thing in this world I hate, it's waste."

"I don't expect you to understand. Your sister wasn't butchered by your enemies."

"I'm the one who found her, remember?"

"And you're also the one who kept me from avenging her."

"You saw what happened to the men who did it. You saw the pictures."

"Vengeance by proxy isn't my thing, mate. She wasn't your sister. You had no right to…"

"They knew you'd be coming after them. You never would've gotten within a thousand yards of them before they saw you coming. I handled it and now they're dead and that's what matters. You saw the footage. You saw they died worse than she did."

Rahul blinked hard and steadied himself with a drunkard's resolve. "When it fit in with the University's plans, of course."

Hicks watched the Zamboni roll out onto the ice. "Everything happens on someone's timeline, Rahul. It's the business we're in. Or at least it's the business you used to be in before you crawled into a bottle."

"Spare me the AA bullshit. Roger told me he wanted to talk about a job. If you've come here to lecture me instead, you might as well quit wasting time and fuck off. I've got drinking to do."

"You might have drinking to do, but you're the worst imitation of a drunk I've ever seen." Hicks watched the ice machine begin its slow circuit around the ice. "I've made a career out of working drunks for information and setting them up to take the fall. They were all dead men at the end of their line with nothing to look forward to except the next bottle. You're not there, not yet. All you're doing is slumming while you wallow in your own misery. The tragedy is an excuse for you to fuck yourself up. I've seen it happen to people like us before. I'm seeing it happen now with you."

Hicks saw the drunkard Rahul had become ebb enough to reveal the talented counter-intelligence man beneath. The man Hicks needed him to be again. "Careful, mate."

Hicks grinned. "A drunk wouldn't have been insulted because he wouldn't have given a shit." He lightly tapped him on the chest. "You still want to be part of the Game, mate. You're too proud to ask and you're too afraid of letting go of your grief. Moving on isn't the same thing as forgetting her. If anything, moving on is the best way you can honor her memory."

Rahul looked down at the ice surface, too. "I suppose this is the point in the conversation where you try to talk me into coming back."

"I'm not going to talk you into doing a damned thing. If you want in, we keep talking. If not, I go find someone else and you go back to your barstool and wallowing in your misery. Makes no difference to me whatsoever," he lied.

"If I wanted back in, I could ask for my old job back in Mumbai."

"Good luck with that. They owe you too much to outright

fire you, but they don't trust you enough to bring you back in. Not the way you are. But, maybe I can do something about it."

"Maybe? Why? How?"

"Because today, I got elevated to Dean of the University."

Rahul looked up at him and seemed much steadier on his feet. "I'm a drunk, James, not gullible."

"There are some things even I don't joke about. This is one of them."

Rahul looked at him for a few seconds more before looking back down at the rink. The machine had finished one pass over the ice surface and was already beginning its second. "Was it a peaceful promotion or..."

"Peaceful, but I'm not popping any champagne bottles. To tell you the truth, I don't even want the fucking job, but it's not up to me. My predecessor dumped a hell of a mess in my lap, a mess I need your help to clean up if you're interested."

"Me? Even now?" He held up his hand so Hicks could see how much it shook. "Even like this?"

Hicks slowly lowered Rahul's hand. "If you sign on, I'll make sure you get pumped with enough medicine to take the edge off. But I need your commitment to staying sober and on point."

"But why me?"

"Because you've been out of the Life long enough by now to move around without raising too many eyebrows, but not long enough to have lost your edge. You've still got your instincts, and I need people with instincts need right now. Christ knows we're not going to pull this off by sheer manpower alone."

Rahul rubbed his hands across his face as if he was trying to wake himself up. "Sounds serious. What's the job?"

Hicks shook his head. "Not until you sign on. Either you're

in all the way or you're not in at all. Relevance or the barstool. What's it going to be?"

Rahul's eyes narrowed as he drummed his fingers on the concrete wall surrounding the rink. "If you're serious, so am I. When do I sign up?"

"Congratulations." Hicks pulled out his handheld and called Scott. "Bring the car around. We're ready to go."

Rahul protested as Hicks took him by the arm and led him to the curb. "You must be joking. I have to get clearance from my bosses back home first."

"I already called them." Hicks saw his expression and grinned. "I'm the Dean now, remember? Influence comes with the job. As of right now, you're in charge of University field operations in Europe. You'll be based out of London for the moment."

"Europe? The University doesn't have any field operations in Europe."

"Which is why we need you, Ace." Hicks steered him through the clusters of tourists roaming through the plaza. "I need you to spend your entire flight over to England reorganizing some of your old go-teams to help you with your first mission. I'm not talking about mercenaries, either. We need the best teams available, and you're the only one I know who can pull it together practically overnight."

Rahul got a little sturdier on his feet as he kept pace with Hicks. "Does this have anything to do with the outbreak two weeks ago?"

Hicks wouldn't tell him all the details while they were out in the open. "All your questions will be answered as soon as you're on the plane. But this will be a closed operation. No interference or assistance from other agencies. No one to get in your way, either. This will only be you, the people you bring on and the people we're supposed to stop."

Rahul stumbled when Hicks pulled him to a stop at the curb. "Sounds wonderful, but you still haven't told me who we're after and what I'm supposed to do."

Scott's black SUV pulled up to the curb. Hicks opened the back door and waited for Rahul to get in. He kept the details to a minimum. In this case, a single name should be enough to tell the whole story. "Jabbar."

Rahul stopped half way into the back seat. "For fuck's sake, Hicks. Jabbar's a pipe dream. He's some ghost story ignorant hajjis tell themselves around the campfire to keep their nerve up. No one even knows if he even exists."

"I need you to fly to London and prove it one way or the other. All the information you'll need on your target has already been uploaded to a tablet and secure phone waiting for you on the plane. Follow the security procedure prompts on the devices and it'll work out fine."

Rahul ducked into the back seat. "It's your dime, mate, but it's a waste of time if you ask me."

"And what if it's not?"

"It's a big 'if,' James."

"Big enough of an 'if' for you to see for yourself." Hicks shut the door. "Now get going."

"You're the boss," Rahul said through the open passenger window. "I'll need to go back to my place and get a few things and…"

"I've already had a few things taken from your place and loaded on the plane. Anything else you need, you can buy in

London."

Rahul spoke over the rising window. "You were pretty sure of yourself, weren't you?"

"Talk to me when you get to London."

As Rahul's window rose, Scott lowered his. "Sounds like I'm taking him to the airport."

"Sounds like it."

"I would've lost that bet."

"That's why you're not in charge, remember? Make sure he gets on the plane, no stops. Head home after. Tomorrow could be a busy day."

Scott rolled up his window and pulled the SUV into eastbound traffic.

As he watched the SUV pull away, Hicks realized he had given his first official order as Dean. He had given orders to people before, especially in the field during operations, but never as the person with complete authority for the University before. The act should have meant more to him than it did, but it didn't. The Carousel of Concern in his mind only grew larger and spun even faster.

Jabbar. Shaban. Stephens. Roger's operation. Tali's demands. And now *Rahul.*

He decided not to dwell on the hundreds of other ongoing operations and plans other University Faculty Members and Adjuncts were planning and executing even now as he watched Rahul drive away. Jason would brief him on all of those in due time. For now, he'd taken the first decisive strike against Jabbar's operation. It might not amount to anything. Rahul could fall off the wagon. Shaban might only be another run of the mill street corner revolutionary.

But he'd done something. And he'd done it as the Dean of the University. And he decided to savor the moment because it might be the last win he would have for a hell of a long time.

Hicks decided to check his handheld as he began walking west. OMNI still hadn't detected any abnormal secure signals in the area, but he saw hundreds of emails had filled his in box in the last hour. Status reports from Istanbul: a possible Asset willing to turn in Moscow, a proposal to fund a safe house in Tehran, and approval request from a Ringmaster in Venezuela who was convinced he could seduce an important trade minister's wife if he received enough financing to buy her a string of pearls she'd always wanted.

But of all the messages he had received only one killed his reasonably good mood. The several messages from Tali Saddon. She had sent him a text at fifteen minute intervals for the past hour from her secure University device. The message was the same each time:

PLEASE PROVIDE TODAY'S UPDATE ON THE PRISONER BRIEFING.

Her final message was especially terse:

I DEMAND AN IMMEDIATE MEETING TO DISCUSS ACCESS TO THE PRISONER.

He knew he couldn't delay telling her about Bajjah's death for much longer. Agent Tali Saddon of the Mossad had many virtues, but patience wasn't one of them. He knew she must already be furious he hadn't responded to her messages. Telling her Bajjah was dead over the phone or via text would make things even worse. He'd have to tell her in person. He hoped telling her he's been named the Dean would calm her down a bit, but doubted it.

CHAPTER 16

TALI LOOKED MORE concerned than surprised when she watched him step off the elevator into her apartment. He was glad she'd decided to lower her nine-millimeter when she saw he had come alone.

"Where the hell have you been?" she said. "I have been trying to talk to you all day. What's going on with Bajjah? Are you okay?"

Hicks surprised himself by taking her in his arms and kissing her. He was even more surprised when she kissed him back. She didn't struggle as he swept her up into his arms and heeled the door shut as he carried her into the bedroom. He'd barely given her a chance to breathe, much less protest, though he knew she could've stopped him if she'd wanted. The Mossad trained their field personnel well.

For Hicks, it was almost as though he was outside his own body during the course of the lovemaking, as if he was watching it instead of doing it. He watched himself pull off her clothes as she pulled off his, kissing each other deeply as he made frantic love to Tali. She climbed on top of him right after to begin a second round. For the second time that evening, he surprised himself, this time by being ready again so quickly. He didn't complain. He didn't plan. He simply let it happen.

Hicks knew it was happening, but he knew this wasn't him. He was never this uncontrolled, this hungry. It was a desire which had come over him somewhere between the elevator and the sight of her holding a gun at her apartment door. But as foreign an emotion as it was, it was also natural and real. It was a swirl of emotion and panic and fear and he didn't dare try to stop it. And neither did Tali.

Tali arched her back and moaned through her climax, her head sagging so her hair fell across his face before she slowly collapsed on top of him. As the two of them lay panting from the effort, Hicks slowly returned to normal. A shiver went through both of them at the same time and he surprised himself by laughing.

He looked over at Tali, who was panting as heavily as he was. She was laying on her back now, her lean body slicked with sweat. She rolled on her side and propped up her head so she was looking down at Hicks. Her tan skin was flushed; her green eyes bright in the afterglow of their lovemaking. He liked the way a thick black strand of hair fell across her face. "Would you mind telling me what brought all of this on?"

Hicks began to return to normal and found he was a little embarrassed. "I'm sorry if I was too...forceful. I..."

She smiled as she laid a finger on his lips. He had always seen her as more striking than beautiful—dark-haired and light olive skin with high cheekbones and green eyes one might not expect an Israeli girl to have.

Those same green eyes looked at him now like he was the biggest asshole in the world. "We both know you didn't do anything I didn't want you to do."

He knew she was right. Tali Saddon was one of the most effective Adjunct Faculty members in the University system. She was one of the best agents the Mossad had produced in the past decade. She was as deadly in hand-to-hand combat as she was with a sniper rifle. In University parlance, she was called a Snake Charmer, an agent who seduced targets for information. Hicks had never liked to know the details about how far Tali went to obtain the information she acquired. He had never ordered her to sleep with anyone, which eased his conscience a little whenever he remembered the kind of intelligence work she did and how she did it. The Israelis had made her into a weapon long before she'd come to work for the University. He used her skills the same way he used Roger's flair for compunction.

At least, that's what he'd always told himself until now.

She had brought down over a dozen plots since she'd worked for the University and she had always lived up to her word.

Tali and her supervisors in Tel Aviv had heard the rumblings in the intelligence community following the shootout in Philadelphia. They'd deduced Hicks had been involved and, in exchange for their silence, Hicks had agreed to give them access to Bajjah after the University was done questioning him. He knew she wouldn't take the news of Bajjah's execution well. He hoped he'd figure out a way to tell her the truth. He hoped she didn't try to kill him afterwards.

They were having such a pleasant evening.

"You didn't answer my question," she said. "What brought this on?"

Hicks hoped his news was enough to distract her from asking about Bajjah. "I was named Dean today."

Tali sat up. More strands of dark hair fell over one eye and she didn't make any effort to push it behind her ear. He felt himself stirring again.

"Don't joke about something like that, James. It's not funny."

"Who's joking? The Dean handed over authority to me this afternoon a few hours after Jason sent out the alert. I'm now in charge of the whole damned show."

He hadn't expected her to react and she didn't disappoint. Her only emotion was to tuck the loose strand of hair behind her ear. "How does this kind of thing work? Did you meet the old Dean? Did you…"

Hicks saw no reason to go into details. The more he told her, the more she could report back to her supervisors in Tel Aviv. The University and the Mossad had always had a cordial relationship based more on mutual benefit than trust. "It happened for a lot of reasons, but none of them are important now."

If she was impressed, she hid it well. "Did he resign because of the alert from earlier today?"

"No. I issued the alert because someone tried to grab me on the street."

"Why would someone try to grab you out of the blue?" Hicks could practically hear her mind working. "Bajjah. It had something to do with Bajjah, didn't it?"

Hicks decided to dodge the question with humor. "Stop worrying about me, will you? I'm fine. They didn't even leave a mark on me."

He jumped when she punched him in the side. Not as hard as she could have, but harder than he'd expected. "Imbecile. I know you're fine. I asked about Bajjah. Did they take him?"

Hicks honored an old University custom. He didn't lie. He simply framed the truth. "He wasn't involved in the attack that triggered the alert."

She seemed to buy the excuse for the moment. "But how did they find you? You've always been so careful."

He knew she wouldn't let it go until he gave her an answer. She and her supervisors had been smart enough to figure out he had been responsible for grabbing Bajjah when news broke about the shootout in Philadelphia. He'd already been through the story so many times that day, he kept it brief. "The DIA was conducting passive surveillance of Bajjah in Philly when I grabbed him. They got a lock on my face from a security camera our Operators missed and traced me back here to Manhattan."

She moved further away from him. The only emotion he'd ever seen her outside of their lovemaking was self-preservation. "Are our covers safe? Do they know who we are? Are you being watched now?"

"They know what I look like, but not who I am or who I work for," he told her. "They don't know anything about the University, either, but suspect I've got Bajjah for some reason but they don't know why. I got away clean and spiked their remote surveillance. No one is following me and there's no proof they know anything about me, the University, or our operatives. But the Barnyard will be hyper-vigilant for the time being, so everyone should keep a low profile for the next few days. Avoid people you know or suspect might be working for the Barnyard. I don't want anyone's cover blown on a lucky guess by a nervous CIA asset. Jason will give the all clear sign when we can go back to normal."

"I don't care about normal. I care about debriefing Bajjah. Your last report said Roger was going to attempt new techniques to get him to talk. Did they work?"

Hicks chose his words carefully. Israel already had a ten million Euro bounty on Jabbar's head for masterminding dozens of terrorist acts against the country. The slightest mention of Jabbar would get Tali on the phone to her superiors back in Tel Aviv before Hicks' feet hit the bedroom floor.

The mere possibility of grabbing Jabbar would become the entire focus of the Mossad. They would dedicate all of their resources to finding the elusive mastermind, including bringing in their allies in other intelligence agencies around the world. The CIA, British Intelligence and other agencies. Their quest for Jabbar would disregard the University's need for secrecy and discretion. The Mossad wouldn't care who they pulled down in their quest to get one of the most wanted terrorists in the world.

Hicks needed to give Rahul enough time to investigate Shaban in London. Even though there was a slight possibility Bajjah's money man might lead them to Jabbar, it was enough reason to stall Tali.

Hicks suddenly regretted coming to Tali's apartment at all. He should've sent her an email before going home and taking a cold shower.

"You are stalling me again," Tali said. "You always stall when you are trying to hide the truth."

"Who's stalling?" he stalled. "I told you Bajjah didn't react well to Roger's enhanced tactics. He had a setback, a stroke, to be specific, but we're going to take a second run at him as soon as he heals. We plan on taking another crack at him tomorrow morning."

Tali's green eyes narrowed. "No. You're lying."

Shit. "What?"

"Yes, you are lying. You did that thing with your face. You always do that thing with your face when you lie."

Hicks had been schooled by some of the best interrogators in the world. He'd had any giveaway gesture, any 'tell,' trained out of him a long time ago. He knew Tali was fishing. His face hadn't changed. "I tell lies for a living. How the hell would you know what tells I have?"

"Because you've never lied to me before, but you did now." She moved even further away from him in bed. "Bajjah finally told you something, didn't he? You've had Bajjah for two weeks and I know Roger must have gotten something out of him by now. She looked at him closer. "Bajjah broke last night, didn't he?"

He decided lying to a trained assassin while naked wasn't in his best interests, so he told her a version of the truth. "He didn't exactly break, but he gave us information on parts of his network."

"I knew it. What parts?"

"We're in the process of vetting the information as we speak. If we uncover anything that even remotely affects your country, you'll be the first to know."

"We will not wait for your analysis," she said. "Whatever Roger got out of Bajjah, my people will be able to get more.

We will talk to him as soon as possible. I demand access to the prisoner immediately. Tonight at the latest."

"You're not in a position to demand anything. He's my prisoner. I granted you access to him after we're finished with him as a courtesy."

"A courtesy you extended in exchange for our silence about your possession of him," Tali added. "If you refuse us access to the prisoner, I see no reason why we should not inform the CIA you are holding Bajjah. So, either allow me to interrogate the prisoner in my own way or face the consequences."

Hicks knew he couldn't delay the inevitable any longer. He braced himself for the storm he knew would follow when he said, "I can't do that."

Tali bolted off the bed and stood over him. The muted lamplight showed the lines of her lean body. She was stark naked and angry and gorgeous all at the same time. A few minutes before, Hicks would have found it erotic. Now, it was something else, something closer to dangerous than enticing. "You can't or you won't?"

Hicks puffed up his pillow and tucked it behind his head. Since any possibility of romance was gone, he decided to make himself comfortable. "If you want to talk to him, be my guest, but you're going to need a Ouija board to do it. Your prisoner is dead."

Her body went rigid. "How?"

He decided another amalgamation of omissions and the truth might smooth it all over. "We'd finally broken him when he began to hold back. Roger hit him with a little more voltage than normal, but it turned out to be too much. Bajjah had a stroke and died early this morning."

"No. I don't believe it. Roger may be a vile deviant, but he is not incompetent. He has never been careless with his prisoners."

"It's not about carelessness, my love. It's about how much he was able to take at a particular moment. We'd put him through a lot in the past two weeks." Hicks remembered Roger's explanation and used it. "It happens."

Tali walked away from the bed. He watched her pace back and forth at the foot of the bed, mulling over all he'd told her. He didn't know if she had believed him or not until she stopped and faced him. "I demand to see his body."

"We cremated his body this morning. You can have his ashes if you want, if Roger didn't already dump them."

"How convenient." Tali crossed her arms. "You knew this when you got here and still you fucked me."

"I didn't do anything you didn't want to happen, remember? Besides, Bajjah's got nothing to do with what happened here tonight. I told you I'm in the process of vetting the information he gave us. I'll send you a full report by this time tomorrow. I know I promised you'd get the chance to work him over yourself, but this is the best..."

"This is unacceptable. We demand complete, unrestricted access to OMNI's research. We demand full disclosure in real time."

Hicks may have enjoyed the sight of a naked woman giving him orders, but not enough to make a fool of himself. "Give a foreign agency direct access to OMNI? Never going to happen."

"You don't want to force a confrontation with us, James. Not with so many of your own country's agencies working to take you down. It would be a shame if Langley learned who you were and about your association with the University."

Hicks hadn't expected her to take Bajjah's death well, but he was surprised she was pulling out the sharp knives so soon. "Threats are more effective when they're believable, my love. Anything you tell Langley about the Mossad's agreement with the University will ruin your credibility with them. You'd be further out in the cold than you already are. Their distrust of you is why our organizations have worked together for so long, remember?"

She balled her fists at her bare sides.

But annoying her could only complicate his life even further, so he quickly added, "I'm not going to give you raw data without vetting it first."

"Why?"

Because I know everything I give you will go straight to your bosses back in Tel Aviv, who will try to vet it through their contacts at the CIA or another agency. Hell, I might as well post it on WikiLeaks myself at that point. I've given you my word on this, Tali. The word of the Dean of the University himself." He tried a smile. "Come on. That has to count for something, doesn't it?"

Hicks couldn't tell by her reaction how much it counted, but it was enough to make her open her fists.

He took it as an encouraging sign and held out his hand to her. "Enough shop talk for one night. Come back to bed."

Tali snatched her silk robe off the end of the bed and pulled it on as she walked out of her bedroom. "No. The lid stays on the honey pot until you make good on your promise. You have exactly five minutes to get dressed and get out."

Hicks swore as he dropped his head back on the pillow. So much for romance.

AFTER HE'D GOTTEN dressed and was ready to leave, he found Tali on the sofa in her living room typing away at her laptop. Her back was to him. Her laptop had a screen guard, so he couldn't see what she was typing, but he didn't need to. He knew it was most likely an email to her bosses back in Tel Aviv, reporting every detail he had told her about Bajjah's death.

Her email might lead to an order from her bosses to lean harder on Hicks for more information. They also might order her to wait for Hicks' report and see what it said. It was nearly impossible to predict how the Mossad might respond to bad news.

He wanted to resent her for sending the email, but he couldn't. She was on loan to the University and she was getting paid by the University, but she was still technically and legally an agent of the Israeli government. Hicks had always been mindful of the loyalties of University Faculty Members from foreign governments. Now he was the Dean, he would have to be even more careful. Tali was the kind of woman where a smart man had to keep a lot of things in mind or risk losing himself in her charms. Seduction was one of the many reasons why she had been such an effective agent. Hicks knew he wasn't immune.

Perhaps that was why keeping the details about Jabbar's network from her had bothered him, though he couldn't explain why. He knew it wasn't love. Tali was a tough woman to forget and nearly impossible to love.

But while they had been together in bed, he had sensed something different between them, something real and deep even though it had only lasted for the briefest of moments. Something in her gasps or a flutter of her eyes, something unguarded and real they had never shared when they had made love in the past. Something more than lust, but shy of love.

And as he stood by the door and watched her fingers snap away at her laptop, knowing she was betraying him with each keystroke, he forced himself to remember Tali Saddon wasn't a castoff like Rahul Patel or a lifer like him and Roger. Part of her loyalty would always lie elsewhere, just as Hicks' loyalty would always lie with protecting his country.

He made a point of zipping up his jacket, hoping the sound might make her stop typing and look at him. He knew she had heard him. She kept typing anyway.

But he knew she must have trusted him on some level. After all, she was typing with her back to him.

It wasn't much, but it was all he could take with him into the close hours of a chilly March night.

CHAPTER 17

As soon as Hicks got to the lobby, he checked his new handheld for any secure federal signals in the area. The scan came up empty. On the street, he looked for watchful eyes, but all he saw were parked cars. No signs of exhaust betraying a running motor to keep the heat on. No fogged up windows, either. Only the odd pedestrian walking a dog, or stumbling home after too many drinks.

A number of yellow cabs glided by, slowing at the sight of a possible fare walking alone. Hicks let them all go, deciding to walk back to Twenty-Third Street instead. Staying on foot was a calculated risk, especially with The Barnyard still on the hunt. But after burning down their facility earlier that evening, Stephens and Avery had other things on their mind right now.

He needed the walk and he needed the time to himself.

Each moment of the past twenty-four hours had seemed to be a constant barrage of information or crisis or danger. He'd either been rushing to something or running away from something or struggling to comprehend a new turn of events. Even his love making with Tali had been ruined by work. He needed to allow his mind to decompress, especially since the Carousel of Concern had suddenly gotten a little bit larger.

Jabbar. Stephens. The University. Roger's plan. Shaban. Rahul. And now, *Tali.*

The sky had brightened to a dark blue as dawn was only an hour or so away. The streetlights were still on and the crosswalk signals blinked warnings to empty streets. It seemed like the whole city had been turned on for him and he decided to enjoy the illusion while it lasted.

He crossed the street and checked his email on his handheld. He scanned the hundreds of alerts he saw from dozens of Faculty Members sending updates on dozens of operations from all over the world. There was a report from a Faculty member keeping tabs on a joint Russian-Chinese mission to Antarctica. Hicks smiled. Not even penguins were safe from the University's influence.

He checked to see if Rahul had given him a status report. According to OMNI, his jet had landed in London over an hour ago. Rahul's handheld device showed he was now in his suite at the Mayfair Hotel, where a University Adjunct was babysitting him. No girls and no booze, not even through room service. The Adjunct wasn't skilled enough to trail Shaban, but keeping an eye on a hotel room was a fairly easy task.

As Hicks kept walking south, he checked Rahul's activity log from the tablets and handheld he'd been given on the flight.

Hicks had expected him to sleep through the flight but the log showed Rahul had opened over seventy percent of the files Hicks had downloaded onto Rahul's devices. What's more, he had read a good amount of each file and used his tablet to email former Indian intelligence contacts he knew to be living in London.

Rahul appeared to be hitting the ground running in his investigation of Shaban, but it was still too early for Hicks to rest easy. The University was entering dangerous, uncharted territory. The organization had always positioned itself as a clearinghouse feeding information to other agencies around the world. The University's strength had always been in its technological capacity.

But hacking computer and camera networks could only tell so much of the story. Not even high definition images could detail the subtle nature of a situation. A furtive look of a target. A damp upper lip or a twitch at the mention of someone's name. The way a woman stood when she spoke to you or something she did with her hair when she lied. The way a man either played with the change in his pockets in a crowded elevator or didn't. The way tension could build between two people or in a room full of traitors. These were subtleties no camera could see. Only a trained operative could catch them and use them to flesh out the narrative crafted by OMNI's email searches and web search histories of a target.

Appreciating such subtleties was a world unto itself; a world where people like James Hicks and Roger Cobb and Tali Saddon had made their home. It was a world where organizations like the University thrived.

Hicks was already halfway to Twenty-Third Street when his

phone began to buzz in his pocket. It was Jason. He answered the phone anyway.

"I apologize for calling so late," Jason began, "but I saw you were on the move. Is this a good time for us talk? There are some details we must discuss following your selection as Dean." Jason's voice sounded heavy, like a combination of sleeplessness and alcohol. Hicks didn't even know if Jason drank and didn't care.

"I should've called you earlier," Hicks admitted, "but something always got in the way. Roger, Rahul, and…" It sounded like he was apologizing and stopped. He remembered he was the Dean now. He didn't have to apologize for anything, especially not to one of his own people. His predecessor never had. Hicks would keep the practice alive. "Anyway, I know you're running the New York Office and the Dutchman duties at the same time. I know it's a lot, but I'd like you to continue doing both for the time being. In fact, it would be a good idea if we began looking for a replacement for the New York Office so you can focus on being the Dutchman."

"I was expecting you to say the opposite. I know we haven't always seen eye-to-eye, but…"

"But we don't need to. The mission is more important than the men. Always has been and always will be." Talking to Jason about a non-University related topic felt odd, so he quickly changed gears. "Have you been following the fire in Weehawken?

Jason seemed just as eager to get back to business. "I was able to confirm it was the same building where they were holding Roger. Local fire officials have been pressured by the feds to wrap up their investigation quickly. Since there were no fatalities, the fire will be written off as vandalism or rats chewing threw wires or something. No one will be filing any insurance claims and no firemen were hurt fighting the blaze, so this is being crafted to fade away as quickly and as quietly as possible."

Which was exactly how Hicks would have handled it. "Has OMNI been able to discover if Stephens and the others have relocated elsewhere?"

"There's no digital signal of them anywhere in the area, but we have a new group to worry about."

When it rains, it pours. "Who?"

"The Mossad. It's one of the reasons for my call. I couldn't help but notice your OMNI signals have overlapped with Tali's signal for the past several hours. I assumed you briefed her about the Bajjah situation."

Hicks didn't know if the 'over-lapping signals' line was a literal reference or a dig. He let it go. "We hadn't sent her a daily progress report on Bajjah, so she demanded to interrogate him personally. I had to tell her he's dead, but spared her the details. I told her he'd accidentally died during questioning, but left out the link to Jabbar. Why?"

"Because she's been burning up the lines between her laptop and Tel Aviv in the past hour. Mossad encryption is tricky, so I haven't been able to see all the information she's sending out, but I can see her online activity has spiked since you left. I hope you know she's relaying anything you discussed with her as we speak."

Hicks knew it, but hearing it only made it worse. "Yeah, I know. Have OMNI monitor Tali's bosses in Tel Aviv. Her boss used to be a man named Schneider. He might not be her handler anymore, but he's a good place to start."

"I will," Jason said, "but remember their email encryption programs are almost as difficult for OMNI to crack as the Russian programs. We can do it, but it usually takes a couple of hours per email and Tali is sending a lot of emails."

"Don't only focus on her emails. Keep an eye on all travel requests into and out of New York from Tel Aviv for the next forty-eight hours, particularly civilian carriers and private jets capable of trans-Atlantic flight. Cross-reference them with known Mossad agents and aliases. Bajjah's death might be enough to get one of her bosses on a plane here to New York. I'd like to know about it first before they knock on my door."

"Consider it done." Hicks heard Jason's fingers on the keyboard. "Might I also suggest we also monitor Tali's OMNI activity closely? We don't have direct access to her laptop, but there are other methods we can use. Even if she decides to turn her handheld off and lock it in a drawer, it will tell us something."

Hicks hated the idea, but watching allies as closely as enemies in this line of work was necessary. "Do it, but don't bug her apartment or conduct direct surveillance of her yet. Conduct all observation through her handheld. Keep her on all of her current assignments, but don't give her anything new until further notice."

"Understood. There's also another development you need to know about." Jason cleared his throat a couple of times. "He's gone."

Hicks stopped walking. They may have been only two little words, but they were heavy enough to stop him cold. "He? You mean…"

"He had made arrangements for one of the Trustees to notify me after he passed. I don't know how it happened or when or where. I only know he's gone."

Hicks had known it was coming—the Dean had said it himself—but it didn't make the news any easier to take. "Which Trustee told you? I don't know anything about them."

"I don't know much about them either," Jason admitted. "All I know is the email came from a secure email address labeled Trustee Number Five on the OMNI system. The sender and location was redacted and classified, even for me. There will be a small memorial service held for the Dean early tomorrow evening in Savannah, Georgia. The Trustee also made it clear your attendance at the service is mandatory."

Jason went on. "The jet is still in London because of Rahul and won't be able to make it back to New York in time to bring you to Savannah, but I'll be able to make any other travel arrangements you wish. I'm sorry for your loss, James. I know you two were close. If you need me for anything, you know where to find me."

Jason ended the connection, which Hicks didn't mind. He didn't have anything more to say, anyway.

Hicks felt winded and leaned against a light pole to get his balance. He pocketed his handheld before he dropped the damned thing. He had known the Dean's condition was terminal, but finality of his death still hit hard. He had lost people in his life before, both before the University and since. The University had never replaced the family he had lost, but it had come closer.

And now the stranger who had been the closest thing to a mentor and a friend was gone. And it was up to Hicks to occupy the void he had left in the University system.

Alone.

As alone as he was on a deserted New York street an hour or so before dawn. Since solitude was all he had, he decided it was time to make it work for him.

CHAPTER 18

A S HE DROVE the Buick down to Savannah, Hicks tried to ignore the Carousel of Concern beginning to turn once again in his mind.

Stephens. Jabbar. The entire University operation. Roger's plan. Rahul. Shaban. Tali. The Mossad. And now: The Trustees.

Hicks kept one hand on the wheel as he thumbed open the lid on a bottle of Advil, shook out three tablets into his mouth and necked them down. He took a swig of water from the bottle in the center console to make sure they went down. He hoped they would be enough to dull his headache enough for the long drive ahead.

The OMNI GPS system on the Buick's dashboard screen told him the drive to Savannah would take at least twelve hours if he was lucky. He didn't mind. The time on the road would keep him from constantly checking his handheld, which was exactly the kind of break he needed. The events of the past two days had happened too fast for his liking. He needed to slow things down because in the intelligence game, speed often killed.

He could have cut his travel time to a fraction if he had decided to fly, even commercially. But air travel left a trail, even when it was covered up in the airline's system, and he wouldn't have been able to take his Ruger on the plane. With three angry federal agencies on his trail, going unarmed would have been foolish.

He could have had Jason rent a private jet, but such flights had a tendency to conveniently crash, especially when they carried people like him at times like these. The anonymity of the open road was the best choice.

Hicks' Buick LaCrosse was already tied into the OMNI system, so he could still do most of his work as he drove. He was also much safer in the Buick than he would be in a jet, especially this particular Buick.

About a year ago, he had the Varsity technicians overhaul the entire automobile and replace all the windows with bulletproof glass. They had also re-enforced the frame, installed armor plating, and upgraded the electronics so the car was tied in to the OMNI system.

The technicians had also swapped out the Buick's standard V6 engine for an AM 29 V12 engine taken from an Aston Martin he had seized from an Asset: a real estate mogul who had made some unsavory deals with the Iranians. It was a choice between the man going to prison for the rest of his life or allowing Hicks to take his car. Hicks cut him a deal: he could keep the car, but Hicks got the engine. He wasn't a total bastard.

Hicks had stashed the Ruger in a hidden compartment in the console in case he needed it. If a cop happened to stop him on the way, he'd never find it. Hicks wanted the pistol close since it might come in handy before this was over.

As the miles rolled by, Hicks was able to check how OMNI was monitoring the actions of all the names in the Bajjah/Jabbar network. The scope had expanded to include names not already on his list, but Hicks' primary focus was still on Rahul's progress in following Shaban, Bajjah's supposed money man in London.

Hicks had hoped the fire in Weehawken would sideline the Barnyard's interest in him for at least a day or so. Stephens and Avery would have to answer a lot of questions about losing a black site that wasn't supposed to exist on American soil. The bureaucrats of the Barnyard were still bureaucrats. They would demand answers while they covered their asses. He figured Avery and Stephens would come back at the University with a vengeance, but he'd worry about it when the time came. From now on Stephens would need to be far more cautious, if he was still in the game at all.

Maybe by that point, they would be willing to listen to reason. Maybe he could find a way to work with them and get them to back off, the way he'd tried with Tali and the Mossad. He remembered the Dean's directive, but Hicks knew the University couldn't fight off three government agencies and the Mossad and investigate Jabbar's network all at the same time without something getting fouled up.

And if Roger's plan worked, Stephens and Avery would find themselves on the bench permanently.

Hicks hit the voice activation button on his steering wheel and said, "Call Rahul."

"Calling Rahul," the female voice repeated.

He was glad Rahul picked up on the first ring. "Funny you should call. I've got some news for you."

Hicks was glad his voice sounded clear and strong. It was a big difference from the way he'd sounded in Rockefeller Center. "Good or bad news?"

"A mixed bag, I'm afraid. I've already tried to establish contact with my former assets in the Middle East. They're all still alive, but they've been a bit slow to respond. It could be from an abundance of caution at my sudden reappearance or it may be due to other things. I'll keep you updated on how it turns out."

"Make the Middle East names a distant priority," Hicks said. "They're already being watched by several foreign agencies and a few of our own. OMNI can track agency surveillance on them remotely. I'm more concerned about Shaban."

"Which brings me to my good news. You'll be happy to know I've not only located Shaban, but I already have a team in place watching him right now."

Hicks was impressed, but kept it to himself. He knew complimenting a drunk too early in an assignment could lead them into a false sense of security and right back to the bottle. Guarded optimism was best. "Tell me more."

"If Shaban is Bajjah's money man, he's doing a hell of a job covering it up."

"Explain."

"Shaban has a reputation as a street corner revolutionary. I had OMNI dig deeper into his real identity and discovered his real name is Mohammed Shaban Ispahani. He's Iranian by birth and goes by the name of Shaban in his day-to-day life.

He's managed to get himself a job at a local Islamic community center under the impressively vague title of 'Community Events Coordinator,' whatever the hell that is. Gets paid a pittance as a salary for the largely a no-show job since Shaban never seems to be there. The owner of the center also happens to own the building where Shaban has a flat in Whitechapel, so he's living practically rent free."

Hicks was glad his instincts were proving to be right. Even if Shaban wasn't the money man of Bajjah's organization, there was more to the London side of Bajjah's network than met the eye. "Anything on the owner of the center and the flat?"

"Another aged zealot," Rahul said. "Believes in the cause and funds young people like Shaban who carry forth hatred. You know the type. He likes the warmth of the fire but never gets close enough to get burned."

Rahul went on. "Shaban is a real hellfire-and brimstone type, though. Likes organizing protests against Israel in public squares on the weekends, hands out leaflets and gets himself on camera. Posts his venom on several blogs, so he's attained something of celebrity status online. I learned the local police suspect him in having a hand in organizing some attacks during the London riots back in 2014, but there's no solid evidence against him at this point. He's a crafty one, our Shaban."

"How many pairs of eyes do you have on him already?"

Rahul said, "I used part of the money you put in the account to hire some of my old colleagues from the NIA. In fact, I have two of them watching him as we speak. There'll be two shifts of five before I'm done, bringing the total number to ten in all. And before you warn me about leakage, they've all been separated from the NIA under less than ideal conditions. None of them will be reporting back to anyone in New Delhi or anyone else. Good men through and through. They aren't trigger happy, but each one of them is a stone killer if it comes to it."

Hicks was encouraged, but he wasn't turning cartwheels yet. "Email me whatever OMNI has on each of the people in your team as soon as possible."

"Why? Don't you trust me?"

"I do. But I trust OMNI more."

Rahul laughed. "You'll have all of their records within the hour. I'll have ten men watching his flat in Whitechapel around the clock in two-hour shifts so I'll always have five bullyboys ready to strike at a moment's notice. All ten if we have to respond to something heavy."

"Where is Shaban now?"

"At his flat. According to the calendar on his phone, which we've hacked, he's due to go on his weekly trip to Mantes-la-Jolie tomorrow. It's a town outside…"

"Paris. I know where it is." Over the years, Hicks had tracked a lot of persons-of-interest in Mantes-la-Jolie's active Islamic community. Like most Islamic communities, an overwhelming majority of the residents were peaceful. But terrorists didn't need large numbers. They only needed a few zealots to accomplish their goals. "Any idea who Shaban is meeting there?"

"According to what OMNI was able to find, he's been helping to organize a network in the areas around Paris. My men are still trying to uncover what he's up to here in London, but it is slow going. We're trying to move cautiously so we don't tip our hand and scare him off. I'll make sure one of my men trail him to France while we dig deeper into his operation here."

"I want reports on this son of a bitch twice a day. I want

images of whomever he meets and audio of what he says. I want to make sure we keep track of every keystroke on every device he has and funnel all of it into OMNI for analysis. I don't want any surprises if we can avoid them."

The dashboard screen changed from a map view of his location to an alert of another call coming through the OMNI system. It was a call from a University extension, but the caller was listed as **UNIDENTIFIED.**

Strange. Hicks knew all extensions on the University system were labeled, even the Dean's.

"I'll have to call you back," Hicks said to Rahul. Hicks killed the connection and answered the incoming call. "Who is this?"

"Hello, James." A woman's voice came through the Buick's speakers. The voice was familiar, but he couldn't place it. "I am one of the Trustees our mutual friend discussed with you before his untimely demise."

That explained the unidentified extension. This must be the same Trustee who had contacted Jason. "Our mutual friend mentioned you."

"I know he did. You and I need to talk before the funeral service this afternoon. There are a few things I want to make clear to you about your new position from the outset. I want to make sure we get off on the right foot and all."

Although Hicks had been expecting to be contacted by a Trustee, he had no intention of simply rolling over for one. "I don't take blind meetings, especially given the current difficulties we're facing right now. If you are who you say you are, you'll appreciate why. If you want to talk, let's talk now. It's a secure line."

"And someone in your position should appreciate the idea

that some conversations are best held face to face."

"And polite conversations begin with introductions. You already know my name. What's yours?"

"Even if I told you my name, it wouldn't mean anything to you. You have never heard of me, and we have never worked together. You also wouldn't find my name in an OMNI search because all mention of me has been scrubbed clean from the system. The fact I'm calling you using a University device should be enough to prove my identity. The fact I know the Dean told you about the Trustees during your last conversation should prove I'm an ally, not an enemy."

Hicks couldn't argue with her logic, but logic hadn't had much of a place in his life the past few days. "Fine. Send me the address of where you want to meet and I'll see you there."

She killed the connection and Hicks activated the OMNI voice prompt button on his steering wheel. "Trace the location of my last call."

OMNI's electronic female voice reported, "Call was from an unnamed University extension."

Hicks figured such would be the case. "Location of the call?"

OMNI responded, "Call originated from proximity of Savannah, Georgia."

A second later, an appointment alert popped up on his dashboard screen. It was scheduled for twenty minutes after OMNI said Hicks was due to arrive in Savannah according to his current rate of speed. Whoever had made the call and sent the appointment knew when he'd arrive in Savannah. They only could've known that if they had access to the OMNI system.

He hit the voice prompt again. "Map the address of the appointment."

The voice said, "Working," as it produced a map of Savannah on the screen. The location was Columbia Square, one of the dozens of quaint green spaces dotting the city. It was public enough so as not to be a set-up, but private enough for two people to talk.

It was exactly the kind of spot Hicks would've picked for such a meeting.

But his instincts told him something was wrong. He sensed a connection that shouldn't be there. He played a hunch and hit the voice prompt button again. "Retrace the previous call."

Again, the female voice responded, "Call was from an unnamed University extension. Call originated from Savannah, Georgia."

Hicks damned near drove onto the shoulder of the highway.

OMNI's computerized voice was the same as the woman who had just called.

CHAPTER 19

HICKS PARKED THE Buick and pulled on his black suit coat as he walked toward the Columbia Square. There wasn't much of a breeze, so he kept the jacket unbuttoned. The Ruger under his left arm would be easy to reach if he needed it.

He spotted the Trustee sitting alone on a bench in the middle of Savannah's Columbia Square. The thick branches of four ancient trees planted at each corner of the square spread out high above them, casting the entire park in rich shadow. An ornate fountain gurgled in the center of the square, successfully drowning out the noise of the early evening traffic.

Hicks noticed the Trustee was the only other person in the square. He didn't know if she had arranged things this way or if the benches were empty by coincidence. Since coincidence was rare in their world, he figured there was a good chance she had arranged it somehow.

The closer he got, Hicks judged the Trustee to be a woman in her late sixties, maybe a little older. She had long white hair streaked with gray beneath a black hat. She was painfully thin and may have looked frail if one looked at her quickly.

But Hicks never looked at anyone quickly. He had been trained to observe, and he could see this wasn't some little old lady sitting on a bench. Her back was ramrod straight and her black shoes had a decent heel to them, something an older woman with balance problems would never wear.

Even in the shadow of the trees, he could see her eyes were large and strikingly blue. They locked on Hicks for the briefest of moments as he approached before she looked away. She had looked at him long enough to see whatever she had needed to see. There was no reason to look at him any longer than she had. She had obviously been trained, too.

Hicks thought her pale skin and overall bone structure belied an Anglo-Saxon origin, the type who could be a descendent from a moneyed family of old-line breeding, maybe all the way back to the Mayflower.

Her attire supported his assessment. She wore a simple black suit carefully tailored to accentuate her delicate frame. The pearls around her neck were obviously cultured and didn't come cheap. She had a black, gold trimmed clutch on her lap that might have been big enough to conceal a .22, but he couldn't tell if it was.

She was smoking a cigarette with a black-gloved hand, flicking the ashes on the ground with a single definitive tap of a long, crooked finger.

She didn't react when Hicks sat next to her on the same

bench. A thick ornate iron armrest was between them.

To anyone who might be passing by the square, the woman seemed more interested in her cigarette than the man sharing her bench. No one was within earshot when she said, "You look younger than the picture taken upon your enrollment at the University, James. Remarkable, considering how long ago the picture was taken and the life you've led since. Our way of life seems to have agreed with you far more than your service in Coast Guard Intelligence."

Hicks smiled. "I was wondering which factoid from my past you'd use to break the ice. I figured you'd call me by my real name."

"I hate being predictable. Besides, 'James Hicks' suits you much better than your given name."

Hicks understood why having his past thrown in his face had disturbed Roger. Some things were better left buried, especially things about ourselves. He tried not to let the casual reference to his file get to him by focusing on his training instead. He surveyed his surroundings.

A few buildings were close by but all the windows were closed. No one seemed to be watching them. In fact, nothing looked out of place. Birds sang overhead. The fountain drowned out everything else. It would have been a pleasant late afternoon scene if it hadn't been for the nature of their discussion or the reason for their meeting.

"Okay. You've proven you have access to my records and asserted your influence. Let's dispense with the bullshit and jump to the part where you tell me why I'm here."

Her gray eyebrows rose, revealing more lines in her forehead than were already there. "Not very polite, are you?"

"Not very patient, either. I've spent twelve hours in a car driving down here to bury one of the few friends I have. My ass hurts, my legs are stiff, and I'm short on manners. So you've got five seconds to convince me why I shouldn't walk away right now."

She allowed a long stream of smoke escape through her narrow nostrils. "I suppose you have a right to be cautious. Being hunted by no less than three intelligence agencies is enough to fray anyone's nerves, even yours."

"Four seconds."

"I am one of the University Trustees our mutual friend mentioned to you yesterday before his unfortunate passing. My fellow board members have asked me to speak with you on their behalf so I might gauge your mettle for myself. They want to make certain you are up to the task of being Dean."

Hicks decided the woman had bought herself thirty additional seconds. Maybe a minute. "My predecessor already put me through a dry run by selling out me and my people to the Barnyard. I passed and got the job. If you've got the access you claim you have, you and your board can read twenty years' worth of information about me with a few keystrokes. There's no reason for a face-to-face like this."

"You're a cautious man, aren't you?"

"I haven't lived this long being reckless. And I never heard much about the Trustees until yesterday."

"You were never Dean before," the woman said, "so there was no reason for you to know about us. I wanted to meet you in person because I believe the only way to be certain about a thing is to see it with my own two eyes."

"Kind of an old fashioned notion for a high tech organization like ours."

She smiled. "This coming from the man who sent Rahul to London so he could give Shaban personal scrutiny instead of simply relying on remote surveillance. There's still a place for the personal touch in the modern world, don't you think? You still can't email a handshake to close a deal." Her smile faded a bit. "Or a bullet into someone's brain should the need arise. At least not yet, anyway. I hope I'm long dead before such an eventuality occurs."

She looked at him for the first time since he'd sat down. She had a shade of clear blue eyes that could be mistakenly described as kind. "My associates wanted me to see you with my own two eyes so I could see your soul or a lack thereof. Do you still believe in the notion of souls, James, or are you the jaded type who believes such notions are quaint superstitions? There's no right or wrong answer, I assure you. All I ask is you tell me the truth because if you lie, I'll know it."

Hicks laughed for the first time in days. "You're kidding, right? I haven't had to pass a psych evaluation in a long time."

Her eyes stayed on him. "Answer the question."

Hicks could tell she was serious, so he decided to answer. "For the Dean's sake, I'd like to believe souls exist. I'd like to hope he has a shot at enjoying peace or something like it."

She flicked the ash on her cigarette. "He's not the Dean anymore. That title has fallen to you."

"I don't intend on letting it fall anywhere."

"I'm glad to hear that but it remains to be seen. You didn't know him, did you? Your predecessor."

The question hardly even made sense to him. "I've spent the past two decades speaking to him on the phone through a voice-modulating program. On his orders, I've crippled people, blackmailed people, assaulted and killed people without even laying eyes on him until two weeks ago. Yesterday was the second and last time I had even seen the man. So, no, I never knew him because he never wanted me to know him. Not until the end."

"I suppose you have a point," she allowed. "Al was always afraid of getting too close to people out of fear they may betray him one day, either intentionally or unintentionally. I always saw it as one of his greatest strengths, his ability to fear not only people's dubious intentions but also their honest carelessness. Al was his real name, by the way. Al Clay. Not Alfred or Albert. Just plain Al. It says so right on his birth certificate. Fitting for a man like him, don't you agree?"

Hicks had never spent much time thinking about what the Dean's real name might have been. He had always been so distant, it would have been pointless to try. The man on the phone and behind the emails had always simply been the Dean. That had been enough for Hicks because that's all of him there was.

But now he finally had a name to go along with the man. Al Clay. Hicks was surprised by how little it mattered to him. Al Clay had been the Dean of the University and now Al Clay was dead.

And Jabbar's network was still trying to kill people. And Mark Stephens and the intelligence community were still hunting the University. And Hicks still had a job to do.

Life stopped for no one. Dead or alive. Cemeteries were filled with indispensable men.

Hicks stood up to leave but didn't button his coat. "Thanks

for the stroll down memory lane, but since you're plugged into what we do, you know I've got things to do. You already know about Rahul being in London, so..."

The woman's blue eyes flashed. "Sit back down, James. Now. You have a rather large red spot on your tie. I happen to think it's a very nice tie. It would be a shame to ruin it."

Hicks looked down and saw a red laser dot moving up his tie to the center of his chest. He followed the path of the red beam to an open window of an old building across the street. It was too dark inside to see the shooter, but the beam was clear enough.

He knew the window had been closed when he'd first sat down. He should've seen it open, but hadn't.

The woman took a final drag before allowing the cigarette to fall to the path. She crushed it beneath her shoe. "Don't make any sudden moves—especially for the Ruger—or my associate will pump two high velocity rounds into your chest. Politely sit back down and all will be forgiven."

Hicks sat back down. "Well, this is a first. I've never been mugged by an octogenarian before."

"Don't be insolent," she snapped. "I'm not even seventy and you're not being mugged. You're being briefed."

"At gunpoint."

She smiled. "It got you to sit back down, didn't it?" She reached into her clutch and produced a slim gold cigarette case. She opened it and held it out to him. "Your file says you prefer cigars, but I'm afraid these will have to do under the circumstances."

He looked at the cigarettes in the case—Dunhill's, of course—then back at her. "A final smoke for a condemned man?"

Her smile remained unchanged. It was no kinder than her eyes had been. "See it as a peace offering between new friends."

Hicks took one and the book of matches she offered. He struck the match and lit the cigarette. He drew the smoke deep into his lungs before letting it out. She was right. It wasn't a cigar, but it helped calm his nerves.

She discarded her old cigarette and selected took a new one for herself and lit it. She didn't look to Hicks to light it for her and Hicks didn't offer. She said, "The other Trustees and I appreciate the challenges you face and we agree with Al's assessment. You're exactly the right person for the job at hand. Al was a programming genius who gave the University a technological edge in the digital age. OMNI was his idea and its creation helped keep us relevant. I dare say it has kept us several steps ahead of the federal agencies who are only now beginning to catch up to our capabilities."

"I guess it was his idea to make your voice the voice of OMNI, too?" Hicks said.

The Trustee offered a vague smile. "He called it his tribute to his predecessor."

"You were Dean once?"

"I was," she admitted, "but that was long ago and doesn't matter anymore. Al built on an underlying network we'd always had, but he put us decades ahead of the other agencies. While people were discussing building the 'information superhighway,' Al had already mapped it out and planned ahead. He was the right person the University needed at exactly the right time. He brought us into the twenty-first century back in the nineties. Your tactical experience will ensure we remain relevant in the years to come."

"Thanks for the vote of confidence, Mom. I'm all choked up."

Despite Hicks' sarcasm, the Trustee didn't skip a beat. "We appreciate how challenging the investigation of the extent of Jabbar's network may be, but we believe you are making excellent progress. We agree with your decision to concentrate all of your efforts to such an end, despite the ire it has drawn from our friends in Tel Aviv."

Hicks took a drag on his cigarette. "Why do I feel a 'but' coming on?"

"But," she continued, "as your investigation strains your resources in the days ahead, you may be tempted to forget about your predecessor's directive to keep the Barnyard and the others at a distance. However, this directive is one of the few directives we insist you follow. You are absolutely forbidden from opening a dialogue with any other intelligence agencies until you discover the full extent of the intent, influence, and involvement of Jabbar in Bajjah's network. You must only share information once we have a firm grasp of what we are dealing with, not before, preferably with Jabbar captured in Roger Cobb's infamous Cube."

Hicks didn't like it. "Al told me, as Dean, my word is final. He said no one can challenge it, including the Trustees."

"This is largely true. You decide the path the University takes. But like all decisions, they are not without consequences. You'll find we don't voice our opinions often except in matters where University sovereignty is threatened. The Bajjah/Jabbar investigation qualifies."

Hicks looked down at his tie to see if the red dot was still there. It was. "A bullet to the chest is a hell of a consequence."

"A visceral reminder of what is at stake, a reminder that failure is not an option, James."

"Meaning?"

"Meaning it is impossible for the University to stop all of the threats we uncover. We have managed to prevent a good number of plots and attacks throughout our history thanks to your efforts and the efforts of other Faculty Members like you. But we won't be able to stop anything if we do not have sufficient autonomy to operate. Sharing information of your Jabbar investigation with the likes of Mark Stephens or the Mossad is not an option under any circumstances. We would become the focus of their interest, not Jabbar."

She continued. "Your entire career has been built on influencing people to work against their own interests in order to further the University's aims. We are concerned you may decide to feed Stephens or the Mossad only enough information in the hope they will back off and possibly leave us alone. You may even threaten them or blackmail them, as is your forte. We wanted you to know it will not work in this instance and we forbid you from doing so."

"Christ, you guys are good, aren't you?"

"Not all of us are guys. So, to be clear, if it's a choice between allowing one of Jabbar's plots to succeed or risking University autonomy through sharing information, you are ordered to allow Jabbar to succeed."

Hicks almost dropped his cigarette. "You can't mean that."

"The University cannot function if it is compromised or infiltrated or split apart by several of our own intelligence agencies. Our effectiveness lies solely in our ability to influence events. Your rash actions in seizing Bajjah in Philadelphia raised our profile, which has caused a great deal of inconvenience, but the damage isn't irreparable. Not yet. The Barnyard still doesn't know exactly who you are. They don't know you work for the University. You must make sure they never do."

She went on. "Unfortunately, your ill-advised rendezvous with Agent Saddon caused her to contact her superiors in Tel Aviv, which has led them to come to New York to pressure you into giving over all the Bajjah information. She tried to dissuade them, if it's any comfort."

He wasn't surprised, but hearing the Trustee tell him made it sting more than it should.

"All you've done since I've gotten here is give me orders and made threats. Are you bastards doing anything except watch from the stands and armchair quarterback?"

"We can do plenty and we already are," she said. "We are using our influence to dampen the Mossad's zeal for the Bajjah information. Tali's supervisor Schneider is coming to New York to hold your feet to the fire, but we made sure his superiors are less enthusiastic. In fact, he is making the New York trip without their permission or consent. We have also thwarted the Barnyard and NSA attempts to involve other agencies in the hunt against you, such as the FBI and the ATF. The Barnyard still has sufficient resources of its own, but at least they don't have the resources those other agencies could provide."

Hicks was impressed, but he knew it wasn't enough. "With all the pull you keep telling me you have, you still can't get Stephens to back off?"

She looked away. "Stephens and the Barnyard are a more complicated matter. Direct involvement in their operation would expose other Trustees to undue scrutiny, especially because they have your identity and now Roger's as well. Avery's decision to burn down the Weehawken facility was made without authorizations and has caused a great deal of internal strife within the joint operation. This strife has slowed their progress considerably. We will use our influence to slow them even further, but you still need to be careful. I don't believe they'll give up so easy."

For once, they agreed.

He smoked his cigarette and thought about what she had told him. And what she hadn't told him. She'd said he couldn't share information with Stephens. She hadn't mentioned anything about his plan to use Roger to knock Stephens out of the game. It meant she most likely didn't know about it and couldn't forbid what she didn't know. It gave him all the wiggle room he needed. If protecting University autonomy was paramount, that's what he'd do. But she might not like how he did it.

"I guess all the terms you've given me are non-negotiable?"

She looked down at the red dot on his chest. "No, James. I'm afraid they're not."

Hicks took another drag on his cigarette. "It's nice to have clarity, I guess."

"You're a most capable man. Al made a convincing case to name you as his successor and all of us agreed. But we all answer to someone eventually. And you answer to us."

Hicks looked down at the red dot on his chest. "Do I have a choice?"

The woman offered a smile. "The best choices are made when we know the consequences." The smile went away. "I'll need you to agree to our terms before we can leave here and go on with our mourning of our dearly departed colleague."

Hicks decided he might have liked this woman if she didn't have a sniper aiming at his chest. "I promise I won't involve other agencies until I know more about Jabbar's network. I'll also clear it with you first."

She kept looking at him. Waiting.

Hicks added, "And I will not sacrifice University autonomy for the sake of stopping an attack by Jabbar."

The woman looked across the street and held up two fingers. The red dot disappeared from Hicks' chest.

She smiled again. "I'm so glad you listened to reason, James. We have high hopes for you as Dean. Killing you so early into your tenure would have been such a waste."

Hicks began to breathe again. "Yeah, thanks."

"You're not in this alone, my friend. You have the support of a great number of important and influential people. For now, at least. Don't squander it. And don't test it, either."

She slipped her cigarette case back into her clutch as she stood. "You've had such a long drive from New York. Why don't you stay here for another five minutes and enjoy the view?"

"Another threat?"

"We don't make threats, James. We don't have to." She looked around the empty square and inhaled deeply. "This is one of my favorite places in the world. The elms are so tall and dignified and they cast such lovely shade. I learned one of the most invaluable experiences of my life in this same plaza a long time ago. 'Sometimes, you can't appreciate the true nature of a thing until you see how the shadows play across it.'" She gave him a little wave. "See you in church."

Hicks finished his smoke as the sound of her heels clapping against the pavement echoed through the deserted plaza.

He dropped his cigarette on the ground and crushed it beneath his shoe. The goddamned Carousel of Concern had gotten even bigger.

CHAPTER 20

THE DEAN'S MEMORIAL service was appropriately solemn and mercifully short. Some mourners were clustered in the front pews while various other people were sprinkled throughout the chapel. He didn't see the Trustee anywhere, and he wasn't surprised. She looked like the type who had made a career of always being present, but never seen. Al Clay hadn't been a field operative. The Trustee had been at one time and a skilled one in her day.

He spotted Jason sitting alone in a pew in the middle of the church. He looked visibly shaken, but Hicks saw no point in trying to comfort him. He had no idea if Jason and the Dean had been close or if the Dean had been a voice on the phone for him, too. It didn't matter. The dead were gone. The living had problems of their own.

As the preacher began his sermon, the Carousel of Concern fired up again in his mind.

Stephens. Jabbar. The entire University operation. Roger's plan. Rahul. Shaban. Tali. The Mossad. The Trustees.

Hicks considered using the rare opportunity of his presence in a church to ask God for some help, but God had never been one to return his calls. He decided to skip it and use the occasion to try to clear his mind.

The preacher spoke in general terms of loss and redemption and of a life well spent and of the eternal reward awaiting his loyal servant, Al Clay. It didn't sound like the preacher knew Al any better than Hicks did. Hicks found some measure of comfort in that. The Dean was nothing if not consistent.

Hicks decided to duck out before the final 'amens' were said. He had paid his respects to the memory of a man he had hardly known and decided it was time to leave. He knew he hadn't paid his respects to Al Clay, merely the version of the man he had called the Dean for so long. It hadn't brought him any sense of closure. He didn't believe in closure anyway. Closure was for romance novels and movies of the week and head-shrinkers who made money off the fantasy it existed. In his world, holes remained. It was how he navigated around them that counted.

He had a long drive back to New York and a lot of University business to catch up on along the way.

AFTER GETTING SOMETHING to eat at a quaint diner off the highway, Hicks filled up the tank, got back in the Buick, and began the long drive north. The left lane opened up in front of him and he hit the gas. The V12 engine hummed as it slowly came to life. It was built to go fast and Hicks was happy to oblige.

When his new handheld began to vibrate, he checked the dashboard screen. He expected to see an incoming update from Rahul or Jason.

Instead, he saw two words: **PROXIMITY ALERT.**

OMNI had detected a secure federal bandwidth within the Buick's scanning range.

Hicks kept one hand on the wheel as he tapped the dashboard screen to bring up a tactical map of his immediate area. One icon on the map showed his Buick heading north on the highway. A second icon several hundred feet behind him was actively sending and receiving signals via a known secure NSA bandwidth.

Maybe Stephens was back in the hunt after all.

Hicks hit the voice command button on the steering wheel. "Overlay map with a live satellite image."

The electronic voice of the Trustee repeated the command as the road map was replaced by a live image taken from a satellite miles above the earth.

It showed a bird's eye view of Hicks' Buick in the middle of dozens of cars all heading north along the highway. The icon showing the secure signal was still at the bottom of the screen, but the vehicle was out of the current view.

Hicks commanded OMNI to zoom out five percent and the vehicle appeared at the bottom of the screen. "Zoom in on the source of the secure signal."

The screen re-centered on the vehicle as it magnified the image. The signal was coming from a black Ford Expedition barreling north at seventy-five miles an hour.

Hicks checked his rearview mirror, but there were too many

cars between him and the Expedition to get a visual fix on it. He was more curious than worried. It might not be Stephens. It could be a couple of FBI men on their way home or a secret US Marshal prisoner transport. It could've been a couple of Treasury men on their way to a stakeout or any number of other benign reasons, none of which had anything to do with him.

Hicks decided to find out.

He slowed down as he shifted into the center lane before moving to the right. He hoped the SUV would pass him, giving him a better look at the vehicle.

But when the Expedition also slowed and moved into the right lane, he knew this wasn't some federal vehicle on a milk run. He was being followed.

Hicks knew he couldn't simply gun the engine and try to outrun them. Speed might have been enough in the old days, but a clean escape was damned near impossible under the watchful eye of the Barnyard satellites above. Besides, traffic was too heavy. He bet Stephens had a satellite locked on his Buick and was tracking him remotely. He didn't know how or when they had acquired him, but it didn't matter anymore.

Hicks knew Stephens had to be in the car. This had become personal.

And it was time to show Stephens exactly who he was dealing with.

The day before, he would have needed an Operator to help him execute his next move. But yesterday, he wasn't the Dean. He decided to put his newfound access to the test. He double tapped the icon of the Expedition on the screen and activated OMNI's voice prompt. "Tap into the secure signal of the target vehicle."

A spiral appeared on the dashboard screen, showing OMNI was working to hack the frequency. A few seconds later, a new prompt appeared on the bottom of the screen: **FREQUENCY ACCESSED.**

Another window popped up which allowed him to contact the car trailing him. He selected the option and spoke over the secure frequency. "I guess you're not too good at taking hints, are you, Ace?"

Stephens' response was quicker than Hicks had expected. "I don't take hints, asshole."

"You don't take advice, either. I told your boss Avery to leave me alone."

"Must've been some kind of mix up," Stephens said. "I didn't get that message."

"Too bad. How about we pull over so I can deliver it to you personally?"

It sounded like Stephens laughed. "You read my mind. There's a place off the next exit…"

"I've got a better idea." Hicks steered the Buick onto the wide shoulder on the right side of the highway and hit the brakes, kicking up gravel as the car skidded to a stop.

He watched the dashboard screen as the icon of Stephens' SUV slowly passed him. With his own eyes, he watched the black Expedition pull onto the shoulder about a hundred feet ahead. The move also drew a lot of horns and screeching breaks and curses from the drivers moving north at a good clip.

Hicks rolled the Buick forward to close the gap between them. He stopped ten feet away from the back of the Expedition and put the Buick in park. He kept the engine running and the headlights on. He got out of the car—leaving the driver's side door open—and leaned against the hood of his Buick and waited. He made sure his suit jacket was open, too.

The sound of the cars buzzing past them on the highway reminded Hicks of angry bees. Roger's retort of Stephens' past came to mind. Buzz, buzz.

He watched Stephens get out of the passenger side of the Expedition and walk back toward him. He was taller and broader than Hicks remembered from the street and the video feed from the warehouse. The Trustee back at Columbia Square in Savannah had been right once again. Seeing things with your own eyes gives the truest perspective.

Stephens was wearing a blue suit, a white shirt, and a blue tie. His jacket was open, too. He stopped by the back wheel of the Expedition, about ten feet away. His hands were at his sides.

Hicks smiled. "Don't you look pretty? All dressed up in a nice suit. Guess you got called on the carpet by your bosses for the Weehawken thing."

Stephens didn't smile. "You, my friend, have been one gigantic pain in my ass."

"I'm not your friend. Tell the driver to roll down his window and keep his face in the side view mirror where I can see him."

"And if I refuse?"

"You saw what I did to your people on the street yesterday. Figure it out."

Over his shoulder, Stephens said, "Roll down your window and stay visible. Let's see how this asshole plays this."

The driver's window rolled down and Hicks saw a woman's face in the side view mirror. She had a short haircut bordering on pixie style.

Hicks remembered how Roger had goaded Stephens into

losing his temper. He decided to do the same. It might give him an edge. "Holy shit. Is that Sandy Duncan?"

"Who the fuck is Sandy Duncan?"

"Doesn't matter." He looked at the driver again. "She's cute, though. You fucking her?"

"The only one who's going to get fucked around here is you, little man. Spent the whole day in meetings talking about what to do about you."

"No shit? What did you come up with? A resolution to write a memo and schedule a meeting to review the memo?"

"We're way past that stage," Stephens said. "Playtime's over and now you're coming with us."

"That's not going to happen, Ace. It's been a long day, so the only place I'm going is home. You should go home, too. You look tired as hell."

"Only place you're going is a holding cell. Orders from the Director himself. He's had enough of your shit and he wants you in custody. In the back seat of my truck or in a rubber bag in the trunk, it makes no difference to me."

"I don't believe that," Hicks said. "If he wanted me picked up this place would be swarming with Quantico farm boys right now. He'd never send only two people after such a high value target. I don't doubt you had a lot of meetings about me today, but I'd wager your wings got clipped and you're banking on the idea that bringing me in is the best way to get back in good graces with your bosses."

He waited for Stephens to answer, but he didn't. Hicks went on. "You still don't get what's going on here, do you? I've already beaten your group twice and today I hacked your own communication line while you were tracking me. I've been one step ahead of you every time, and I still am. Bringing me in is only going to bring you more trouble than you've already got. I warned you once to leave me alone. I won't warn you again." He remembered some personal details from Stephens' file. "No reason for your daughters to grow up without a father."

Stephens shifted his weight, like he was getting ready to make a move. "You're the second asshole in the past twenty-four hours who has threatened my family. Your friend back in the sweatbox told me the same thing when he grabbed me. Whispered my girls' names and birthdays in my ear while he had me on the table. That how you bastards operate? By threatening men's families?"

"I didn't threaten them and neither did he. I threatened you. Each time you've tried to jump us, you've gotten slapped back. Consider those warnings a professional courtesy because they won't last forever."

"Professionals get paid, little man. Who's paying you?"

Hicks shook his head. "We're not there yet. First we need to get along before you get to go along."

"How about we try building up some trust," Stephens said. "Tell me where Bajjah is. I know you grabbed him and his accomplice down in Philly. At least confirm you've still got him or he's still in the country. I know you're plugged into the game at some level. I'd bet we're playing for the same side. Give me something to bring back to my bosses and maybe I can buy you a little more time."

Twenty-four hours before, Hicks might have taken that option. But a lot could change in a day. A lot had. Maybe the Dean and the Trustees were right. Men like Stephens never took no for an answer. It wasn't in their DNA. If he cracked the door

212

open, they'd kick it in and burn the house down, especially now that pride was involved.

He remembered the Trustee's threats, but she wasn't in the field calling plays. She wasn't responsible for protecting the University. He was and that's exactly what he was going to do. His way.

"How about I make you a deal instead?" Hicks offered. "Back off now and in a week, you and I will have a sit down where I answer all of your questions. Show a little patience and good faith today and in a few days, I'll make you look like a hero. Make your bosses forget all about your Weehawken embarrassment. Hell, maybe you'll get Avery's job instead."

"That's the deal?"

"Yep. And it expires the minute I drive out of here."

Stephens leaned toward him. "What makes you think you're driving out of here?"

"There's no question about me driving out of here, Ace. Either you listen to reason or you and your girlfriend end up as chalk outlines on the side of the highway."

Stephens left hand flinched.

Hicks had the Ruger in his hand before Stephens' hand reached his belt line.

Stephens stopped when he saw it. "Damn, old man. You're fast."

"I'm not old." Hicks didn't want to attract the attention of any cops who might be driving by, so he kept the Ruger at his side. "A Beekeeper's greatest asset is supposed to be his patience. You'd be wise to keep that in mind the next time you try to crowd me. Give me a week unobserved and unobstructed and I'll give you answers to questions you're not even asking yet. But if you keep pushing me, it'll cost you."

Hicks feased himself off the hood and began walking backward toward the driver's side of the Buick.

Stephens stayed where he was, hands visible. "Why should I trust you?"

"Because you're still alive, Ace. That's got to count for something."

Hicks kept the Ruger free as he got behind the wheel and fired up the engine. The windshield and the windows were all bulletproof glass. The doors and body were armor plated. If Stephens or the driver fired at him, Hicks would be safe and respond accordingly.

But the DIA Beekeeper didn't go for his gun. He simply stood and watched Hicks pull the Buick back into traffic and drive away.

CHAPTER
21

HICKS KEPT CHECKING the dashboard screen to see if Stephens was following him. The icon for the Ford Expedition stayed on the shoulder of the highway. The distance between them grew, with the SUV's icon moving toward the lower edge of his screen until it was off the map.

Hicks was encouraged. Maybe Stephens had listened to reason after all.

The left lane began to slow as the traffic in the center lane began to speed up. A narrow space next to him cleared, so Hicks decided to put the V12 to work.

He checked his mirrors before signaling he was going to change lanes. He was almost in the center lane when a black Peterbilt truck seemingly came out of nowhere and slipped into the spot from the right lane. It wasn't pulling a trailer, so it easily fit into the narrow space.

Hicks cursed, aborted the move and steered back into his the slower left lane. His Buick might've been a big car with an even bigger engine under the hood, but the freight hauler was a hell of a lot bigger, even if it wasn't pulling any cargo.

Hicks noticed the center lane traffic was still moving well, but the black Peterbilt didn't speed up to match the flow of traffic. It was keeping pace with Hicks, boxing him in against the concrete highway divider on the much slower left lane.

Something was wrong.

He glanced over at the rig. It was riding too close and too high for him to see up into the cab. All he could see was the side of the chrome bumper and the big front wheel churning as the truck moved along beside him. He looked for a company name or some kind of identification on the door, maybe even a design or a logo. Nothing.

Impatient drivers stuck behind the slow-moving rig saw the wide space opening up between the Peterbilt and the other cars ahead of it. Hicks heard them hit their horns and, in his rearview and side view mirrors, saw them flashing their lights and gesturing for the truck to get out of their way.

But the truck held its speed.

Hicks checked his rearview mirror again. The car behind him was cruising more than a car-length back. He decided to test a theory. He took his foot off the gas without hitting the break. His engine geared down as the Buick began to gradually lose speed.

But so did the Peterbilt. Only now, it was beginning to slowly drift into his lane.

Instinct kicked in and Hicks slammed on the brakes. The

Peterbilt narrowly overshot him as it crowded in front of him into his lane.

The truck banged into the concrete divider separating north and southbound traffic sending sparks and bits of concrete into the air. Traffic in all lanes behind him swerved to avoid the dangerous situation unfolding in front of them.

Hicks cut the wheel to the right, glided into the center lane, and gunned the engine. The V12 roared to life as the Buick darted past the semi.

But the Peterbilt bounced off the concrete divider and careened to its right, bunting the Buick into the left lane. The big car skidded over onto the shoulder, but Hicks managed to keep both hands on the wheel, fighting to maintain control and speed without hitting the concrete retaining wall along the narrow shoulder of that portion of the highway.

Hicks floored it and raced up the shoulder lane. Cars in the other three lanes honked at him as he sped past. He hoped another car hadn't broken down or was getting a ticket somewhere ahead of them. If they were, it was about to be a bad day for a lot of people.

In the rearview mirror, he saw the Peterbilt glide onto the shoulder and fall in behind him; closing ground fast. Hicks may have had a V12 under the hood, but the big engine needed space to maneuver. He saw the shoulder lane was narrowing as there was an onramp ahead.

Hicks was running out of room.

And with the Peterbilt closing in fast, he was running out of time.

Since he didn't have the space to outrun the Peterbilt, he would have to find a way to stop it. And with traffic beginning to thicken ahead of him, he'd have to do something fast before the semi smeared him against the concrete divider.

He lowered the passenger window as he pulled the Ruger from his holster. An ad for the Ruger .454 boasted it had once stopped a charging Alaskan grizzly. He hoped it worked as well on American steel.

With the passenger window open, Hicks heard the Peterbilt's engine shift into a higher gear as it lurched ever closer. He jerked the wheel to the left and brought the Buick across two lanes into the center, then into the far left lane as panicked drivers all around them began to speed up or slow down to stay out of the way.

The Peterbilt's engine geared down as it came off the shoulder and careened toward the Buick.

Now.

Hicks aimed the Ruger at the truck's front tire and began firing through the open window. The revolver boomed as he jammed on the brake, pumping all eight rounds of the modified Ruger into the bulk of the Peterbilt as it raced by. The Buick's tires screeched as round after round punched through the semi's front left tire, the engine block, and finally the driver's door before the gun clicked empty. At such distance, it was impossible for Hicks to miss.

The recoil from firing eight rounds from the big Ruger deadened his right hand. He dropped the revolver on the passenger seat and tried to control the wheel one-handed. He saw the massive front left tire of the Peterbilt shred as it sped past him, sending thick chunks of rubber bouncing off the Buick's bulletproof windshield. Hicks moved from the brake pedal to the gas, pulling the wheel to the right as the truck skidded in front of him, buckling forward on its left side like a wounded animal. The Buick narrowly missed the back end of the Peterbilt as Hicks skidded back into the center lane.

Hicks struggled to control his car as he sped past the dying truck. The front left side of the Peterbilt crumpled against the concrete divider. Sparks and smoke and shattered glass poured out onto both sides of the highway before the truck's momentum caused it to flip over the concrete divider and onto the other side of the highway.

Hicks brought the Buick under control and ducked into the right hand lane, hoping to slide back into anonymity with the traffic merging onto the highway. He checked his rearview and side mirrors. Smoke and flame began to flicker out from the overturned Peterbilt's engine block. Cars had stopped on both sides of the barrier as drivers ran to the truck to free the trucker before it exploded.

He figured someone back there was bound to remember his car or a passenger may have even had enough time to take his picture with their phone. OMNI could always take care of that later. For now, he needed to put as much distance between himself and the burning Peterbilt as possible.

He hit the voice command button on the steering wheel. "Call Jason."

The Trustee's voice repeated the command as the dashboard screen flashed red. It was a warning he had never seen before. He looked at it for a full two seconds to make sure he was reading it right. Unfortunately, he was:

WEAPONS SYSTEM LOCK. DRONE INCOMING.

CHAPTER 22

Hicks pounded the steering wheel. These fuckers didn't give up.

He hit the voice command button on the steering wheel. "Show tactical map with drone."

The map switched to a tactical view, but a red line blinked at the bottom of the screen: **DRONE OUT OF VISUAL RANGE**

Hicks knew how drones worked. By the time the damned thing was in scanning range, he'd be dead. He would need more help than his onboard computer could give him. It wasn't designed to track incoming threats from above. "Connect me to Jason."

Jason picked up on the second ring. With danger imminent, both men forgot about the standard security protocols. "I got back home and saw what's happening via OMNI. Are you okay?"

"Hell no. Did you see the drone warning?"

"Hold on." He heard Jason's fingers on the keyboard. "I see it now, but it's a local alert from your handheld, not the OMNI system."

"I don't care where it's from. The damned thing is inbound and I can't see it yet."

"Let me try to get a fix on its position. Hold on."

Hicks continued to thread in and out of traffic, doing his best to try to confuse the drone's guidance system. He knew it was no use. The damned things could kill a moving target from miles away, but the maneuvers made him feel like he was at least doing something more than waiting to die.

He had no idea how the drone was tracking him or if the pilot had been assigned to visually target him. Until he knew for certain, he had to keep moving among vehicular herd moving north.

Jason came back on the line. "OMNI's showing it's a CIA drone piloted out of Arizona. It's five miles out of your current position and closing fast. The signals are consistent with Predator class drone. A prototype known as 'Valkyrie.' I'm not familiar with that particular class. I'm looking it up now."

But Hicks knew all about Valkyrie. "It's a Predator drone designed to rake me with bullets or drop a fucking missile on my head." Hicks punched the steering wheel again.

The Valkyrie had been designed in response to popular civilian criticism that drone strikes were too imprecise. The taxpayers had grown tired of seeing the bodies of dead Middle Eastern civilians on the nightly news and wanted a more precision weapon. Civilians didn't grasp the notion that there wasn't anything precise about war. The drone's systems had been designed to take out a single terrorist vehicle in a convoy full of school buses without hurting a single child in the explosion. The idea of a surgical strike was a misnomer, but Valkyrie got as close to surgical as a such weapon could get.

Stephens obviously wasn't taking any chances. Since the semi had failed to kill him, he had gotten Langley to authorize a drone strike as well.

"Isn't your Buick bulletproof?" Jason asked. "You should survive if they open fire."

"Against automatic rifle and gunfire," Hicks said, "not against explosive rounds or a goddamned missile." Hicks kept threading through traffic, running through all of the feasible alternatives. He couldn't out run it and he couldn't bring it down. There was only one possibility that might work. "You're going to have to get the drone to land."

"How in the hell am I supposed to do that? I can't fly a drone!"

"Hack it and whack it," Hicks said. "None of the Varsity's Operators have any experience with piloting drones either, so you've got as much of a chance of pulling this off as any of them. Have OMNI lock onto the drone's remote control frequency and hack it." He swerved to avoid a car that had drifted into his lane.

He heard Jason's fingers on the keyboard. "Will it work?"

Hicks knew drones usually had command protocols to automatically land if they detect a malfunction or tampering. If OMNI could either hack it or confuse its systems, it might throw the drone off course, it's the only shot we've got.

Hicks dashboard screen began blinking again. **WEAPONS ALERT. INCOMING DRONE WITHIN STRIKING**

DISTANCE.

Hicks looked for a way off the highway, but all he saw was cars and overpasses. No exits in sight. "Give me some good news, Jason. I'm running out of options here."

"OMNI has locked onto the guidance controls and is working the hack right now," Jason said. "But I don't know if we'll be able to bring it down before it catches up to you."

Since the hack was the best chance they had, Hicks was going to have to buy himself some time.

He spotted a pair of overpasses about a quarter of a mile away. The shoulder lane ran directly underneath them. Since he didn't have the space to outrun the drone, he might be able to hide from it.

He waited until he was under the dual underpass before he jerked the wheel to the right and skidded to a stop on the shoulder. The Buick stopped before the edge of the second overpass. He threw the car in reverse and backed up so the car couldn't be easily seen from the air.

He put on his hazard lights so passing motorists would assume he was in some kind of trouble. Most would drive by without stopping. If a cop happened to pull over, he'd have to deal with it somehow.

He lowered all his windows and tried to listen. The constant sound of the cars speeding by echoed beneath the overpasses above, but not enough to drown out the high-pitched sound of the drone speeding by overhead. He heard the whine of the engine die off in the distance. He looked at the dashboard screen to see if OMNI had been able to track it on the map, but no luck. The damned thing must have been flying too high for his handheld to track accurately. The device's sensors weren't set up to track an aerial threat. He would make sure that changed when he got back to Twenty-Third Street.

If he made it back.

Hicks raised all the windows again to block out the traffic noise so he could better hear Jason over the speakers. "I need an update, Ace."

"Stopping beneath the underpass threw them off. OMNI is tracking the drone heading north. It's two miles away now and still going."

"Whoever's flying it knows what they're doing," Hicks said. "They'll double back to reacquire me. It won't take them long to figure out where I'm hiding. If a cop spots me here, he'll radio in my position. The Barnyard will hear it, and I'm dead. You've got about three minutes before shit gets complicated."

More clicks from Jason. "OMNI is hammering away at the source code for the drone's navigation system, but it's encrypted and complicated." He heard a series of beeps on Jason's end of the call. "Damn it. The drone is reversing course. It's coming back your way."

Hicks knew he was the perfect target for the drone. He couldn't run. He couldn't fight back, either. All he had was the Ruger. Even if he had a fifty-caliber sniper rifle in the trunk—which he didn't—he'd be dead before the drone was within range.

He lowered the windows again and heard the whine of the drone's engine over the sound of the traffic. It was a sound most people would have missed if they didn't know what to listen for. Unfortunately, Hicks knew what one sounded like.

The engine sounded louder as the drone flew lower. Not low enough to skim the roofs of the cars but low enough to get a closer look at the roadway.

"Come on, Jason. The damned thing just buzzed me. It's bound to have a visual on me after the last pass."

More clicks. "Get out of there right now," Jason said. "The drone's targeting systems have gone live. Current trajectory shows it will be making a tight turn and coming in low. It may try to launch something at you under the underpass. Move now and confuse the targeting array."

The Buick's wheels spun and kicked up gravel as Hicks threw the sedan back into drive and hit the gas. The car lurched ahead and Hicks kept it on the shoulder. "Give me a bearing. Is it still heading south or has it banked north yet? Does it have a visual on me?"

"No visual yet, but it's beginning to bank back north toward your previous location. OMNI's still trying to hack it, but it's not looking good."

Hicks sped along the shoulder until he saw a wide enough space on his left and ducked back into traffic. He hoped he'd look like any other car on the road, at least long enough for OMNI to hack the drone's system. "Get that bird on the deck, Jason. I've got a lot of people around me who'll die if you don't."

Hicks' dashboard screen flashed red again, faster than he'd ever seen it flash before. **WARNING. WEAPONS LOCK.**

The far left lane was moving faster now. Hicks cut across two lanes of traffic and floored it. He knew he couldn't hide any longer. He knew he couldn't outrun the damned thing or even fire back. All he could do was hope he might make it miss.

And Valkyries weren't designed to miss.

His windows were still down so he could hear the whine of the drone's engine as he finally saw it in his side view mirror. Its narrow profile looked like crosshairs in the sky. He watched it barely clear the top of the overpass he'd been hiding beneath as it closed in for a strike. Whoever was piloting it wasn't taking any chances on a remote hit. They wanted him dead, and they wanted to be sure about it.

A space opened up in the center lane in front of a Greyhound bus and Hicks glided over toward it. He imagined the civilian vehicles were the only reason why they hadn't fired on him already. If he stayed in the thick of traffic, it might buy him more time.

Hicks had cut in front of the bus when he saw a small orange cloud explode high in the night sky behind him. He cut past the bus into the right-hand lane. In his rearview mirror, he saw headlights zigzagging in all directions as fiery debris rained down on the roadway.

Jason and OMNI had hacked the drone's system after all.

"Nice going, Ace."

"I had OMNI flood the drone with conflicting commands as it was ready to launch on your position," Jason said. "The missile must have activated before the drone launched it."

Hicks didn't care about details. He was still alive. "Search for any other secure signals in the area. These bastards have already tried to kill me twice. Third time's the charm."

"I'm not picking up any in your immediate area. Civilian emergency frequencies are going crazy about the semi and now the drone explosion, but nothing seems federal. Do you want me to direct OMNI to wipe out all traffic cameras in your vicinity?"

"No. If you make them all go dark at once, it'll raise too much suspicion. Have Omni louse up their feed as I approach at random times. I don't want Stephens to get an exact fix on where I am on the road."

"Understood. I would advise you get off the highway as soon as possible, James. I know it'll be slower going for you, but it'll be harder for Stephens' people to acquire you on local roads. I doubt even they can muster another drone so quickly."

"I'm already on it. I'll be in touch when I'm close to home base. And thanks for what you did back there, Jason. You saved a lot of people now, not only me."

Jason was quiet for a moment. "Wow. That must've hurt to say."

"You have no idea."

Hicks killed the connection and got off the highway at the next exit. His onboard GPS told him he'd added two hours of travel time to the trip back to New York, but he didn't care. Anything beat the deathtrap of the highway.

Hicks gave himself a few miles to calm down before he made the call he knew he needed to make. He'd narrowly escaped being killed three times in the past hour. Sweat popped on his forehead and back. He gripped the wheel as tightly as he could to keep his hands from shaking. He remembered his training and controlled his breathing. He wanted his voice to be clear and strong when he made his next call.

He used the back of his sore right hand to wipe away the sweat on his forehead.

When he was finally ready, he cleared his throat and hit the voice prompt button on the steering wheel. "Connect me to the previously hacked frequency."

The Trustee's female electronic voice responded, "Connecting."

The dashboard screen showed the call had connected. He could hear Stephens talking. He sounded like he was on the phone. And he didn't sound happy.

"You're sure he got away?" Hicks heard Stephens say. "How the hell is that even possible? How the hell could he have taken down a drone? He was driving a fucking Buick for Christ's sake!"

Hicks hadn't hacked their system to listen in. He'd hacked their system to deliver a message. "Hey, Stephens."

The sounds from within Stephens' car went silent.

Hicks didn't wait for a response. "You missed. You're dead."

Hicks killed the connection.

The left lane of the two-lane road opened up, but he stayed where he was. The slower pace of traffic suited him fine.

He'd had enough excitement for one night.

CHAPTER 23

As soon as he got back to the Twenty-Third Street facility, Hicks killed all the lights in the bunker and meditated.

It had been a long time since anyone had tried to kill him twice in a single day. It was the first time anyone had tried to kill him with a semi. He'd survived errant drone strikes before, but this was the first time anyone had ever directed one at him. It was enough to give him pause. He needed peace and distance for a few moments before the rush of all of his responsibilities as Dean crushed him. *Speed kills. Haste kills.* He was outgunned and outmanned. Clarity was his only weapon.

What happened has happened. It was in the past. Focus on the present. Focus on the future. Get Jabbar. Burn Stephens. Keep the University intact. Stay alive.

Having cleared his mind as best he could, he turned on the

lights and went to his desktop.

He ignored the hint of panic spreading in his belly at the sight of hundreds of priority alerts and search notifications in his inbox. Although the operations concerning Jabbar and Stephens were incredibly important, they were still only two of the hundreds of active operations happening throughout the University system.

Faculty Members positioned all over the globe were still gathering intelligence on white-collar criminals, drug lords, and weapons dealers. Dozens of University Faculty Members, Assets, and Adjuncts were extracting information from a variety of targets for a variety of purposes. Many of them had never had any direct dealings with the Dean and most never would. They didn't care the previous Dean had died and Hicks had been named to replace him. Their missions continued no matter who was in charge as long as the money kept flowing from the Bursar account into their own.

Hicks was glad Jason had taken it upon himself to prepare a morning and evening breakdown of all the key reports and activities of all Faculty and Adjunct members. The report was categorized by region and importance, which made the information easier to digest. He may not have liked Jason, but he had to agree he was a pretty effective Dutchman.

After scanning through the more immediate highlights of Jason's broader update, Hicks decided most of the projects could wait. He dug into Rahul's evening report about Shaban from London. He wanted to know what their only link between Bajjah and Jabbar was up to.

"Our men trailed the suspect to the Paris suburbs via train where he met with a group of local radicals. A list of these radicals is attached at the end of this report. We learned French Intelligence has also been watching this group for over a year. None of the members have done more than spout rhetoric. They have supported terrorist actions carried out by other groups throughout the world, but have never directly participated in terrorist activity."

"The meeting between Shaban and the group lasted a little over three hours where the suspect delivered parcels to some of the attendees. A later examination of the parcels by my men proved said parcels contained pamphlets against Israel and the West. No other paraphernalia was found. No other messages passed. A small bundle of one thousand Euros was the only thing out of place. Shaban was followed back to his London flat, where he remained alone and without incident on his computer for the rest of the night. OMNI's standing surveillance of his computer provides details of his online activities and are attached to this report. It should be noted the suspect did not receive or make any calls or text messages on any devices upon returning from Paris."

The report went on: "While the suspect was out of the country, our forces conducted an extensive search of his flat. Other than standard anti-Israeli/anti-capitalist literature, nothing out of the ordinary was discovered. If he was Bajjah's money man, he's doing a hell of a job hiding it. I don't know where he got the thousand Euros for the French group. Maybe the community center where he works? We'll keep digging."

Hicks had been hoping Rahul would find something in Shaban's flat to prove he was working with the Jabbar network. Bajjah had said Shaban was the network's money man. There had to be something there.

Hicks toggled to the next screen to review OMNI's hack of Shaban's home computer. His online activities were surprisingly mundane. He had paid some bills online and written emails to a few family members. He had even sent an e-card to his cousin in Liverpool wishing her a happy birthday. Hicks suspected it might be code for something else, so he checked the recipient. Shaban did, indeed, have a cousin in Liverpool who was about to turn eight years old. It appeared even Islamic extremists had a sentimental side.

But a further search of Shaban's laptop hard drive revealed something interesting.

Shaban had pulled a hack of his own. He'd done his best to erase it, but OMNI picked up enough fragments of activity to piece it together.

Shaban had accessed the network of a shipping company based in Toronto called Regent Shipping. Shaban didn't focus on payroll records or emails, but on the activities of one ship in particular called The Regent Sea. He had accessed the company's internal GPS system to track the location of the ship, which, according to the company's internal records, had left Toronto four days before. The destination on the manifest was Harwich, England. It was due to arrive the day after tomorrow.

Shaban had not accessed any other information on the company's servers. Not payroll records or bank accounts. Only the manifest and the list of the ship's crew.

Why?

Hicks forwarded the results of the hack on Shaban's computer to Rahul. He attached the following message: "Keep an eye out for any further interest Shaban shows in this particular ship, especially his activities around the time when the ship is due to arrive in England."

Hicks directed OMNI to conduct its own hack of Regent Shipping's system. He wanted to view the full manifest of the *Regent Sea*. He wanted to know about the crew and about what the ship was carrying across the Atlantic.

The hack was almost complete when he heard his handheld begin to buzz.

Tali was calling him. And she was calling from her University handheld. Interesting.

He answered the phone. "This is Professor Warren."

"This is Dr. Andros," she replied, using the code to prove she was not in any danger and in a secure place. "I need you to come to my place immediately, James. It's important."

Tali had been one of the most calm and capable field agents Hicks had ever worked with. He wasn't sure if her sniper training in the Israeli Defense Force had made her that way or if her nature had made her an effective sniper. But Tali never made urgent statements, even when they were necessary.

"What's wrong?"

As she came up with an answer, Hicks went to his desktop and had OMNI locate her handheld's signal. She was at her apartment. But was she alone? He ordered the OMNI satellite to scan the area for additional secure signals.

"Nothing's wrong," she said. "My Uncle has made an unexpected visit to New York and is most anxious to see you. The sooner, the better." She tried to put a smile in her voice to take the sting out of her words. "You know how impatient he can be sometimes. I'm afraid he won't be in town for long, so we'd like to know when we can expect you."

'Uncle' was the University term for a foreign agent's

supervisor from their home agency. Tali's Uncle from the Mossad was a thin, humorless man named Emanuel Schneider. Hicks figured Schneider's unscheduled visit to New York was due to the email Tali had sent about Bajjah's death. The Trustee had been right once again.

He wished she hadn't alerted them. He wished he hadn't gone to her apartment. He wished Bajjah and his friends hadn't launched a biological attack in the first place. But all the wishing in the world wouldn't change a damned thing. Only action could do that.

OMNI's scan of Tali's apartment showed Mr. Schneider hadn't come alone. Three secure signals known to be used by the Mossad were currently being emitted from her apartment. One belonged to Schneider and maybe another to Tali, but most likely to two other people.

OMNI also picked up four additional secure signals on street level in front of Tali's apartment. Hicks switched OMNI's scan to a live satellite feed and zoomed in on the source of the signals. They were coming from a van parked across the street.

Hicks almost laughed. A van for surveillance. Jesus. Why don't you hang a neon sign on the side?

Hicks knew Tali was aware of the University's technical abilities, but he had never explained OMNI's capability to her. She believed her handset was simply part of a secure, closed communications network. Time to use her ignorance against her.

He activated the camera on her handheld device to get a better look at who was in the room with her. "I'm in the middle of a couple of things right now, so I can't make it over to your place. How about we meet somewhere else a little later on?"

She hesitated. Her device's camera was facing the fireplace in her apartment. No one else was in frame, but he caught the shadows of two people on the wall.

The OMNI scan was right. Tali wasn't alone. She was leading him into a trap.

She went on. "We must insist on meeting here, James. It's safe and secure and we can talk freely."

There was no way he was walking into a room full of Mossad agents. "Can't do it now, but I've got an idea. Put me on speaker so Uncle Manny and I can chat." He knew Emanuel Schneider hated to be called 'Manny.'

"I am afraid this is unacceptable. He insists on seeing you here in my apartment as soon as possible."

"If it's so important, you won't mind telling me why." He was curious how she'd answer.

He could hear the combination of annoyance and embarrassment in her voice. "Why are you being so difficult?"

"Because I'm busy. Either he talks to me now over the phone or we don't talk at all."

Hicks saw the camera feed jump as her handheld was taken from her. She came into frame, looking drawn and exhausted as Emanuel Schneider's gravelly voice came on the line. "Schneider here. A belated congratulations on your deserved elevation to Dean, my friend. Well deserved, I'm sure."

The two men weren't friends and never had been. Schneider had been a bureaucrat from the IDF who had found his way into the Mossad through patronage, not competence. But what Schneider lacked in ability, he made up for in appearance and ambition. He was tall and thin and still had most of his hair even though he was on the north side of fifty. He wore custom shirts and suits made from London's finest haberdashers. He looked and acted like a spy, which was one of the many reasons why Hicks had never fully trusted him. And neither did the CIA, hence his Mossad unit's awkward relationship with the University.

"I found myself in town for a couple of days," Schneider went on, "and I believe it might be a good idea for us to chat."

"So chat. You've got my full attention."

Schneider hesitated. "This is the kind of chat best conducted while sitting across from each other."

Hicks saw no reason to keep fencing with him. From the camera on her handheld, Hicks could see Tali was holding her head in her hands. She looked like hell. Schneider had obviously put her through a lot already.

Time to do the same to him. "Depends on what you want to talk about."

"The nature of things," Schneider said. "Details about certain operations and agreements between our two organizations."

"Meaning Bajjah."

Schneider forced a laugh. "Perceptive as always, James. Yes. We'd like to get clarification on what happened to our prisoner and why."

At least all the cards were finally on the table. "I've already given Tali a full briefing on what happened. I know how thorough she is, so I'm sure she has already passed the information on to you."

"I want to hear it from you."

Hicks obliged. "Bajjah died during questioning and we cremated him afterwards. He gave us some raw information we're currently researching and, as soon as we have a full picture of what he told us, we'll give you a detailed report. Tomorrow or the day after at the latest."

"It seems like an inordinately long time to wait for results from an organization with your abilities."

"I've been Dean for a little more than twenty-four hours, Manny. Things are a little more hectic around here than normal. But I promised Tali we'll get you the report as soon as possible, and I'm making you the same promise. I know it's not what you want to hear, but under the circumstances, it's the best we can do."

Schneider sucked his teeth. "What a shame. I'm surprised to hear the new Dean of the University could not make an exception for old friends with long memories."

Hicks normally enjoyed a veiled threat as much as anyone, but today was not a normal day. "The University's memory is as long as the Mossad's, Manny. The University also has connections and influence much older than your country. You should remember that when making polite threats."

"I have no intention of forgetting," Schneider countered. "If anything, our long association is the reason why I have given you the courtesy of contacting you about our Bajjah concerns first before I contacted my colleagues at the CIA. Or the NSA, or even the DIA."

Hicks wasn't surprised Schneider had gone for the jugular so soon. Emanuel Schneider believed that when diplomacy failed, be vicious. "Revealing our long association would be as dangerous for you as it was for me, my friend. Those agencies would trust you less than they already do."

"Normally I'd agree with you," Schneider allowed, "but circumstances changed. I've heard many things about a remarkable young man they have working for them right now. A man named Stephens, who is making great progress hunting down the mysterious man who snatched Bajjah right out from under their noses." Schneider laughed. "It would be a shame if Stephens learned who took the Moroccan and why."

"I guess Tali didn't tell you everything. Stephens tried grabbing me yesterday and failed. He failed again today, too. If you're looking for a horse to back, you'd better keep your money on me."

"There are others in Washington—and elsewhere—who would like to know who took Bajjah and why. They know it was you, but they don't know who you are or why you took him. And, until now, the University hasn't even been brought up in conversation. I can make sure all stays as it has always been as soon as you give up this ridiculous fiction and tell me the real reason why you killed Bajjah."

"I didn't kill him. He died during questioning."

"So you told Tali. She is a marvelous field agent, but she is, ultimately, only a field agent. She focused on the event of Bajjah's death itself whereas I had the luxury of distance from the information. I focused less on the event and more on the reason."

Hicks' gut tightened. Schneider might not have been much of a field agent, but he wasn't a fool. He was rumored to do the New York Times crossword puzzle each morning in pen. He prided himself on solving problems. "Bajjah died because we hit him with too much current at the wrong time. It happens."

"Yes it does, but it's also convenient in how his death coincides with your elevation to Dean and all the increased attention Stephens has placed on you and on the University. A terrible coincidence and none of us believes in coincidence, do we?"

Schneider didn't give Hicks a chance to respond. "I know your interrogation methods, James, or should I say, the methods of Roger Cobb. And while I despise him as a human being, there's no denying he is a first-rate interrogator. I don't doubt Bajjah is dead, but I don't believe Roger accidentally killed him, either. I believe you intentionally executed him to keep us from talking to him because he gave you something valuable. I want to know what that something is."

Fucking Schneider. "You've got a suspicious mind, even for our line of work."

"No, only a logical one, for if Bajjah had died during questioning, why didn't you tell us immediately? Instead, you refused to answer Tali's messages and only told her a version of the truth when she pulled it out of you in her own inimitable way. Once I decided you must have intentionally killed him, I began to ask myself why. Why didn't you want us to question Bajjah?"

Schneider paused.

Hicks stayed silent. The bastard was getting close enough to the truth on his own. No reason to help him.

Hicks heard Schneider snap his fingers. The Israeli had always had a flair for the dramatic. "And that's when it hit me. The only thing worth the risk of drawing our ire was if Bajjah gave you someone important. Some like, say, Jabbar or someone who could lead you to Jabbar or someone close to him. Tell me, James. How did I do?"

Hicks knew denying it at this point was useless, but the truth could be dangerous right now. Shaban was the only lead he had to Jabbar and a poor lead at that. If Schneider knew about Shaban, they'd try to abduct the kid. Rahul's people wouldn't let that happen and a lot of people would get killed. The operation would be blown and it wouldn't take long for the other agencies to piece it all together.

But if Hicks kept denying it, he risked leaving Schneider no option but to contact the Barnyard with his concerns. A prize like Jabbar was worth the risk of burning down the University to get.

Hicks decided to do what he did best. Split the difference and tell a half-truth. "If Bajjah had told me where to find Jabbar, you and I wouldn't be having this conversation right now. I'd be dragging Jabbar's ass onto a private jet to a black site somewhere off shore."

"Perhaps," Schneider allowed, "but Bajjah gave you something to lead you to him, didn't he?"

"He gave us the names of nine people in his network," Hicks allowed. "Five were within the United States and the other four were in the Middle East. That's the information we are trying to vet. Some of those names appear to have loose ties to Jabbar, but there's nothing solid yet."

"Good. So you can give us those names immediately."

"I could," Hicks said, "but I won't."

From the feed from the handheld's camera, he saw Tali pick up her face from her hands and look at Schneider. She looked worried. Her boss was getting annoyed.

Good.

"Why?" Schneider asked.

"Because I need to know what I get in return for giving them to you."

"The University enjoys our continued silence about its involvement in the Bajjah matter. And I don't give Stephens a full dossier on you, James."

"Not good enough. I'll agree to give you the names Bajjah gave me, and I'll keep you apprised as to how our investigation moves along. But I'm going to need more from you than your silence, Manny. A lot more."

"Fine. What do you want?"

The seed of a plan took root in Hicks' mind. Maybe Schneider could be more than an inconvenient pain in the ass after all. Two birds. One stone. "Corroboration, my friend. Now, if you've got a few minutes, I'll explain what I need you to do."

CHAPTER 24

A FEW HOURS LATER at The Jolly Roger Club, Hicks allowed himself to sink down far enough so the cool leather of Roger's couch hit the back of his neck. The dull headache he had been fighting for days was threatening to turn into a full-blown migraine. Almost getting killed twice on his way back from Savannah hadn't helped. His unexpected sparring session with Schneider had only made it worse, though it looked like the Israelis might prove to be more useful than he'd expected.

He tried to focus on the operation at hand. The reason why he had come to The Jolly Roger Club was to hear Roger's plan to stop Stephens, but thoughts of Tali kept creeping back into his mind. He didn't want to dwell on her betrayal. Hell, it wasn't even a betrayal. She was an avowed agent working for a foreign government. Telling her superiors about Bajjah's death had been part of her job. She didn't owe him anything except to follow orders and he couldn't order her to keep Bajjah's death a secret. She wasn't his wife or his girlfriend or even his paramour.

But they had saved each other's lives so many times, Hicks had come to see her as more than a colleague, but less than a lover despite having slept together. The closest word he could use to describe her was a friend. Maybe he didn't have a right to see her that way, but he did. His disappointment in her bothered him. Sometimes, humanity found a way to poke through the cracks of his line of work. Disappointment was among the most basic human of emotions.

He looked up when he heard the door to Roger's sitting room open.

A young woman strode toward him with the elegant confidence of a fashion model on a runway, though she had neither the build nor the poise for it. She was too curvy for her small frame, but was strikingly pretty.

She had applied the right amount of eyeliner to draw focus on her eyes and her black curly hair flowed down in tendrils to her slender shoulders. Her black tank top showed an obviously enhanced bust line. Roger liked to keep his chamber on the chilly side, so it was clear to Hicks the girl wasn't wearing a bra. Her black leather mini-skirt showed off the rest of her curves and toned legs. Hicks was amazed she could walk a straight line in such high heels, but Roger Cobb knew a lot of talented people.

From the doorway, Roger beamed with a showman's pride. "Please allow me the great honor of presenting my dear friend and colleague, Cindy. Her stage name is spelled 'Syndy' with an 'S,' but we can dispense with show business monikers for the moment." To the girl, he said, "Cindy, this is my client whose name isn't important, remember? We're all friends here, so we can speak freely amongst each other."

"Nice to meet you," Cindy said as she lowered herself into the couch across from Hicks with the grace of a debutant. He guessed she was either a stripper or sex worker, but moved with a more practiced fluidity than a common streetwalker. Her wry smile showed teeth too white to be natural. "I like you. You're cute."

Hicks looked at Roger. "This is what you've been working on? This is the plan you've been putting together? A honey trap? It's the oldest trick in the book and our boy will never fall for it."

Roger clapped his hands and hugged himself. "I'm so glad you said that because Cindy isn't merely a pretty face, my friend. She's oh, so much more." To the girl, he said, "Show him our surprise, my sweet."

Cindy flashed a stripper's smile as she opened her legs, revealing she not only was not wearing underwear, but had also been born a male.

An extremely well-endowed male.

Hicks closed his eyes as his headache bloomed into a full-blown migraine. When he opened his eyes, he looked at Roger until Roger got the point.

Roger offered his hand to help Cindy stand. "Give us the room, my love. My friend and I have much to discuss." He kissed her on the cheek and whispered something in her ear. She gave Hicks a little wave over her shoulder as she walked back to the outer room. If she had noticed Hicks' disappointment, she didn't show it.

Roger took Cindy's seat on the couch and sighed. "Ah, still

warm." His eyes flashed. "Impressive, isn't she?"

"Roger, for fuck's sake…"

"Now, now. Don't get all Republican on me before you hear what I have to say."

"I don't have to hear anything. I saw. A lot. I asked you to come up with a way to stop the biggest intelligence combine in the world and you bring me a goddamned tranny?"

"The face that launched a thousand ships didn't belong to a king, old boy, but to a woman," Roger said. "And Cindy isn't some goddamned tranny. She doesn't get her kicks prancing around her apartment in women's underwear, not that there's anything wrong with that. Cindy happens to be a pre-operative transsexual who is also a skilled sex worker."

"A tranny hooker." Hicks' migraine spiked. Two days wasted on a half-assed plan. He began to massage his temples. "Jesus. I need ice."

"What you need is to listen to me for a change. Cindy may have been born a man, but thanks to modern science and convention, she is a woman. She's had implants, hormone treatments, and has endured more pain and alienation than either of us have ever known in order to become what she was born to be."

"Great. My heart goes out to her. I admire her, but she's got no role in our plan."

"Of course she does. You had no idea she'd been born a male until she opened her legs, did you? Don't lie."

Hicks conceded the point. "Yeah, but…"

"And if you—a trained operative who is unfortunately stone sober—couldn't tell the difference, you can bet our target won't, especially at the end of a long night of strong cocktails."

"I was hoping you'd dig up something in his past we could use. Something we could blackmail him with. Not…this."

Roger pressed on. "I didn't bring Cindy here tonight on a whim, you know. I have spent the last two days delving into every aspect of our target's life. OMNI even helped me pull together a full psychological profile on this guy. Believe me when I tell you Cindy is exactly the right type, the right size, and the right kind of girl he loves. And I will guarantee he won't know about her little secret until it's too late." Roger smiled. "Well, it's not such a little secret, but you know what I mean."

Hicks felt any argument he had against Roger's plan evaporate. Roger's scheme was so unexpected, so low, so old school that it might work.

But he wasn't convinced yet. "Has she at least been to the River?" Hicks asked. 'The River' was the University term for Assets who had received some field training.

"Not in the same way you and I have been trained," Roger admitted, "but what difference does it make? We're not asking her to parachute behind enemy lines or steal files or enroll an Asset. She's an experienced escort who happens to be popular among those who prefer a more unique sexual experience."

Maybe it was the migraine, but Hicks was beginning to doubt the whole idea again. "Shit, Roger, I was hoping you'd find something in his background we could use against him. This is…"

"Our Target is a boy scout, and I mean literally. He was in the Scouts until he was in is twenties. He pays his taxes and doesn't cut corners at work. Even his enemies like him. The only weakness is for cheap girls at the end of a night of drinking, a failing common to us all. All we're asking Cindy to do is pick up a drunk in a bar at the end of the night and convince him to take her back to his room. What you and I might call a challenge, she calls another Tuesday at the office. We point out the mark to her and the rest is in her hands." Another smile. "Or preferably in his if we get the camera angle right."

Hicks found massaging his temples was beginning to cut the pain. "Can we can trust her to keep her mouth shut afterwards?"

"I've known her for years and she owes me a couple of favors," Roger said, "but I'm not taking any chances. She doesn't know who the mark is or why we want her to entrap him. I told her he's an influential man we need to help have a good time. Even after he tells her his name, it'll mean nothing to her. All she cares about is watching anime and having enough money to buy nail polish. Girlfriend loves her nail polish. She hasn't the slightest idea about politics and couldn't care less. She's exactly as ignorant as we need her to be."

A couple of dozen things could still go wrong with Roger's scheme, but he couldn't come up with anything better. Like the Dean had always said, 'complaint without resolution was whining and whining never got anyone anywhere.'

Roger obviously sensed Hicks' resignation. He tapped him on the knee. "Trust me, damn it. Corruption and vice are my areas of expertise, remember? It's like they said in the Bible, 'a willing pre-op transsexual prostitute can be an invaluable asset to any extortion plot.'"

"You read one fucked up version of the Bible."

"I'm paraphrasing, of course. So you approve?"

Normally, Hicks would've rejected the idea. But after a few days of being hunted, nearly kidnapped, killed by a semi and wiped out by a drone, he decided the scheme was crazy enough to work. "I don't approve, but go ahead with it anyway."

Hicks allowed himself to sink further back in the couch. He let the back of his neck rest on the cool leather cushion. His migraine was finally beginning to subside, if only a little. "I never expected everything in this business to run smooth, but I never expected it to be all so fucked up all the time."

Roger got up from his chair and headed for the wet bar. "If you couldn't take a joke, you shouldn't have joined. Scotch?"

He wanted one. He needed one. But he needed a clear head more. "No thanks. I'm scheduled to get a briefing from Rahul on Shaban in a bit."

Roger rolled his eyes. "In that case, I'll pour you a double. You'll need it."

This time, Hicks didn't argue.

CHAPTER
25

"I'M AFRAID THERE's been a change of plans," Rahul told Hicks on the phone later that night. "The Regent Star is due to dock this morning, not tomorrow as we'd thought."

Roger's double scotch hadn't dulled the impact of the news. "How the hell is that even possible? Weren't you were tracking the goddamned thing?"

"I have been tracking it," Rahul explained, "which is why I know about the change in the arrival time. The harbormaster's office is expecting heavier than usual outbound traffic tomorrow, so they've decided to bring the *Regent Star* in this morning."

Hicks knew operational details changed on a dime all the time, but he didn't like it had happened during this particular operation. There were too many moving parts and too many people who could have said the wrong thing at any time along the way.

But speculation wouldn't solve anything. He focused on the problem at hand. "How are you handling the change?"

"Half of my men are on their way to the port as we speak. The remaining half is here with me, watching Shaban's flat. He looks like he's getting ready to go somewhere."

"My money says he's going to meet the ship."

"As does mine," Rahul agreed. "OMNI caught him hacking the Regent Transportation servers again last night. And he focused on the *Regent Star's* position at sea. My guess is he's getting ready to meet the ship in port. He also accessed full details on the ship herself, and I mean all of it. Technical specifications on the ship, engine speed, fuel capacity, cargo capacity, and the like. He'd also accessed the complete cargo manifest and a list of all the crew members. In fact, he seems to have done this several times, especially the crew list. I don't know why. There's no reason for it to have changed since the ship put to sea, but it holds some fascination for him."

Why was Shaban was so damned curious about a common freighter out of Toronto. Was he part of a plan to attack it? Was there something in the cargo he was waiting for? He'd ordered OMNI to generate a detailed analysis on the cargo, but he hadn't had the time to review it yet. He hoped Rahul had. "What kind of cargo is the ship carrying?"

"Spare parts for American cars sold in Europe. There rest is odds and ends, including some sensitive seismology equipment used to monitor earthquakes. It seems they don't like to ship such equipment by air because the flight turbulence could ruin the equipment."

Why would Shaban be interested in seismology equipment?

"Did you check the manifest with the shippers?"

"I did and each bit of tonnage is accountable from the source. I can't imagine there's anything of interest to Shaban on that ship."

As soon as Hicks seemed like he was making progress, he slammed into yet another brick wall. "What did you find out about the crew?"

"Now we're getting to the good part," Rahul told him. "The captain's record is clean as is most of the crew. Some have been arrested in the past, some even for assault, but nothing to be concerned about. I was ready to give up when one name practically leapt off the page."

Finally, a break. "Who?"

"A crew member named Feyyaz Arap. He's a Turkish citizen who has been working for the company for over five years, but his last name struck a chord with me. Now the name 'Arap'..."

"Is the Turkish term for 'Arab,'" Hicks said. "I pulled a couple of tours in the University's Istanbul office. Tell me more."

"It's not an alias, by the way. Feyyaz's real last name is Arap. But our boy wasn't born in Turkey. He was born in Birjan in the South Khorasan region of Iran. His family immigrated to Turkey when Feyyaz was a teenager. And guess who else was born in Birjan?"

Hicks didn't have to guess. He had seen Birjan a couple of days ago when he'd first run a search on Shaban. He had been born in Birjan also. "Son of a bitch."

"I'll admit a common birthplace isn't much to go on, but given Shaban's interest in the ship Arap is on, it's enough of a coincidence to give one pause. I was going have OMNI do a deeper dive on Arap's background, but when the change in arrival time happened, I had to react to that instead."

"I'll worry about Arap," Hicks said. "You concentrate on watching the ship and tracking Shaban. I want as many eyes on both of them at all times from now on. Something is about to pop and we'd better be ready for it when it does."

A FTER SENDING SCHNEIDER a carefully redacted report of the information he had retrieved from Bajjah, Hicks reviewed the OMNI search results on Fayyad Arap's life.

The merchant seaman was thirty years old and had been on and off several international watch lists over the years. His activities in Iran, even as a boy, had troubled SAVAK, the Iranian secret police. Records showed SAVAK had detained and interrogated Arap during his last trip back to his homeland about a year before. OMNI wasn't able to locate any written records in SAVAK's files on the results of the interrogations, which wasn't unusual. The Iranians usually didn't keep records of such sessions.

But a detailed search of Arap's medical history upon his return to Canada told Hicks all he needed to know about the results of their interrogation: pain killers and penicillin.

Outside the normal immigration documents, the Turks didn't have any many records on Arap either. He seemed to behave himself in his adopted country. However, The Royal Canadian Mounted Police (RCMP) had conducted tight surveillance on him for a time. They had tied Arap to various vocal radical Islamic sects in Canada. RCMP records showed Arap liked to attend meetings and rallies and hand out pamphlets on street corners, like Shaban. He'd been arrested five times in the past three years, charged with inciting riot and mayhem during various protests throughout Canada.

Hicks directed OMNI to access RCMP surveillance files on the cell phones Arap was known to have used while he was in Canada. Records showed Arap had used several devices during his various times in Toronto. Many had been used once, then discarded. They looked like obvious 'burner phones' to Hicks.

Arap was a man with a secret.

Hicks ran all the numbers through OMNI and did an extensive search on the activities of each number. RCMP records showed Arap had sent text messages from several burner phones to a jumble of numbers Hicks had seen in other OMNI searches he had conducted over the past few days.

Next, he cross-referenced Arap's numbers with OMNI's ongoing search of Jabbar's network.

As OMNI's search began, an innocent white line appeared from Arap's numbers to other numbers OMNI had been tracking. The white line grew scarlet and began to blink.

Hicks pushed himself away from his desk.

Arap had direct contact with numbers directly associated with the Jabbar profile.

Arap's texts with Jabbar had been to numbers located in Toronto.

Jabbar had been in Toronto after all, as OMNI had predicted.

One number was a year old, the other six months old, but OMNI should still be able to hunt down an approximate location. OMNI accessed local cell carriers in Canada and showed both signals had bounced to the same general location on the map: an office park area on Toronto's west mall.

OMNI had long calculated a high probability of Jabbar

being located somewhere in Canada.

Hicks had a lock on where the most wanted man in the world might be.

Jabbar.

It was a thin lead, but it was more of a lead than he—or anyone else in the world—had ever had before. It was something. And it was all his.

Hicks began setting protocols for OMNI's detailed search and analysis of all digital traffic in the office park on the map. He knew it would give him more data than he could ever use, but he was looking for something specific. He was looking for a match to all numbers and accounts used by Jabbar.

Arap was tied to Jabbar. Arap was on the *Regent Star.* The *Regent Star* was of great interest to Shaban, a member of Jabbar's network.

And with the *Regent Star* about to dock in London, he didn't have a moment to lose.

Hicks flinched when he saw a new traffic alert from OMNI appear on his screen. Shaban had received a text message to his cell phone.

HOME EARLY. COME NOW.

Hicks' handheld began to buzz. The screen on the desk set said it was Rahul.

"My man at the port called." Rahul sounded winded. "He said the *Regent Star* is already in port. He doesn't know how long it's been docked, but there's a chance Arap may have already left the ship."

CHAPTER
26

"**S**HABAN GOT A cryptic text message from a number we haven't seen before," Hicks told Rahul. "Another burner phone, but the message is real." Hicks read it to him.

"That must be why the little bastard popped downstairs so quickly. He's on the street now, and I'm following him on foot. I've got a man and woman cover team backing me up. Three others are trailing us in the van."

Hicks checked the time. It was one in the morning in New York, so it was six in the morning in London. He hoped there was enough commuter foot traffic at that time of the morning to prevent Shaban from realizing he was being followed by three people and a van. But there was no record of Shaban receiving formal field training from any terrorist network. And Hicks knew Rahul was one of the best at this kind of work. He had to believe Rahul wouldn't get burned.

Hicks pulled up the tactical map for Rahul's handheld on OMNI and saw he was heading east. "Any idea where he's going?"

"Heading for the Marble Arch tube station," Rahul said, using the British term for their subway. "If he does, I'll let my cover team ride the train with him. He'll be less suspicious of a man and woman following him."

Hicks couldn't argue with Rahul's logic, but it was time to change tactics a bit. "Switch to visual surveillance. I want everyone on the ground to activate their glasses now."

A few seconds later, Hicks received an alert on his screen telling him Rahul had activated the video feed from the camera mounted on his glasses. He was watching Rahul's visuals of Shaban on one screen while the other showed the view from Rahul's B Team at the *Regent Star* in Harwich.

"What about the other agents?" Hicks asked. "You told me you had ten in the field."

"I do, but you only provided me with two sets of glasses, old boy," Rahul said. "But don't worry. I'll be receiving reports from my people in the field. I'll pass them on to you as I get them."

Hicks knew a lack of glasses was the result of a hastily planned op. Normally, he would've provided Rahul with enough glasses to outfit his entire team. But Scott could only spare two sets of glasses from the Varsity team, so Rahul only had two pairs to work with. At least Rahul's people could communicate with Rahul via phone. It wasn't as seamless as Hicks would've liked, but it was better than nothing.

The feed from Rahul's glasses showed Shaban walking down the street. He looked similar to the photos OMNI had found of him in various British Intelligence databases. He was a light-skinned Iranian who looked like he was in his early twenties, though Hicks knew he was thirty. He didn't dress like a jihadi. He wore a denim jacket and designer jeans the manufacturer had torn to make them look distressed.

OMNI's searches into Shaban's background showed his family had money and gave their boy a monthly stipend. His father was an exiled general of the Iranian Army who had fled the country with plenty of cash. Hicks supposed it was easier to be a radical when Mom and Dad help pay the bills. He bet they had no idea what their son was up to. Radicals had forced his father to leave Iran in the first place, so he doubted the father would approve of his son's extremism. Shaban's hatred of the west might have even been some kind of way of rebuking his father. The University's profilers would eventually enjoy delving into Shaban's psychiatric background if they took him alive.

As Hicks watched the walk along the street, he saw Shaban looked like any other kid on his way to work or college. He wore a black ski cap and had a beat up black backpack slung over his right shoulder.

Rahul began providing a running commentary through a microphone in one of the earpieces of his glasses. "You'll notice the backpack on Shaban's right shoulder. He brings the damned thing with him wherever he goes. Our observations show it contains a laptop, his cell phone, and little else. We didn't see him put anything else in the bag before he left his flat, and it doesn't look any heavier than normal. Searches of his apartment prove he doesn't have any weapons, but we're still proceeding with caution."

Hicks saw Shaban turn a corner and disappear from view.

Rahul gave him the play-by-play as it happened. "The cover team confirms the suspect is heading down into Marble Arch tube station. Our signal is spotty underground, so we won't be able to reliably track them once they're underway. But there's enough of cell signal bleed-through on the platform at the Marble Arch station where they should be able to tell us what train they board."

Hicks felt himself balling his fists on his armrests and made himself stop. He was used to being the man in the car or on foot tailing the suspect. Quarterbacking an op from thousands of miles away would take some getting used to. He wanted to be doing more than simply listening, but knew he could only do more harm than good by interfering in Rahul's operation. He'd chosen Rahul for his expertise. Sometimes, the best way to help was by staying out of the way.

But there was plenty he could do behind the scenes. He had OMNI access the closed security camera feed of the London Underground and opened the feed from the Marble Arch station. He spotted Shaban standing in the middle of dozens of other commuters waiting on the eastbound platform. He knew the eastbound platform was serviced by the train to Harwich.

The same place where the *Regent Star* had docked.

"I've got visual confirmation on the suspect heading east," Hicks reported as he checked the Underground's service map. "He's waiting for the train to Stratford where he'll switch to the train to Harwich. Looks like you were right, Rahul. He's going to meet Arap."

"Of course I was right," Rahul said. "When have you ever known me to be wrong? I'm back in the van and we're making our way to Harwich. We should arrive in about two hours or so, depending on traffic. We should be there before the suspect arrives, but not by much."

Hicks saw Rahul's male-female cover team appear in frame behind Shaban. They were close, but not close enough to alert Shaban. They were fumbling with a map of the Underground, like any other tourists trying to navigate the British train system. Shaban had his ear buds in, but OMNI's surveillance of his phone showed he wasn't using cellular data. He seemed to be listening to music.

Whatever Shaban must be planning with Arap, he seemed awfully cool about it. *What are you up to, you son of a bitch?*

Hicks knew there was no point in continuing the dialogue with Rahul. "Get back in touch with me when you arrive in Harwich. And have your B-Team at Harwich locate Arap. I want eyes on him as soon as possible. Something doesn't feel right."

"Yes, I know."

CHAPTER
27

HICKS KNEW THE next ninety minutes would be hell because there was nothing to do but wait. Waiting was the Job and it was the one part that Hicks had always hated. Waiting was nothing but time and time often led to doubt and second-guessing.

Should he have left Shaban on the street this long? Should he have had Rahul grab him and try to turn him? Should he have had Shaban interrogated so they could find out what he was up to? Rahul could've broken him easily. Had he left Shaban in the wind too long?

Hicks shut down all of his doubts as soon as they stirred. He had already decided on the best course of action. Rahul had concurred. Even if this whole thing ended up going sideways, he had played the cards he'd been dealt the best way he could.

But doubt never stopped being part of the Job, even for a Dean.

Hicks checked the clock time on his monitor. It was almost one-thirty in the morning here in New York. Time to check in with Roger.

Back when he'd run the New York office, he usually liked to schedule his major operations so he could follow one at a time. Developments with Shaban and Arap hadn't given him such a luxury. He knew Roger's operation with Cindy should be in full swing by now, so he should have some kind of an update.

He was glad Roger answered his phone on the second ring. Murmured bar sounds and the rattle cocktail shakers were in the background. "Hello, mother. How are you?" It was his code phrase he was safe and able to talk. "I suppose I should switch to 'Dad' now, given your ascendancy to the throne."

"Knock it off and tell me how it's going."

"Our girl is giving an Oscar-worthy performance. She looks especially radiant this evening. Simple black dress and diamond studded earrings. Alluring and accessible, but not in an obvious, cheap sort of way. She's all dressed up with someone to blow."

"Good. What's the mark doing?"

"Awash in boozy glory. He and his buddies have been drinking martinis since they got here around eight this evening. Vodka martinis, of course, the bourgeois little fucks. They didn't even have the decency to drink gin."

"Focus, Roger."

"I am focusing. The Mark and his friends have been talking shop all night and appeared to be pleased with themselves. Real suave, Mad Men stuff. But once Cindy walked in, the Mark has had eyes for no other. His friends stumbled out of here about thirty minutes ago to allow love to take its course. Cindy and the Mark have been chatting for an hour now, getting closer and closer as time goes by and the drinks keep flowing. They've already kissed once and our friend seems none the wiser. I told you she's good."

At least one operation appeared to be going according to plan. "Keep an eye on them..."

"Gotta run, ma. Love is in the air and it looks like our boy is ready to close the deal on fetching young Cindy. He's got his arm around her waist and he has asked for the bill. I should have a complete package for you within the hour, if not sooner. Let's hope our young man is ready for his close up."

"Make sure he doesn't get so fucked up he misses his train tomorrow morning. None of this works unless he's at his desk tomorrow afternoon."

"He'll be there, don't worry. I'll pour him into his desk chair myself if need be." Roger paused. "What's the matter? You never mother-hen like this."

There was no point in telling him about the London operation. Best to keep separate operations separate. "Don't worry about it. Just take care of things on your end."

Roger laughed. "Of course, darling. It's my best feature. I'll be in touch."

Hicks killed the connection. *Fucking Roger.*

ICKS SPENT THE next hour watching OMNI's tactical map tracking Rahul's progress on the road. Shaban's train was still underground, so he was in and out of OMNI's scanning range. At least he could track Rahul's progress toward Harwich via satellite. He didn't bother trying to contact him. Rahul would not be able to tell him anything he couldn't already see from above.

He killed time by checking the daily activity summary Jason had prepared for him. Results on searches Faculty Members had run and operations they were looking to plan. Progress reports on ongoing operations and requests for funding increase on half a dozen more schemes and plans. There were plenty of requests for his approval, but he shelved them all. There would be time in the coming days to look at them closer.

He stopped reading when the words in the reports began to blur. He wasn't in any state of mind to approve or disapprove anything.

Because Shaban was going to meet Arap and Arap was their best link to Jabbar.

Their only link.

An hour and a half after dropping out of contact, Rahul pinged Hicks. A visual of the port's parking lot came into view on the feed from B Team. "My people have canvassed the town and there's no sign of anyone matching Arap's description anywhere."

"So Arap may still be on the ship?"

"If he left the ship, he's done a damned fine job of hiding himself. They're unloading the cargo now, so there's a good chance he's working on the docks as we speak. My cover team on the train is still tracking Shaban. They switched trains at Stratford as scheduled. Shaban has shown no sign he's aware he's being tailed. My team is in the next car over from him, so it's not obvious he's being followed. They're due to arrive in Harwich in about ten minutes."

Hicks felt his blood pressure begin to rise as things came

together. Arap's location was still an unknown, but the clock was ticking. He knew there were still a dozen ways the entire operation could turn to shit the closer the train got to the station. "If the B-Team spots Arap, I want them to observe him, but they are not to interfere unless they're in direct danger. Let whatever plays out between him and Shaban play out. But they are under no circumstances to allow Arap to leave their sight. He is our main target now."

"Understood. I'll advise my people. Hold on." The line went quiet as Rahul spoke to his team.

Hicks used the time to do some advance work on his own. He tried to access the security cameras at the port, but the firewall was surprisingly complicated. He knew OMNI could eventually hack it, but it would take a few minutes. Close to when Shaban's train would arrive in the station.

In the meantime, he directed OMNI to access the train station's camera feeds. The hack was accomplished in a matter of seconds. The cameras appeared to be ancient, maybe as far back as the early part of the new century. He couldn't zoom in effectively and the cameras couldn't pan back and forth the way more modern systems could. The images were low definition, but OMNI was able to boost them to give a bit more quality.

He scanned the train platform, which was mostly empty except for a few travelers milling around waiting for the train to arrive. He activated OMNI's facial recognition system, which began analyzing each face in frame. None of the people on the platform appeared to be on any known watch lists anywhere in the world.

And none of them were Arap. *Maybe he was still on the ship after all?*

Hicks toggled over to the station's interior cameras to see who might be milling around inside. A few men were obviously cab drivers, clustered together, sipping coffee while they talked. They were all doughy men whose bodies had begun to sag from so many hours spent behind the wheel and eating vending machine junk food while waiting for fares at the station. OMNI scanned them as well, but they came up negative. One had a local warrant for lack of child support payments, but Hicks kept looking.

Hicks toggled to the security cameras outside the station. Several cars had already lined up along the curb, undoubtedly ready to pick up various passengers coming off the train. OMNI automatically scanned the faces of all the drivers and all the license plates in camera range.

The system pinged when it stopped on one face in particular. OMNI had made a match between a face in one of the cars and someone already in the network.

The ping came from a driver in the third car from the front of the line. An old blue Ford Escort with deep dents along the hood and side. The front bumper looked like it had been replaced as an afterthought.

OMNI pinged because it had come back with a fifty-four percent match between the driver of the Escort and the most current photo they had on Arap.

Hicks tried to zoom in on the driver for a better look but remembered the station's ancient camera system was one of the old static types.

Shaban's train was seven minutes out.

To Rahul, Hicks said, "I have a nearly positive match on Arap from the cameras outside the station."

"Shit. He must've gotten off the ship before my men got there. Where is he?"

"He's in a blue Ford Escort outside the train station." He checked OMNI's search on the license plate. "The plate is registered to an Econoline van. He must've swiped the plates and put them on the Ford. You need to get B Team over to the station now."

"Hold on."

Hicks watched Arap's blurry image on the security camera feed. He toggled over to the tactical screen and had the OMNI satellite focus down on Arap's Ford. Given the current angle of the satellite's orbit, all he could see was the rusted top of the Escort's roof. All he could see was the driver's hands on the steering wheel.

And those hands disappeared from view and a new window opened on Hicks' operations screen: **TARGET PHONE IN USE.**

OMNI had detected Shaban had finally turned on his phone and was making a phone call to a number OMNI didn't have in its system. Most likely a burner phone Arap was using.

The call went through and Shaban and the other man began speaking to each other in Farsi. OMNI performed a live English translation of the conversation. The computerized voice of the female Trustee repeated the words as they appeared on Hicks' screen:

Subject One: My train is almost at the station.

Subject Two: I am on my way. I will meet you at the car park across the street from the station.

The call ended.

Hicks told Rahul, "He's lying about being at the car park

across the street. The son of a bitch is parked right in front of the station. Get your people on both ends of the road to the station. If something happens, I want the area shut down and both suspects contained."

"I'm roughly five minutes away," Rahul said. "B-Team is en route. Standby."

Hicks toggled back to the satellite view of the station. He pulled back and watched the blue icon showing Rahul's van making its way along the highway to the station. Given traffic conditions and traffic light frequencies, Rahul looked to be about ten minutes out.

The red B-Team icon was approaching the north end of the station. To Rahul, Hicks said, "B-Team is on site, but tell them hang back. I don't want Arap to smell a trap and take off."

"I'll let them know."

Hicks felt the adrenalin kick in big time. Even on a video feed from thousands of miles away, the rush of the hunt was real.

A black icon showing Shaban's phone and computer appeared less than a minute away from the station as the train rolled in to the security camera's frame.

Hicks checked the exterior camera again. Arap hadn't moved. He hadn't gotten out of the Ford. He looked like any other driver waiting for a passenger to arrive at the station.

OMNI's satellite image showed Rahul's was still at least five minutes out but closing in. "How we doing on time, Ace?"

Rahul's mic muffled as the image from his glasses became unsteady. "B-Team is already in a supportive position at the car park across the street from the station. They are out of Arap's line of sight but will fan out once the train arrives. Three of us are now on foot running toward the station. My driver will provide backup with the van once he gets closer."

Hicks' screen showed the frame moving as Rahul ran toward the station. "Make sure you're not running in a pack. I don't want Arap or Shaban…"

"This isn't my first op for fuck's sake. We're in a scattered formation. One of my people ran ahead with a bag like he's trying to catch the train."

Hicks saw the scene from thousands of miles away unfolding before him on his screens. It was all rushing together again and he felt himself gripping his armrests once more. This time, he didn't stop.

CHAPTER 28

HICKS WATCHED SHABAN'S train pull into the station.

Hicks split his screen between the exterior camera and the platform camera.

The doors opened and a few weary passengers shuffled off the train. Some pulled wheeled luggage behind them while others lugged heavy shoulder bags. They paused on the platform and looked around for signs pointing toward the exit.

Shaban stepped off the last car of the train. His black ski cap was pulled lower on his head than when he'd been on the street. He slung his backpack onto his right shoulder as he headed up the stairs to the overpass. Two people Hicks recognized as Rahul's cover team—a tall dark-skinned man and a much shorter, lighter-skinned woman with a black ponytail—went up the stairs behind him at a reasonable distance. Close enough to see Shaban, but not closer than any of the other passengers.

Hicks toggled one screen to the station waiting room while keeping the other locked on OMNI's satellite view of the exterior of the station. Arap still hadn't moved, but now he could see exhaust coming from the back of the car.

He checked the other screen for Rahul's icon. He was on foot and making good time, but still half a block away. He was getting closer, but still wasn't close enough.

Shaban came into frame on the station's waiting room camera as he came down the steps from the overpass. The cluster of taxi drivers spread out as potential customers streamed down the stairs into the station building. There was no audio on the station feed, but the drivers were obviously asking if anyone needed a taxi.

Shaban walked past the milling crowd with his head down. Rahul's cover team came into frame just as Shaban reached the front doors of the station building.

Hicks switched to OMNI's satellite feed from above the station. The automatic front doors of the station building opened and closed as people went to waiting cars or followed drivers to their taxis.

He watched Shaban move through the crowd at the station entrance, but stopped when he spotted the Escort, as if surprised to see Arap was there. *Of course he's surprised. Arap told him he was in the car parked across the street.*

Shaban bent low to look inside and offered a tentative waive to the driver.

Hicks saw Shaban's body twitch as bullets fired from inside the Ford began striking him in the face and chest. From thousands of miles above the Earth, Hicks watched the silent impact of each shot passing through his body and shattering the glass doors behind him.

The satellite feed may not have audio, but Hicks could practically hear the gunfire and the screams of the passengers as they scattered amidst the sudden violence.

From over three thousand miles away, Hicks watched his entire op turn to shit. And there wasn't a goddamned thing he could do about it.

Hicks heard Rahul curse as the images from his glasses became even harder to see as he broke into a flat out run. He knew the gunfire had kicked the agent into high gear.

Hicks relayed what he saw on his screen. "Shaban is down. Shooter is in a blue Ford Escort and armed."

It was easy for Hicks to spot Rahul's operatives on the OMNI satellite feed from above. They were the only people running toward the Ford while the rest of the people were running away from it. He saw the members of B Team trying to close in on Arap, but they were buffeted by the panicked crowd of humanity stampeding away from the gunfire.

Arap threw the Ford into drive and veered left, crunching into the rear bumper of the car parked in front of him. He put the car in reverse and crashed into the front fender of the car behind him. The impacts from both collisions had damaged his car, but had also cleared enough space for him to pull away clean.

Via the visual from Rahul's glasses, Hicks could see Rahul had turned the corner of the station building as Arap worked his car free.

Hicks heard Rahul yell at Arap as the Ford swerved wildly for the exit. A cab trying to flee the melee accidentally t-boned the Ford on the driver's side. The Escort's airbags deployed as Arap scrambled out of the car through the open passenger window.

Rahul and his partner ran up the roadway as Arap scrambled to his feet. Hicks heard Rahul shout a warning at Arap as the shooter brought up his weapon. Hicks saw the semi-automatic's slide of Arap's gun was locked back.

The gun was empty.

Hicks screamed into his microphone. "He's empty! Don't shoot! Take him alive! Don't shoot! Don't..."

But Rahul and his partner had been too well trained. An armed man was about to point a firearm at them. They both fired on the Iranian as Hicks shouted his warnings.

From the feed of Rahul's glasses, Hicks saw Arap's body buck with the impacts of multiple rounds striking his head and chest. The son of a bitch was dead before he hit the roadway.

Hicks yelled and ripped off the headset, throwing it onto the desk.

The one and only lead he had to Jabbar was lying dead outside an English train station.

All of this had been for nothing.

Hicks watched the chaos of the scene unfold from OMNI's satellite feed. Rahul's B- Team had finally been able to filter itself through the panicked crowd—guns out looking for any secondary shooters who might be backing up Arap. But the only people in frame were Rahul and his people. Most of the passengers had forgotten their luggage as they scattered to safety. Some of them had run back into the station building in a blind panic, but most had put as much distance between them and the shooting as possible.

A few brave or curious passengers had gathered around Shaban's body, obscuring his corpse from OMNI's view. Hicks didn't need verification from Rahul that Shaban was dead. The amount of blood pooling onto the pavement around the feet of the onlookers told the story.

Hicks was glad to see the female member of Rahul's cover team had managed to push her way through the crowd and rejoin her male colleague as they walked away from the scene. She had Shaban's bag over her shoulder.

Hicks could tell by the view from Rahul's camera that he had slipped away unnoticed as well. He grabbed his headset when he heard Rahul speaking to his team in his native tongue. Rahul gave Hicks his report in English. "Shooter and suspect are both dead. All ten members of my team are accounted for and moving away from the scene. B-Team is falling back to their vehicle and will meet us at the rendezvous point in London. Only Arap was armed."

"His fucking gun was empty, Rahul."

"We didn't see it until after we put him down." Hicks could hear the growing wail of distant sirens through Rahul's earpiece. "In the meantime, if you could do something about the surveillance video..."

"I'm already on it." With a few keystrokes, Hicks directed OMNI to erase a week's worth of footage from the camera's servers. One day of missing footage would raise eyebrows, but five days' worth would be written off as a technical glitch, especially on such an antiquated system. "Were your people able to search Shaban?"

"We retrieved his computer and cell phone and will examine them on the way back to London. We'll perform a more in-depth study of them in my hotel room later."

Hicks had wanted Arap and Shaban taped to chairs in an interrogation cell somewhere. He wanted Roger pulling the truth out of them. He wanted to feed them to Tali and the Mossad when they were finished. In the end, all he had was two more corpses, a cell phone and computer OMNI had already hacked.

It wasn't much, but it was something. "What else did you find in his bag?"

"Nothing," Rahul said as he jogged across a quiet intersection. "I checked Arap and the car, too. The trunk had popped open when it struck the cab. There was nothing in the trunk, nothing in the back seat and nothing on his body, either. He either left his bag on his ship or he stowed it elsewhere. I couldn't grab his phone because there were too many people paying attention and taking pictures."

Hicks wanted to order him to go back and tear the Ford apart. He could always have OMNI erase the pictures taken by bystanders later. There had to be something back at the scene to justify all this. A message, a letter, something to link Arap directly to Jabbar. Something more powerful than a common number between burner phones. Something to explain why Jabbar had sent one of his best people to kill Shaban.

He didn't know exactly what they should look for, but all of his instincts told him there had to be more to this than two dead Iranians outside an English train station.

Rahul must have taken Hicks' silence as a cue, because he added, "If there was something else to find at the scene, we would have found it, James. This looks like a simple textbook hit to me."

Hicks sank back in his chair, because he saw it the same way. But it didn't make any sense. All of this for a simple murder? Had Arap sailed across an ocean to shoot some low-level operative? It didn't make sense.

There had to be something more to justify all of the trouble with Stephens and the Barnyard and the obfuscation and the worry of the past few days. It couldn't boil down to a common hit.

Hicks wanted to throw his monitor against the wall and stomp the fucking thing to bits. He wanted to scream at Rahul for killing a man with an empty gun.

But Hicks no longer had the luxury of emotion or rage. He had a team on foreign soil still in harm's way at an active scene. He set emotion aside and let his training take over. He forced the storm in his mind to calm so the facts could rise to the surface.

His team was getting away clean. They had Shaban's phone and his computer. There was no trace of a biological agent on site. A terror attack did not appear to be imminent. The entire event seemed to only involve two men and both men were dead. He hoped Rahul could find something on the hard drives of Shaban's devices might give them something to help find Jabbar.

"Turn off any device you got from Shaban before you get in the vehicle," Hicks told Rahul. "Remove the batteries if you can. I don't want anyone tracking you on your way back to London."

"Consider it done," Rahul said. "And I'm sorry, James. I know you didn't send me over here to have it turn out like this."

Hicks could hear the police sirens growing louder through Rahul's earpiece. "There'll be plenty of time for regrets later. For now, get your asses back to London and let me know when you're safe. That's your priority now."

Hicks killed the connection and tossed his headset back on to the desk. He watched the silent aftermath of the shooting on his screens. He saw the situation slowly transition from a chaotic killing ground to an active crime scene under the authority of local police. One cop began stringing up crime scene tape to keep the spectators away from the bodies while another checked the dead men for pulses.

Questions began to flood Hicks' mind. Not the Carousel of Concern, but more basic questions.

Arap couldn't have travelled all that way to simply kill *Shaban. And why make it so public? Shaban trusted Arap. He would've gotten into the car without question. Arap could have driven him someplace and killed him quietly. Why gun him down at the train station in front of more than a dozen witnesses?*

It would only be a matter of time before news of the shooting hit the BBC, and eventually newswires around the world. It wouldn't generate any Breaking News bulletins, but it would be covered and the members of the Barnyard would know about it before it hit the newswires. The shooting would be featured on news sites throughout the world and on the crawls at the bottom of the screen on CNN and Fox News and MSNBC. Two Arabs shot dead in a sleepy English port town would make news.

Local police would soon identify Shaban and discover he was on numerous terror watch lists. They'd learn Arap was a Turkish national working on the *Regent Star.* The British intelligence apparatus would begin the process of digging deep into the lives of both men. Those details would be left out of the reports, but the damage would have already been done.

By the next morning—if not sooner—British Intelligence would issue a general inquiry to their counterparts in the intelligence community around the world in an effort to learn what the other countries knew about both men. In a day or two, they may even discover Arap and Shaban had a common connection to the Jabbar profile.

The Barnyard Apparatus and every intelligence agency in the world would join the active hunt for the infamous Jabbar. The only advantage the University had on Jabbar was already dead.

Jabbar would be long gone by then, of course. The second he caught mention of what had happened, he would fry his hard drives and disappear. The terrorist would be twice as careful next time around and he had already proven elusive for more than twenty-five years.

Hicks shut his eyes and ran his hand across his brow. None of this made any sense. Arap was obviously valuable to Jabbar. Using him on a common hit was a waste of valuable resources and Jabbar was not a wasteful man.

Hicks sat up straight.

No, Jabbar was not a wasteful man.

Nothing in his profile showed he had ever acted out of vengeance or anger. Agencies all over the world had tried to lure him out into the open by killing or torturing his suspected associates. He never acknowledged any of their deaths or suffering. He never responded to any kind of provocation whatsoever. He never took revenge.

Jabbar was not a rash man. He was a planner. It was one of the many reasons why he had never been caught.

Shaban's death must have been planned with a specific purpose in mind. It had happened exactly as Jabbar had wanted it to happen. Arap's mission was to publicly execute Shaban.

But why?

Hicks looked at his screen when he heard an alert ping and saw a window open on his tactical screen: **INCOMING TEXT MESSAGE ON SUBJECT PHONE.**

He clicked on the window and saw it was from the hack OMNI had placed on Shaban's phone. Rahul may have turned off the phone and removed the battery, but the account was still live. The message to Shaban's account read:

TO WHOMEVER KILLED MY MEN. WE SHOULD MEET.

Hicks stared at the screen. He directed OMNI to run a quick trace on the source of the text. It was a long shot, even for OMNI's capabilities, but it might give him something.

Whoever had sent the text already knew about what had happened at the train station. Was this one of their handlers? Or was it Jabbar himself?

Of all the questions flooding his mind, Hicks typed only one word: **WHY?**

The reply was almost immediate: **BECAUSE IT WOULD BENEFIT BOTH OF US.**

Hicks decided to push a little to see how far he could get. **HOW DO YOU KNOW WE AREN'T POLICE?**

The first reply came as quick the previous response. **BECAUSE YOU TOOK SHABAN'S COMPUTER AND PHONE BEFORE THE POLICE ARRIVED. YOU ARE TOO ORGANIZED TO BE COMMON THIEVES. YOU ARE TOO STEALTHY TO BE BRITISH. THE ENEMY OF MY ENEMY IS MY FRIEND.**

Whoever this was knew what they were talking about, but they obviously didn't know who Hicks was. He typed out the only response he could: **WHERE AND WHEN?**

The answer: **NOON TOMORROW AT THE BASE OF THE TALLEST LANDMARK OF THE CITY WHERE YOU WILL TRACE THIS TEXT MESSAGE. COME ALONE. DON'T BE LATE.**

One question remained for Hicks: **HOW WILL WE KNOW EACH OTHER?**

The answer came as a photo attached to the text message. It was a screen grab from the ATM camera footage of Hicks crossing Third Avenue a few days before.

A text followed: **I WILL KNOW YOU. SEE YOU TOMORROW – JABBAR**

Jabbar.

Hicks checked the trace on the location of the message. OMNI detected it had been bounced around half a dozen communication towers and satellites throughout North America before it settled on one location.

The CN Tower in Toronto. The same city where OMNI had estimated they'd find Jabbar all along. The same city where Hicks decided Jabbar's office park must be.

Jabbar had contacted him. Jabbar had known to contact him through Shaban's phone. Jabbar knew what he looked like. He had the ability to hack a CIA operation.

He knew what, but he didn't know why.

He hoped he'd find many of the answers he sought the next day.

CHAPTER 29

THE NEXT MORNING, Hicks decided he needed to return to his routine now more than ever.

He had neglected his meditation and yoga sessions for far too long. That morning, he returned to them. The solitude gave him clarity. The yoga routines gave him strength. He shook off the cobwebs of indecision and chaos of the previous days and focused on himself. He focused on what needed to be done. He'd need such a level of clarity to handle what he knew would face him throughout the coming day.

As he was toweling off after his session, he heard his handheld buzz. It was a text message from Roger. **I'M BRINGING OUR BOY TO THE TRAIN. SEE YOU IN TWENTY. HERE'S SOMETHING TO MAKE YOU SMILE.**

The pictures Roger sent in the following text messages

didn't make Hicks smile, but they proved Cindy had achieved her objective.

Hicks hoped he would be able to say the same when he eventually returned to the Twenty-Third Street facility later that evening.

If he returned at all.

He quickly got dressed, pocketed extra speed loaders for the Ruger, and set out for Penn Station.

AT PENN STATION, Hicks checked the main departure board in the Amtrak concourse for the eight-thirty train to Washington, D.C. He saw the track number and went downstairs. He had always hated train stations. No matter the station or where it was in the world, they all smelled of stale angst and train grease. Some people found train travel romantic. Hicks found trains tedious and outmoded and slow.

He found Roger leaning against a support beam on the platform. For a man who had been up all night, Roger looked like he had stepped out of a spa. His tan sport coat was pressed and his matching pocket square was perfect.

Hicks skipped the pleasantries. "Where's our boy?"

Roger inclined his head toward the train car. "The guy with his head against the window. He's hung over as hell and guilty as sin." Roger smiled. "Exactly as you wanted him."

Hicks saw a brown-haired man slumped against the window of the business class coach. He hadn't expected him to look as clean-cut and bright-eyed as he did in his government ID photo, but he still didn't like what he saw. "He looks like shit. I told you this won't work if he's too fucked up to follow directions."

"Stop being such a puritan. I made sure he's only hurting enough to make him pliable for your charms. He's a cocky little prick when he's sober, but right now, he's a mewling mess. He's suffering from the remorse of the indulgent. He doesn't regret what happened, only that he's paying for it now."

Hicks knew better than to argue with him. When it came to drunken depravity, Roger was usually right. "How much does he remember from last night?"

"Not much," Roger admitted, "but that was the point, wasn't it? He's been begging me all morning to give him something to help kill the hangover. I played the helpful drinking buddy and told him I knew a guy who could get him something to help him straighten out." He playfully poked Hicks in the chest. "You're the guy."

Roger handed him a clear plastic baggie full of pills of various shapes, sizes, and colors. "Tell him to take these on the ride home. I've already given him a large bottle of water for the train. I spiked it with some electrolytes to help him recover even faster. Tell him to take a handful of these pills and drink all the water he can before he arrives in D.C. The more water he drinks, the better the pills will work. He'll be functional by the time he gets to the office."

Hicks looked at the bag of multicolored pills. "What are they?"

"They're like vitamins on steroids," Roger explained. "They'll begin to quell the effects of his hangover as soon as he swallows them. A clear mind will help the seeds you plant take root. Like you said, this doesn't work if he's fucked up."

"I'll take it from here." Hicks put the bag of pills in his jacket pocket. "You and I have a full day ahead of us, so you'd better get some breakfast in the food court upstairs."

Roger looked like he'd thrown a dead fish in his lap. "Me? In a fucking food court? Don't be insulting. I'll wait for you here."

HICKS BOARDED THE train and found Dan Finch alone in a three-seater inside the doorway. Even from several feet away, Hicks could smell several hours' worth of vodka seeping through his pores. Finch's head was slumped against the window and he was wearing the same blue suit Hicks had seen him wearing in Roger's surveillance pictures. It was an expensive suit bought from a respectable men's clothing store chain in D.C., but not custom made. According to OMNI's profile of the man, Dan Finch had long dreamed of owning a closet full of custom made clothes. Today may be his first step toward getting it, if he was smart enough to follow Hicks' orders.

Finch had pulled up the collar of his overcoat in an effort to shield his eyes from the invasive glare of the train car lights, even though the lights weren't bright. He'd even tucked his train ticket in the headrest off the aisle seat so he could sleep off his drunk without the conductor disturbing him.

Finch barely stirred when Hicks dropped into the seat next to him and nudged him with an elbow. "I hear you might need some help."

Finch slowly opened his eyes and winced at the light. He was only thirty-one years old, but thanks to a late night at his hotel's lobby bar, looked a hell of a lot older. "You the guy Sam sent?"

Hicks figured 'Sam' must have been the fake name Roger had given him. He dug the bag of vitamins out of his pocket and tossed them on Finch's lap. "If you take a handful of those, you'll get better before you know it. Keep drinking as much water as you can on the ride back to D.C. if you want them to work as well as they should."

Finch slowly pushed himself upright and fumbled to keep the bag of pills from falling off his lap. He blindly pawed around the seat for the bottle of water. He found it between his back and the window. "Thanks, man. I guess I overdid it last night."

Hicks smiled. "Bright lights, big city. It's been known to happen from time to time. Those pills and the water will straighten you out fine."

Finch took a handful of pills and gulped them down with some of Roger's water. He looked at Hicks with heavy red eyes. "No change. My head's still pounding and my hands are still shaking."

"Like most good things in life, it takes time. We'll need you to be in good shape by the time you get to the office."

Finch took another healthy gulp of water. "Office? Are you kidding? I'm in no shape to go near the office today, man. I already called in and told them I'm working remotely."

"Change of plans, Danny Boy, because you need to go into the office today. You've got a hell of a lot of work to do. That's why I gave you those pills."

Finch lowered the water bottle. "You…you know my name?"

"Sure I do. Dan Finch, All-American boy and scholar from the sovereign state of Indiana. Graduated from Butler ten years ago with a B.A. in Political Science. Graduated in the middle of your class, unfortunately, but grades aren't important, not for a man with your kind of ambition."

Finch seemed to forget all about his hangover for a moment.

"Wait a second. Who..."

Hicks went on. "And look at where your ambition got you. Chief of Staff to the senior senator from the sovereign state of Indiana. Mom and dad are so proud. They bore the shit out of their friends on Facebook with updates of how their little Danny is doing out there in Washington. That picture with the president at the Christmas party last year was a big hit, even though he is a Democrat."

Finch tried to push himself away from Hicks, but he was already in the corner of the train seat. "How did you know all this? Who the fuck are you?" He looked around the train car, but no one else was paying attention. "What is this?"

"Who I am isn't important." Hicks removed his handheld from his inside pocket. "You're not important, either. But your boss? He's important. He's the reason why you and I are having this conversation right now because I know you don't want him to see what I'm about to show you."

Hicks tapped the handheld's screen and brought up one of the images Roger had sent him that morning. "That's you and your buddies at the bar last night, slinging that 'House of Cards' bullshit for the drunks and the tourists who don't know any better."

Finch looked at Hicks cycling through the pictures of him and his friends talking to various people at the bar. "Wait. How'd you..."

Hicks stopped at the photo of Cindy standing in the middle of Finch and the others. "But when this girl walked in, politics suddenly didn't seem so interesting anymore. Pretty girl, wasn't she? She's obviously not like those corn-fed girls you've got back home in Indiana."

Hicks thumbed to the picture showing the two of them kissing at the hotel elevator. "I've got pictures of what happened upstairs, too. Want to see?"

Before Finch could object, Hicks thumbed to another picture of Finch performing fellatio on Cindy. "My, oh my," Hicks said. "Look at what you're doing there. What would the folks back in Indiana say?"

Finch made a clumsy attempt to grab the phone.

Hicks gave him a short elbow to the gut, sending him back against the window. The shot wasn't hard enough to break a rib or draw attention from the other travelers, but hard enough to make a point.

"Don't do that again."

Finch cradled his sore belly. "You son of a bitch. You set me up. You and Sam. You drugged me!"

"No one drugged you, asshole. You got drunk all by yourself, just like you made the decision to take her up to your room all by yourself. We baited the hook, but you decided to bite."

"Who the hell are you? What the hell do you want?"

"Those are all the wrong questions, Danno. You're worried about these pictures when you should be grateful I have them instead of someone else. Like someone in the media, for instance. Or a blogger. Or your boss. Personally, I don't see anything wrong with what you did, but the senator's constituents back in Indiana aren't as open-minded as the rest of us. Can you imagine what would happen if these images ever got out? You'd lose your job. Your reputation would be ruined. Your Conservative friends would shun you and your Liberal enemies would love to watch you starve. No hiring manager in any government agency in the country would touch you. All of the political consultants in the business would view you as a liability. You've seen it happen before, so you know I'm right."

Finch groaned as he slumped against the window. He looked worse now than when Hicks had first walked onto the train. "Why are you doing this to me? Who sent you?"

Hicks put the handheld back in his pocket. "You're still asking all the wrong questions, Ace. Don't focus on who sent me. Don't even focus on the pictures. Instead, focus on what you can do to make sure no one ever sees these pictures except you and me. Right now you're between a cock and a hard place, but I've got a way out of this which will benefit all of us."

"Let me guess." Finch's bloodshot eyes got nasty. "Especially you."

"I'm going to ask you to do something I need done. If you do it, you'll come off looking like a hero. And you'll gain a good friend in the bargain. Me."

Finch tried to flatten his ruffled overcoat collar. "I don't know what you want, but whatever it is won't work. I'm not a criminal, and I won't break the law for you no matter what you're threatening me with. I always get caught." He looked at the pocket where Hicks had placed his handheld. "I never get away with anything."

"That's the beauty of this conversation, because I'm not asking you to break a single law. In fact, what I need you to do falls well within the parameters of your job and is one hundred percent legal."

Finch tried to push himself up straighter. "Legal? Then why the…" He looked again at where Hicks had his phone. "Why did you do all this?"

"Insurance to make sure I'll have your undivided attention

to what I need done as soon as possible. In a couple of minutes, you're going to receive an email explaining everything I need you to do and how I want you to do it. You will not deviate from the steps I give you."

"You've got to at least tell me what to look out for."

"You're going to receive an email from an anonymous whistleblower who is sending you damaging information about an intelligence agency over-stepping its authority on American soil. The email will be traceable to an actual person inside the intelligence community. Since your boss is also the chairman of the Senate Intelligence Committee, you will do your level best to make sure he launches a formal—and public—investigation into the allegations. The only thing is, I'm going to need you to make sure this information is leaked to the press this afternoon."

As drunk as he still was, Finch had a few brain cells firing. "You've gone through all this bullshit to leak something to the press? You could do that yourself."

"Sure, but I'm a nobody. Who would publish anything I'd give them? They'd want to vet the material before they ran it and vetting takes time. And if there's one thing neither of us have it's time. Someone might make the material disappear if we wait too long and neither of us can let that happen. Thanks to your contacts in the media, that won't happen. You're an unimpeachable source, so if this information comes from you, they'll run with it. Your boss will look like a reformer taking hold of unlawful government action and you look like the hero for giving him the information. We all win, including me."

Finch blinked hard, as if it might help him hear better. "You're blackmailing me to do my job?"

The words of the Trustee on the bench came back to him.

"This isn't blackmail. It's an incentive to do your job to the best of your ability." Hicks gave him a good-natured elbow as he stood up. "Cheer up, Danny Boy. You got on this train as another drunk with a bad hangover and a heavy conscience. You're going to be stepping off the train in Union Station as one of the most influential men in Washington."

He watched a dozen objections run through Finch's mind and watched each one of them die quickly. "You stink, mister, you know that?"

"So do you. Like a vodka bottle. Look for my email as soon as this train comes out of the tunnel. You'll find both of your phones have already been charged up and should last until you get back to the office. Get yourself some coffee, Ace. You've got a lot of work to do."

Hicks had expected Finch to have some kind of comeback as he watched Hicks step off the train. Most Assets usually did. The Last Word usually gave them the illusion they had some measure of power in a powerless situation.

But Dan Finch didn't say a word. He stayed slumped against the window, looking in the general direction of where Hicks had been seated.

Hicks had seen this look before. Finch had ridden into Manhattan on top of the world. He was the right hand aide of one of the most powerful people in the country. Now, he was riding back home hung over and under somebody's thumb. His fate was no longer in his own hands.

But Hicks had learned long ago that fate never is.

Now Finch knew it, too.

Roger fell in next to him as he stepped off the train.

"I watched some of it through the window," Roger said.

"Glad to see you haven't lost your touch with the carrot-and-stick routine, old friend. I don't know about you, but there's nothing like a successful bit of extortion to put the day on a proper footing."

Hicks wasn't so cheerful. "Nothing's successful unless he does what we're telling him to do."

"He'll do it," Roger said. "His type always does. If he was a tough guy, he wouldn't have gotten into politics in the first place. Now, would you kindly tell me where we're going?

"We're going to Toronto."

"Canada? What the hell is in Toronto?"

Hicks put on his sunglasses as soon as they hit the main terminal of Penn Station. "We're going to find out."

CHAPTER 30

SINCE THE UNIVERSITY jet had finally made it back from London, Hicks decided to use it to fly up to Toronto. He didn't know if the previous Dean had used the jet much. Al Clay hadn't struck Hicks as the jet-setting type, but Hicks had believed the man was a former spy, not the computer geek who had built OMNI. Hicks hadn't even known the University had a jet at its disposal until he had become Dean.

At first thought such a luxury was an unnecessary expense. The funds to pay for the damned thing could be better used to hire more operatives to fight the University's new two-front war.

But now he was on-board the damned thing, he began to see how a private jet might come in handy. The entire operation was a University business. A University flight crew was flying the University jet to a University-controlled landing strip in

Toronto's Pearson Airport. There, a customs official on the University payroll would allow Roger and Hicks into the country armed to the teeth. A member of the University's Varsity squad would meet them at the tarmac in an armored Land Rover and take them to the CN Tower.

Expensive, perhaps, but justifiable under the circumstances.

Hicks had briefed Roger on the Jabbar meeting before the jet took off.

When Hicks was finished, Roger surprised him by saying, "You're not enjoying any of this, are you?"

"Enjoying what?"

"The jet. The power. The access. The fact you're about to meet one of the most wanted terrorists in the world. You're not getting even a little thrill from any of this."

Hicks wasn't in an introspective mood, but knew Roger never let anything drop until he got an answer. "I'll bask in the glory later. Right now, all I care about is Jabbar."

"If there's one thing I've learned in our line of work, James, it's that 'later' is never guaranteed. There's always going to be something going on—another threat to face. Another problem to solve. You've risen from a lowly ensign with the Coast Guard's Intelligence unit to running your own intelligence agency. You deserve to pat yourself on the back a little."

Hicks should've been annoyed at Roger for mentioning his past. He should've been annoyed he knew it at all. But Roger Cobb and he was damned hard to be angry with for very long. "How'd you know?"

"I've known for years, but it was never important until now. You let it slip once during a night of bad sake in Taiwan about ten years ago. You quit talking soon after, of course, but it was one of the few times you acted like an actual human being. It was almost touching."

Hicks remembered Taiwan and the sake, but little else from that night. It was one of the many reasons why Hicks kept a close eye on his drinking. If Roger had kept the secret this long, he would keep it even longer. "Let's not talk about it again. And don't expect me to pat myself on the back anytime soon. I might be the Dean, but I've got all the problems and responsibilities to go with it." Hicks decided it sounded like whining and stopped himself before saying anything more.

"The curse comes with the blessing, but you have still accomplished something important, my friend. Let it soak in and enjoy some of the benefits while you can. Who knows? We could both be dead in an hour or two."

"That's what I like about you, Roger. You always look on the bright side."

"Like the man said, 'In the midst of movement and chaos, keep stillness inside you.'"

Hicks figured out where this sudden burst of wisdom was coming from. "You've been reading Deepak Chopra again. Goddamn it, I told you to knock that shit off."

Roger smiled as he leaned closer. "The less you open your heart to others, darling, the more your heart suffers."

Hicks looked out the window. *Fucking Roger.*

"You're no fun." Roger readjusted himself in his seat. "So, what do you need me to do while you're meeting with Jabbar?"

Hicks was glad they were getting back to the business at hand. "I need you to do the hardest thing I've ever asked you to do. I need you to blend in with the tourists while watching my back."

"I can blend in when I want to, you sarcastic bastard. There's not much fun in being another cow in the herd. You said the meeting is taking place at the CN Tower. Will there be any Varsity bully boys on scene in support?"

"Only the driver. Scott sent him ahead of us late last night."

"I'm surprised he didn't demand to come along. He must have hated sitting on the sidelines for this one."

"I didn't give him a choice. His team is good, but only one of them has ever worked Toronto before and this isn't the type of operation for on-the-ground training. Jabbar told me to come alone, so if he senses a tactical group lurking around, he'll walk away and I'll never find him again. It'll be up to you and the driver to watch my back."

"I'm honored. Ready, too." Roger opened his sport coat to reveal the nine-millimeter Glock in his shoulder holster. Hicks knew Roger's flamboyant nature led most intelligence professionals to write him off as a lightweight. But Hicks had been in enough scrapes with the man to know he was almost as good as Tali when it came to fieldwork. Years of champagne, cocaine and a profane lifestyle had dulled his edge a bit, but he was still sharper than most.

And it was a comfort to Hicks to have him there. "I don't know what we'll be walking into, Roger. Whatever happens, I need you to stay focused and frosty."

"Frosty?" Roger grinned. "Baby, I'm practically a fucking Eskimo. Want to rub noses?"

Hicks looked out the window again. *Fucking Roger.*

A BLACK LAND ROVER pulled up next to the jet as Roger and Hicks got off the plane. A black man with a compact build wearing a black shirt, cargo pants and boots stepped out from behind the wheel and opened the rear passenger door. "Name's Weaver, sir. Varsity Squad. Mr. Scott told me to take care of you today. Pleasure to finally meet you."

Hicks had never met Weaver before. Had he mistaken Hicks for the old Dean? It didn't matter. He didn't speak until they were inside the SUV and underway. "You have our passports, Weaver?"

The driver handed two passports back to them. "Jason got these to me ahead of your arrival. You'll find they've already been stamped and are good to go, sir."

Hicks took the passports and handed one to Roger. He didn't bother opening it up. He knew it would be the Professor Warren identity, a profile he knew cold. Besides, he didn't plan on using it unless they got stopped somewhere on airport property. It would be up to Weaver to get them out of it.

Hicks asked, "Did Scott brief you on where we're going and what we're doing?"

"No, sir. All he told me was to come ready and come heavy, which I have."

Hicks decided to keep the details to a minimum. The less Weaver knew now, the less he'd have to be reminded to forget later on. The Jabbar meeting could be a chat. It could also blow up into something much more. "I need you to take us to the CN Tower where we could be walking into a possible hostile situation."

"Won't be my first one, sir, and it won't be my last." Weaver rolled down the window and waived to the guard at the airport gate. The guard raised the barrier and Weaver drove on. "I've been ordered by Scott to keep you two alive no matter what happens and that's what I plan on doing. Nothing else is my business unless you tell me it's my business."

Hicks liked Weaver already. "Good man. I'll have Jason patch you into his OMNI feed while you're stationed here in the car. Roger will be providing over-watch support for me on the ground, so all communications will go first to him, and from him to me. The less chatter in my ear, the better if things get hot. One voice calling the plays cuts down on confusion."

"Understood, sir."

"I'll need you to watch the eye in the sky from the dashboard screen in here. Be ready to roll if Jason finds something he needs you to investigate. Sound good to you, Weaver?"

Weaver glanced at him in the rearview mirror before keeping his eyes on the road. "Anything you need, I'm here."

"Best let me off a block away from the tower," Roger added. "Circle the block until I tell you I'm in position. That'll give me time to get a sense of the scene before I give you the go ahead to come in."

Hicks closed his eyes and shut out the rest of the world for a moment while he focused on his breathing for the rest of the ride into downtown Toronto. Watching the passing cityscape would only make him more anxious than he already was. He needed to quiet his mind and keep himself on an even keel.

Stephens. The University. The Trustees. Finch's Mission. The Mossad. Jabbar. The Carousel of Concern was spinning faster than ever in his mind, but he commanded it to slow down. Only one item on the carousel mattered right now. Jabbar. It all hinged on him now.

Hicks had walked into hundreds of unknown situations before, but he had never dealt with a terrorist as high-level as Jabbar. He doubted any Western operative had. Most terrorists like Jabbar either got killed or killed themselves before anyone from the West got their hands on them.

This was new territory for him. It was most likely new territory for Jabbar, too. He doubted one of the most wanted men in the world held many face-to-face meetings. Hicks didn't find that encouraging.

One anxious, dangerous man was enough.

TWENTY MINUTES LATER, after navigating the streets of downtown Toronto, Weaver dropped off Roger a block away from the CN Tower, before he pulled back into traffic. He began to circle the block around the tower as slowly as the flow of traffic would allow.

Before taking off from New York, Hicks had Jason divert one of the University's Low-Earth-Orbit (LEO) scanners to move into position over the upper atmosphere high above the CN Tower. It was a fraction of the size of a standard OMNI satellite and not nearly as powerful. It was too high to be considered a violation of Canadian airspace, yet low enough to monitor Hicks' immediate area. It also gave him a more reliable way of communicating with Jason and the team via a secure network.

Hicks checked his handheld to see if the LEO scanner had detected any hijacked camera feeds or if there were any other secure signals in the area. Canada might be another country, but it was still within the CIA's sphere of influence. They could easily track him here as they could in New York, maybe even more so.

He was relieved to see the only signals OMNI picked up were from the Royal Canadian Mounted Police (RCMP). He had expected that, especially around a major tourist attraction like the CN Tower. He bet this was why Jabbar had picked the tower. Sometimes a public location was the best meeting place for two hunted men. Mutually assured destruction could be an effective insurance policy.

He inserted the tiny Bluetooth earpiece in his ear in time to hear Roger's first transmission. "I'm in position at the plaza. All clear. Nothing out of the ordinary."

"Where are you located?"

"Now why on earth would I tell you that? You might look my way and accidentally give away my position, which wouldn't be good for either of us, now would it?"

Hicks hated when Roger was right.

CHAPTER
31

HICKS ASKED WEAVER to pull over when they got closer to the tower. He got out of the Land Rover and threaded his way through the crowd of tourists making their way to and from the skyscraper. He made sure his jacket was open as he moved. The feeling of the Ruger beneath his left arm was comforting.

All the guidebooks said the CN Tower is the tallest freestanding structure in the Western Hemisphere. As if one of the tallest buildings in the world wasn't enough of a draw, the Toronto Blue Jays played next door at the Rogers Centre and a small patch of green named Bobbie Rosenfeld Park separated the two complexes.

It was a warm day for early spring, so Hicks didn't look out of place by keeping his jacket open. The lack of wind meant he didn't have to worry about the jacket blowing open and revealing the Ruger beneath his left arm.

He subtly scanned the crowd for any sign of Roger, but was glad he couldn't spot him. He heard him via the earpiece in his ear. "Jason and Weaver report they're reading you loud and clear on all screens. No obvious hostiles in the area, but we don't know what Jabbar looks like. He could be walking around out here right now and we'd never know it. Jason is also monitoring all secure signals via OMNI. I'll let you know if he suspects our friends from the Barnyard in the area. Stay loose and keep your head on a swivel. We'll handle the rest."

The crowds of tourists in the plaza grew thicker the closer Hicks got to the tower. He didn't know if Jabbar wanted to meet inside the tower or outside, so he split the difference and stood near the entrance.

His skin began to itch as he sensed the dozens of cameras in the area watching him. He doubted Stephens had tracked him to Canada, but he wouldn't be surprised if they had. The Barnyard was not without its own resources, and if one of their computers picked up his image and ran a facial recognition scan, RCMP units would surround him within minutes. His sunglasses should be enough to throw off a casual scan, but if Langley had widened their search parameters, he could draw attention.

But grabbing Jabbar was worth the risk. He only hoped Jason and Weaver would detect any increased police activity before they got too close.

By sending Hicks the screen grab of the CIA surveillance, Jabbar had proven himself to be adept at hacking data systems. There was a good chance he was watching the plaza remotely right now, deciding whether or not it was safe enough to approach.

Hicks knew any one of the dozens of people milling past him could be Jabbar, so he didn't waste time guessing if he was one of them. He hoped the terrorist believed he had followed his directions and had come alone.

The longer he stood at the entrance to the tower, the more Hicks began to conclude all tourists in all parts of the world looked the same. Men, women, and little kids. Tall, short, heavy, thin. Most of them had smart phones. Those who weren't posting something on Facebook or Instagram were taking selfies from the base of the tower looking up. He heard accents and dialects from Pakistan and India, France and Australia. Jabbar could've been any of them and none of them. He didn't try to guess. He tried to keep his mind a blank and make sure the Carousel didn't fire up again. He focused on the task at hand.

Roger's voice came over his earpiece. "On your ten o'clock, a light skinned male in his early sixties. Could be Middle Eastern. Carrying what appears to be coffee. Looks too sweet to be wholesome to suit me. This may be our target."

Hicks spotted the man Roger had described. He fit OMNI's general approximations of what Jabbar may look like: common, unassuming, and easy to overlook. The man with the coffee could have passed for Greek or Persian or Turkish. He was holding a full Styrofoam coffee tray with both hands as he gingerly steered his way through the tourists, making sure no one bumped into him. Hicks noticed he was clean-shaven with a receding hairline. He wasn't carrying a bag or wearing a jacket. He didn't look like a tourist.

Hicks checked the man's ample torso, hips, and ankle for the outline of a weapon. Nothing. Not even a smart phone in his pocket.

The man even smiled as he approached him.

Hicks flexed his right hand and eased it up toward his belt buckle. The grip of the Ruger was only a few inches away.

But the man passed him by. He used his shoulder to push through the revolving doors and enter the CN Tower lobby. He hadn't spilled a drop of his coffee.

Hicks didn't bother to watch the man after he went inside. If the man was Jabbar doing a dry run, he'd know soon enough.

"Shit," Roger said in his ear. "I could've sworn he was our man."

Hicks didn't dare respond in case Jabbar was close enough to see his lips moving. *Keep looking.*

He spotted a plump young woman walking toward him from the park side of the tower. She didn't look much different from the other people in the plaza, but something about her caught his eye, though not in a romantic way.

She looked like she could be a kindergarten teacher or a babysitter or a nurse. She was in her middle twenties and around five feet tall. She had a round face which bore a naturally pleasant expression and dark, almond shaped eyes. Her black hair was tied back in a bun. Her clothes were non-descript and plain—a loose brown jacket over black pants. She had a cheap black book bag over both of her shoulders and her sneakers looked like bargain store knockoffs. Once again, he looked for an outline of a weapon, but her clothes were so loose, it was impossible to tell if she had one.

Despite all of his training, he knew he could have seen this young woman a dozen times and still never remember her. But as she walked closer to him, the more he knew what made her stand out.

It was her eyes. Eyes much older than she was. Eyes that were supposed to be kind, but were not. The kind of eyes that had an intent peace about them, a serenity caused by the contentment of commitment.

Eyes that had seen too much to ever genuinely smile.

The same eyes he saw each time he looked in a mirror.

He knew this woman had to be Jabbar.

"There you are," the young woman said when she was only a few feet away. Her voice was cheerful and without a hint of an accent. "From what I saw on the ATM footage, I figured you'd be taller."

He kept his hand on his belt buckle. "And I figured you'd be someone else."

"I know." She wrinkled her nose. "I'm sorry. You were expecting some dusty old man with a long craggily beard muttering passages from the Koran, weren't you?"

He decided to try to shock her. "No, but I expected you to at least have a penis. You bastards aren't known for empowering women."

"Women empower themselves, if it pleases Allah." She inclined her head back to the park. "Why don't we go over there where it's quieter and less crowded? Don't worry. I'm sure your people will still be able to keep a close eye on you from there. But we should hurry. We don't have much time to chat."

Hicks didn't move.

She held up her hands and opened them. "No wires or trigger device in my hands." She slowly turned so he could look into her backpack, which was open. "No bomb. No AK-47 either. Only my laptop and a couple of granola bars. See?"

Hicks peered inside the bag without touching it. All he could see was a laptop and a couple of granola bars, exactly as she'd said. Her clothes were loose enough to conceal a bomb vest, but he doubted it.

He motioned for her to lead the way and he followed when she did.

The wind picked up as they got closer to the park. She eased aside a few stray hairs from her face. "What does your agency call me, anyway? Jabbar? Abdullah? The Sheik? The last one's my favorite. Makes me sound like a wrestler or something. 'Jabbar' seems to be the most common. It was the name the French DGSE used to identify my uncle, back when he was in charge of things."

Hicks kept scanning the crowd as they walked. No one seemed to be paying them any attention. "How'd your uncle die? Drone strike, I hope."

"Heart attack in his sleep," she said. "After he died, I took up his cause. All of his sons had died fighting the jihad, so I was the only one left to carry on his work."

"Carry on his work," Hicks repeated. "I didn't know terrorism was a family business."

"Living this kind of life is a calling," she said. "On my side and yours, too. I continued my uncle's practice of keeping my true identity a secret from the rest of my operation. My uncle always believed people can never hurt you if they don't know who you are. And, as you said, we bastards aren't known for empowering women. Anonymity makes things easier, doesn't it?"

Hicks knew the Dean would have enjoyed the irony of sharing management styles with the most wanted terrorist in the world. But Hicks hadn't come to Canada for irony. "How about you skip to the part where you tell me why we're here."

"How about you tell me what agency you're with?"

"I'm not with an agency."

"Look at you being modest. I know you have to be part of some kind of agency or department or task force or whatever you call it. There's no other way you could've made the number of hacks I've seen you make. So, which one is it?"

She looked up at him, waiting for an answer, before sighing. "I guess it doesn't matter anymore anyway. At least you're not with any regular government agency. I know the CIA is going to a great deal of trouble to find out whatever they can about you, but they're not having much luck. They know you took Bajjah in Philadelphia, but they still don't know why or where you're holding him. Or should I say 'were?' I assume you must've killed him by now."

"Assumptions can be dangerous."

"A lesson you're about to learn well and soon. I hope you're a quick learner because, like I said we don't have much time."

"You keep saying that." Hicks kept eyeing the crowd as they walked. "Much time for what?"

She surprised him by giggling. "Before I die, silly. Arap's death in England yesterday made my position in the organization untenable. I made a mistake which led to his death, so my life is in forfeit. Balance must be maintained. Which is why I decided to meet with you today so I could set you on the right path before I die."

Hicks stopped walking and slipped his hand under his jacket for the Ruger.

Jabbar smiled at the gesture. "A gun won't do any good

here, silly man. I'm here to help you, not harm you, remember? Drawing your gun will bring a lot of unwanted attention and you'll never know the truth. You see, I knew you'd want to take me for questioning, like you'd done to Bajjah. I couldn't let that happen."

She slowly eased an empty pill bottle from her coat pocket and handed it to him. "I swallowed an entire bottle of sleeping pills right before I walked over to you. I washed them down with an energy drink, which should delay the effects, but we don't have much time before I get sleepy. I won't be much use to you, and I'll be dead soon after. Check the prescription. You'll see I had it filled today."

Hicks read the label. The name had been scraped away, but it was a prescription of sleeping pills that had, indeed, been filled earlier that day.

He'd worked too hard to find Jabbar to simply watch her die. He went to take her arm. "Come on. I'm getting you to a hospital and your stomach pumped right now."

She twisted away from grasp. "No you're not and if you try to touch me again, I'll scream. How long do you think it would take before all of these chivalrous men come to the aid of a young girl in fear for her life, from an armed man nonetheless?" She giggled again. "Imagine. Infidels rallying to my defense. If they only knew. I'd bet a couple of them would be Jews, too, especially one of the doctors in the hospital. The irony of it all is so yummy, isn't it?"

Hicks kept his distance and took his hand away from the Ruger. This young woman was smart. She had planned for every contingency and limited his options. He wasn't surprised. She hadn't led the most effective terrorist organization in the world by accident.

"So why did you call this meeting? You sure as hell didn't do it so I could watch you overdose."

"Of course not. I took the pills because my life is forfeit now. I made a mistake by not being aware Shaban was being watched. My mistake cost poor Arap his life. He was one of my closest aides and one of the few people who knew my true identity. When your people gunned him down yesterday, I knew either you—whoever you are—or the British would begin digging into his life. You might've gotten lucky and found something in Arap's things belongings to lead you to me. My arrest would put my entire organization at risk, so my death is a necessity. But I also wanted to use the time I have left to explain how wrong you've been about almost everything practically from the beginning."

Now Hicks knew the real reason of the meeting. A ruse. "I uncovered your network. I found Shaban and Shaban led me to you. Now you're telling me I'm wrong? If this is wrong, I don't want to be right."

"Yours is a logical foundation built on sand," she said. "A foundation built by information provided by Bajjah, which is your main problem. He is a born liar, or should I say, was."

"He might've been a liar, but he told us the truth. I have some people on my payroll who can be pretty persuasive."

"I'm sure you do, but I'm curious about something. Did he ever utter the name Jabbar once during all of your persuasive questioning?"

She must have been able to see the answer in Hicks' expression. "See? I knew he was loyal, for the most part, anyway." She looked up at the sky as though she was pondering a question no one had asked. "Let's see. I bet he gave you the names of five men in the United States and another four throughout the Middle East. All the men were on watch lists, all with active ties to radical groups throughout the world." She looked at him and smiled. "How did I do?"

"You missed one. He gave us Shaban."

"Yes, I know he did." Her smile faded. "The other nine other names he gave you were all part of an elaborate cover I created for our people to use if they ever fell into enemy hands. I'm sure you've discovered they're all real people, but none of them pose any real threats to anyone. To borrow an American term, they're 'fall guys' for the rest of my organization dedicated to doing the real work of Allah. By giving you those names, Bajjah proved himself to be a loyal soldier until the bitter end."

Hicks leaned closer to her, but not too close. "Maybe the pills are affecting your memory already. You're forgetting Bajjah still gave us Shaban."

She looked down. "I know. I suppose it was his one act of revenge against me for believing I had forsaken him. Perhaps he was right, for I had forsaken him. He told you Shaban was someone high up in the organization, didn't he? Like a money man or his lieutenant or something to make him stand out from the other names he offered you."

Hicks didn't say anything. She continued, "When I learned Bajjah had been captured, I didn't try to find him. I didn't even ask who might have him or where. I treated him the same as I had treated the hundreds of my other brothers who fell under the scythe of the Great Satan."

"You've got a nice way of talking about betrayal."

"Bajjah didn't betray me as much as he made a fool out of

you. For you see, my friend, Shaban and Bajjah hadn't been part of my network for well over a year."

"Bullshit." He was careful to not allow his temper to get away from him and draw attention. "All ten names he gave us checked out as part of the same network. Shaban included."

"Bajjah decided to separate himself from my cause over a year ago," she said. "He had been a legendary fighter in defending our way of life against the infidels, but he had always lacked the patience to devise strategy. Over time, he became impatient with the pace of our attacks. He grew more bloodthirsty as the years went by. I suppose he wanted all of his personal sacrifices to mean something. It's not easy to abandon one's family for a cause greater than oneself, even when such a cause is Allah."

Hicks saw his entire plan, all of the intelligence he had gathered and all of the theories he had formed, begin to unravel like a ball of string. No, she had to be lying.

She went on. "When I discovered his plans to wage his own jihad against the West in his own way, I had no choice but to exile him from the network." She smiled. "As my death will prove, no one person is more important than the network or our cause."

Hicks didn't give a damn about her network. "But Shaban..."

"Bajjah took Shaban with him when he left us," she explained. "Our organization has infighting like any other group, so Bajjah didn't have much trouble getting others to leave with him. Shaban in London and Omar in New York helped Bajjah set up his new network."

It didn't make sense to Hicks. "Networks take money and our intelligence shows you keep a tight hold on the purse strings."

"I do," she said, "which means Bajjah had to find new backers, doesn't it? Those same backers who paid Rachid Djebar to make introductions between Bajjah and the scientists in Madinha who crafted the virus used in the New York outbreak."

"You're not making sense. If you knew all of this was going on, why let him do it? All he would do is bring more heat on your organization."

"We didn't know exactly what he was doing," she admitted, "but we'd hoped whatever he did would draw attention away from our organization. It worked for a long time, too, until he launched his silly bio-attack on New York. We knew such an attack would fail because there were too many variables and it was too limited in scope. But Bajjah was too stubborn to listen. He proved us right, didn't he? The plot failed and he got caught, exactly as we had predicted. Since Shaban had been disloyal and was the only remaining member of Bajjah's organization who could point back to us, I had to eliminate him."

It was beginning to make sense to Hicks. "So you ordered Arap to kill him."

"Shaban was a hot-head who would try to take revenge once he learned Bajjah was dead. So, I bought time by having Arap make contact with him and keep him calm. He promised Shaban he'd be allowed back into our organization and given a place of honor. I ordered Arap to kill him publicly, to show the others in my organization how much we cherish the loyalty of our followers and punish those who stray from the path. If I'd known Shaban was being watched so closely, I would've made other plans."

"When I saw how your people searched Shaban's body," she went on, "and left the scene so quickly, I knew they weren't

British intelligence or undercover police. Not CIA, either. Then I remembered the mystery man who was frustrating their search for Bajjah. I took an educated guess you'd be watching the events at the port and have access to Shaban's e-mail, so I emailed Shaban." She opened her hands and smiled. "And here we are."

"Yeah. Here we are. But you still haven't told me why."

"But I've already told you why, you silly man." Another gust of wind picked up through the plaza. She turned so it was hitting her back, not her eyes. "Haven't you figured it out yet? Bajjah wasn't working for us. Any action he took, any attack he carried out, was without our permission or resources or our money. He was working for someone else."

Hicks leaned closer. "Tell me who."

Jabbar took a step back. "No. I'll do what my uncle would have done and pose a question instead. Ask yourself who benefits from a biological attack on the United States. Iran? Al-Qaeda? ISIS?" She shook her head. "They would have done it themselves before they'd let an outsider do it for them, especially a zealot like Bajjah. They also would have taken responsibility for the attack, which they didn't, did they?"

Hicks knew how Iran and the terrorist groups worked. He knew she was right.

She went on. "A question which only raises a whole bunch of other questions, doesn't it? Like who could benefit from funding Bajjah's zealotry? Who has the resources to finance Bajjah's plans if we didn't do it? Who benefits from American resources being diverted to fight an unseen, unknown enemy within its borders? Who has begun to rattle their sabers recently? I'll give you a hint: they're the same people who are benefitting from an American withdrawal from the rest of the world right now."

Hints of those same questions had been rattling around Hicks' mind since the day he'd broken Bajjah. Questions drowned out by the noise from his Carousel of Concerns. Stephens. Jabbar. The Mossad. The University. The Trustees. He'd been too busy focusing on the perceived threat of Bajjah's network to focus on Bajjah himself.

He'd never asked the most important question of all. Where was Bajjah getting all of these resources?

He had assumed it was Jabbar's network. But with Jabbar's denial of involvement, there was only one group who could be.

And the prospect was far worse than anything he'd considered before.

"Impossible. If anyone found out, it would cause another world war."

"Cold wars are easy to reheat, especially by outside players." She smiled again. "You don't believe me, do you?"

"Believing the Russians or the Chinese were funding Bajjah is a pretty big leap to take."

"Not the Russians or the Chinese, my friend. Not officially anyway. Splinter groups in their intelligence organizations who want to push things along to further their respective countries' interests."

If what she was saying was true, it made sense. But it was a big 'if.'

She seemed to read his mind. "I'm not asking you to believe any of this on blind faith. I know faith comes difficult to men like you. You'll need evidence, which was why I wanted to meet you today. You'll find proof for every statement I've made on the hard drive of the laptop in my bag. Don't bother searching the device for other information on our organization. It's a brand new laptop and only has the information I downloaded onto it from a thumb drive. It's…"

Hicks watched her body flinch a microsecond before the left side of her head exploded outward. The report of a rifle shot echoed through the plaza half a second later.

Instinct and training caused Hicks to draw his Ruger as he dove to his right. Tourists in the plaza were already screaming and running in all directions as he rolled next to a trashcan at the edge of the path.

"Jabbar is down," he reported to Roger and Weaver over his earpiece. "I repeat, Jabbar is down. Suspected sniper in the area." He scanned the plaza for signs of a shooter, looking for a trail of gun smoke, movement, anything to show him where the shot had come from.

He focused on the direction of the shot—a row of planted trees on the other side of the park. But with dozens of people running in all directions, he couldn't see more without breaking cover. With a sniper on the loose, breaking cover was a bad idea.

He hoped Roger had a better view from his vantage point. "Roger, do you have eyes on the shooter?"

Nothing. Not even static.

"Goddamn it, Roger. Report! Do you have eyes on the shooter?"

But all he got was dead air.

Where the hell was he? Had Roger been compromised? Why didn't Jason or Weaver break in? One of them could have overridden the frequency and broken in by now. Where the hell were the others?

He didn't have time to worry about it now. He was pinned

down with a sniper on the loose. A sniper he couldn't allow to get away. A sniper who might be working for the same network that had been backing Bajjah.

He kept his eyes on the tree line as panicked people ran by. He didn't bother to check if Jabbar was still alive. No one could have survived a headshot. But he needed to get to her bag. Her laptop supposedly had the information he needed on who had funded Bajjah.

He judged the distance between where Jabbar had been struck and the tree line was about a hundred yards. Not a world record shot, but impressive in a crowded area with a swirling wind, especially with only one shot.

Hicks continued scanning the tree line, looking for movement among the chaos of the fleeing civilians. The wail of approaching sirens grew louder in the near distance. If the shooter hadn't gotten away yet, he'd have to make a break for it soon or risk getting caught. He'd be at his most vulnerable on the run. That's when Hicks would make his move.

If he got the chance.

The initial chaos died down enough for Hicks to focus on the shadows of the tree line. He spotted a small, dark bump at the base of the left side of a tree slightly left of center of the line. It was the only tree with such a bump. He hadn't seen it when he'd first taken cover, but saw it now.

There you are, you son of a bitch.

Hicks ducked as he saw movement right before a rifle flash from the shadow. A bullet struck the ground several feet in front of him sending dirt and stone into the air. But by ducking right before the shot, he'd caught most of the debris in his hair.

He looked up in time to see a figure darting among the

shadows along the path behind the trees, heading for Bremner Boulevard.

Hicks heard Roger call out to him from the plaza as he got to his feet. He was pointing at his ear as he ran, but Hicks didn't have time for a conversation. He pointed down at Jabbar's body as he broke cover and ran toward Bremner. "Get her backpack," he shouted. "We'll need it."

He bolted across the lawn in pursuit of the shooter, leaping over the people still lying flat on the grass too afraid to move. He could see the shooter was still more than a hundred yards away, well out of his Ruger's range. He had to close the gap before the sniper made it to the crowded boulevard.

The shooter broke into a flat out sprint as soon as he broke free of the tree cover. He was wearing all black from head to toe, making it impossible to see what he looked like. And now the sniper had reached solid ground, he was running even faster. Hicks was still running on soft grass and watched the distance between them grow.

A black SUV with no plates or markings screeched to a stop at the curb on Bremner Boulevard. The back door opened and the shooter dove in as the SUV peeled away.

Since he was still too far to open fire, he pulled out his handheld and aimed its camera at the SUV so OMNI could scan the vehicle's black box frequency. The SUV was moving at a good clip, but he had a clear line of sight, which was all the handheld needed to scan.

But a window appeared on his handheld's screen he had never seen before.

SCAN FAILED.

Was scanning while running throwing off the reading? He

stopped running, locked on the fleeing vehicle, and ran the scan again. The same window appeared: **SCAN FAILED.**

It didn't make any sense. The target was a late model vehicle. It should've had a black box frequency OMNI could read.

Roger stopped running when he caught up with Hicks. He had Jabbar's backpack in his hand. "I've been trying to talk to you over the earpiece, but you didn't answer. The signal is jammed."

OMNI signals never jammed. "Not a chance."

Roger looked down at Hicks' handheld. The screen was still blinking **SCAN FAILED.** "Face it, James. Our signals are jammed. OMNI's been compromised."

Hicks saw traffic was heavy and would only get heavier as the sirens approached and the police began to seal off the area. He turned when he heard Weaver's Land Rover screech to a halt curbside on Bremner Boulevard. Hicks tucked his gun back into the shoulder holster as he and Roger climbed in the back.

Weaver hit the gas as soon as both men were inside. "Sorry, sir, but I couldn't get a fix on their position. Couldn't raise either of you or Jason on OMNI either. I don't know what the hell happened."

"Neither do I," Hicks said.

"The scanners may be down, but we can still catch up to them," Roger told Weaver. "They're only half a block ahead of us around the corner on the drive. They can't have gotten too far in all this traffic. If we hurry, we can…"

But Hicks had a better idea. "Weaver, get us get back to the airport as soon as you can. I want to be as far away from here as possible before the cops close the area. The sooner Roger and I are back in New York, the better. Might be a good idea to get new plates for this thing, too.

"Plates are fakes anyway, sir, but I'll make sure I change them out."

Weaver immediately cut a U-turn across several lanes of traffic and drove back toward the airport, ignoring the angry horns and screeching tires in his wake.

Roger held on as he said to Hicks, "What the hell are you doing? We can still catch them."

Hicks flicked the bits of dirt out of his hair as he looked down at the **SCAN FAILED** window on his handheld device. "We don't have to catch them. I already know who it is. And I know where they're going."

CHAPTER 32

IT WAS AFTER seven o'clock when Hicks saw the Breaking News alert crawl across the bottom of the television screen. He had been watching the television with the sound off so as not to give himself away.

The news for the past hour had been full of live reports from Toronto detailing the shooting at the CN Tower. Reporters were speculating if it had anything to do with the other shooting from the previous day in England.

He hadn't needed to hear what the reporters said about those items. He'd witnessed them first hand. But this breaking news alert was different. He needed to hear this. He needed to see how well his plan was going into effect.

He raised the volume enough to hear the anchor hand it off to the network's Intelligence correspondent; an earnest-looking young man who looked more like a male escort than a news reporter.

"First it was WikiLeaks and Julian Assange, then it was Edward Snowden. Tonight, another major scandal appears to be rocking the intelligence community as reports of illegal black sites on American soil begin to surface. Well-placed sources speaking on the condition of anonymity have informed us that a congressional investigation is about to be announced centering on a suspicious fire that broke out at a Jersey City storage facility earlier this week. The investigation will reportedly focus on the belief that the building was being used as an unofficial base of operations for various intelligence organizations not chartered to operate within the boundaries of the United States. These same sources, including one from a reputable overseas agency, tell us that the facility was a base of operations for several intelligence entities, including the National Security Agency, the Central Intelligence Agency and the Defense Intelligence Agency."

The screen switched to file news footage of a high angle shot from a news helicopter showing dozens of fire trucks pumping streams of water on the burning warehouse as it billowed smoke and flame high into the sky as the Manhattan skyline glimmered in the distance.

The Intelligence correspondent spoke while the footage rolled. *"As you may remember, six firefighters were hurt in that blaze which local fire officials say appears to have been started intentionally. So far, spokespeople from the NSA, the CIA and the DIA have refused to issue an official comment. However, in a statement released only moments ago by the office of Senator Clayton Newbury of Nebraska, chair of the Senate Intelligence Committee, the senator said he was concerned about the nature of these charges."*

The screen cut to a file photo of a pale, corn-fed man of about sixty sporting a bad comb-over. The correspondent read the text of the statement as it appeared on the screen. "We value the efforts of the men and women of our intelligence agencies and owe them a debt we can never fully repay. However, the laws forbidding certain agencies operating within our borders are in place for a reason. Any infraction of those laws must be investigated. I vow my committee will get to the bottom of this as soon as possible."

For the first time all day, Hicks had a reason to smile. Not only had Schneider followed through on unofficially confirming the report, Dan Finch had released the quote exactly as Hicks had written it. Dan Finch was Senator Newbury's chief of staff.

If he'd had a drink he would've toasted Cindy. *Nice going, girlfriend.*

Schneider had lived up to his end of the bargain, but it wasn't enough.

Hicks checked his watch. It was still too early for the other Breaking News alert to hit the media yet, if it hit at all. But if things played out the way he had planned, it was going to be one hell of a busy night for the cable news networks.

He heard the elevator ping from the hallway. He grabbed the remote and turned off the television. The apartment was once again plunged into darkness as Hicks stood up and got into position. He didn't need light to see where he was going. He'd been in that apartment enough times to know how to move around in the dark without bumping into anything.

He moved to the sofa facing the door and pulled out his Ruger as he waited for the door to open.

Set the anger aside. Remain calm.

He wasn't surprised when he heard the key hesitate in the lock. When he'd broken into the apartment a few hours before, he'd seen the thin strand of black hair the owner had carefully placed across the bottom of the door jamb. It was an old school tactic, a poor man's burglar alarm to see if the door had been opened since they'd left.

He had made no effort to replace it. He hadn't wanted his presence in the apartment to be a complete surprise. He wanted to avoid more bloodshed if he could, at least until he got answers from the person who lived there.

As the door swung open, a narrow rectangle of light from the hallway spilled across the carpet. No one stepped inside. Hicks had expected that. Only a rookie would have walked into a room they knew had been breached.

And Tali Shaddon was no rookie.

Hicks called out to her from the darkness. "It's me."

Tali's Glock led her way into the apartment. She elbowed the switch next to the door and the lights came on. She heeled the door shut behind her and kept the Glock trained on Hicks' chest. Hicks remembered heeling the door shut a few days before, but the circumstances had been much different.

He kept the Ruger aimed at her as well. "Welcome home. How was your day?"

She looked down at Hicks' gun before shifting her aim to his head. "What the hell are you doing here?"

"Toronto."

Her Glock twitched. Not by much, but enough for Hicks to notice. "I don't know what the hell you're talking about," she said. "I haven't been in Toronto in years."

He smiled. "Who said anything about you being there?"

Her expression confirmed it, but she covered up fast. "Enough of your games. I want you out of here. Now."

But Hicks didn't move. Neither did his Ruger. "I know a few dozen people who could've made such a shot from that distance in that kind of wind, but none of them would've gone for a headshot. Not in those conditions. I only know one sniper with the guts and the skill to put a bullet through someone's temple in swirling wind at over a hundred yards. The same person who could have figured out a way to jam our connection to OMNI and remove the black box from an SUV to keep us from tracking it. The same person who had the motive to do any of this in the first place. You."

"Are you drunk again?" She readjusted her grip on the Glock. "I don't know what the hell you're talking about and neither do you. You should leave now while you still can."

But Hicks still didn't move. "You're one of the best liars I've ever worked with, my love, but you could never lie to me. I could never lie to you, either, which is what caused this mess, didn't it? Maybe that's why we've always been able to trust each other. Until today."

"We trusted each other until you killed Bajjah to prevent me from questioning him." Her voice cracked. "You broke our arrangement, James, not me."

"So you retaliated by killing Jabbar in a crowded area? You didn't even give me a chance to fully debrief her before you blew her away." He decided telling her about Jabbar's overdose was pointless.

"Jabbar was the Mossad's top target of opportunity for over a decade. I was able to read her lips through my scope. When

I saw she'd confirmed she was Jabbar, I was ordered to fire. I waited as long as I could, but..."

"I was standing less than a foot from her. In those conditions, you could've killed me instead of her."

"I was supposed to kill you, too!" Her hand began to shake as tears came to her eyes. She lowered her weapon and sank back against the wall. "Schneider wanted you both taken out, but I couldn't do it. Not to you. Not when I had to."

Hicks had rarely seen any honest emotion from Tali, if he'd ever seen any at all even in their lovemaking. She had been trained to mask her emotions by some of the best professional manipulators in the world. But there was something in her manner that rang true. After all, he was still alive. "How did you find me?"

"We aren't exactly amateurs, James. Schneider knew you were up to something, so he had people at all of the airports in the area. When a plane we suspected the University had used in the past had returned from London and was preparing to take off again, Schneider ordered us to track you as well. We didn't know where you were heading, but Schneider found out how much fuel your plane had taken on. He put people on alert at all the airports within range, including at Pearson. When we tracked you and Roger to the plane, we took off from the same airport in our own plane right after you."

She wiped away a tear. "It was surreal, like a slow motion car chase in the sky. Our people in Toronto tracked your SUV once you landed. We followed you and I got into position."

Hicks had always had a blind spot when it came to Tali, but he cursed himself for being so careless. And recently, he had been too busy worrying about Stephens to consider the aggression of the Mossad. He should have known Schneider would never take a back seat, not with Jabbar in the picture. He should have had Scott's Varsity squad watching Schneider, but he hadn't. Finch and Jabbar had been his priorities. And now Jabbar was dead.

But there wasn't much he could do about the past. "You jammed OMNI. You gave Schneider your handheld, didn't you?"

"He took it from me, damn you. The technicians he'd brought with him from Tel Aviv figured out a way to jam the signal locally from the SUV. They tried to access the broader network, but couldn't seem to do it."

Hicks' hand began to shake as sweat broke on his brow. "You gave them OMNI, Tali. OMNI is the only advantage the University has. Without it, we don't stand a chance against the other agencies."

"Tel Aviv doesn't have it yet," she said. "They were only able to block the frequency locally using my handheld. They ghosted my phone and gave the original back to me."

He knew the answer to the next question, but he still had to ask it. He needed to hear the answer from her. "But they intend on working on accessing OMNI as soon as they get back home, don't they?"

Another set of tears streaked down her cheek. "They said they would. I don't know how successful they'll be." She blinked and more tears came. "I'm sorry, James. But I didn't have a choice. He ordered me to give him the phone. He…"

Hicks didn't allow himself anger. Anger was almost as useless an emotion as regret and led to mistakes. He removed himself from the equation and focused on the matter at hand.

The Mossad had tried to kill a Faculty Member of the University. The only thing that mattered now was information. "Did Schneider order me dead or did it come from Tel Aviv?"

"Tel Aviv never would have authorized a hit on a senior foreign agent, especially an ally. Especially the Dean of the University. Killing you was Schneider's decision. He said we could no longer trust you after the Bajjah incident. Since the Americans were already hunting you, he planned on using your death and Jabbar's death to help him gain more influence with the other agencies. He said your death would demonstrate how the Mossad would respond to University treachery in the future."

Hicks knew the answer to the next couple of questions, but he wanted to see how Tali answered it.

Her life depended on how she answered. "Where is Schneider now?"

"Flying back to Tel Aviv. He has already called for an emergency meeting with the director of the Mossad and the prime minister tomorrow morning. He's going to brief them on today's operation and the OMNI technology. He practically had to stake his entire reputation on getting all of them to clear their calendars."

From what OMNI had intercepted, he knew she was telling the truth. Second question: "He sent a report in advance?"

"No. He was afraid you could intercept an email and he didn't want you to know what he was up to."

"But you're telling me anyway."

"Schneider and his team are already on his private jet back to Israel. What can you do to him now?"

"You'd be surprised."

He kept the Ruger aimed at her as he stood. OMNI had already supported everything Tali had told him. He knew she was being truthful. He had already decided not to kill her, but there was no reason she needed to know that yet. "But you've got bigger worries than Schneider, Tali."

More tears ran down her cheeks. "I know what I've done and what I haven't done." She tossed her pistol onto the overstuffed chair facing the couch. "I've always been loyal to you and the Mossad and the University. I'm not ashamed of it and I don't want to die, but I won't beg you for my life, either."

He slowly walked toward her. "You gave them OMNI," he said. "You betrayed our entire system when you let Schneider's men have your handheld. You betrayed me and every member of the University."

"The technicians took my handheld and figured out how it worked," she said. "It's not the same thing as giving it to them and you know it."

"It is to me. And to the hundreds of other people you put at risk."

She flinched when he thumbed the hammer of the Ruger. Not to cock it, but to release it.

But she hadn't seen it. Her eyes had been closed and she swallowed hard. "I'm pregnant."

Hicks stopped. "I thought you said you weren't going to beg for your life. That's a pretty cheap lie to tell..."

"I'm not lying and I'm not begging, damn it. I'm telling you what I know is true. I'm pregnant and it's yours."

He was beginning to reconsider his decision not to kill her. Trying to manipulate him like this was low. "It was only a couple of days ago. There's no way you could know so soon."

"But I do know," she told him, "and so do you. This time was different than all the other times we were together. Something happened this time. Something special. I know my body and I know something is different now. So shoot me if you want to, but make damned sure you know what you're doing because it won't only be me who dies today."

He hadn't expected her to act like this. She was a trained assassin. He had expected her to go for his gun or put up some kind of a fight. He hadn't expected her to pull such a flimsy stunt to save her life.

A flimsy excuse strong enough to work. "The Mossad trained you real well, didn't they?"

"This isn't about my training. This is about what we created together. We have the chance to have something beyond all of the deception and the double-talk and the treachery and the lies. Something new and pure and closer to perfect than either of us deserve. If you don't believe me, put the barrel against my temple and squeeze the trigger because I don't want to live in a world where such things are impossible. And I wouldn't want our baby to live in it, either."

Hicks hadn't intended on killing her. He had intended on turning her. He wanted to get her to finally cut ties with the Mossad and work exclusively for the University. She was too good to kill and too competent to allow to work for anyone else. And he knew he'd need her help to face the enemies he'd found on Jabbar's computer.

He had hoped her gratitude for his sparing her life would have been enough to win her over.

But he hadn't expected this. He hadn't expected so much truth.

He hadn't expected her to tell him she was carrying their child. He hadn't expected life to come from so much death.

Hicks tucked the Ruger back into his shoulder holster.

She sagged and her voice trembled. "Okay. Okay."

"I'm going to let you live, but it's not because you're telling me you're pregnant. Maybe you are and maybe you're not. I'll find out for sure in time and deal with it then. But Jabbar gave me some information today."

The spy in her returned as she wiped the remains of tears from her eyes. "Information? What kind of information?"

"The kind that changes things. The kind we've got to move on now. But, from now on, you don't work for Schneider anymore. You don't work for the Mossad. You're no longer attached to anyone out of Tel Aviv. You don't work for anyone but me and your loyalty is to the University. Are we clear?"

She threw her arms around his waist and laid her head against his chest. "Yes, of course, darling, but they won't like it, James. The Mossad, Schneider will never..."

"It's already been taken care of. And Schneider won't have anything to say about this or anything else ever again."

She eased away as she looked up into his eyes. "I know that look." She stiffened as she pulled away from him. "My God, James. What have you done?"

He decided she wasn't beautiful, but something close to it. She didn't flinch when he caressed her cheek with the side of his hand. "You've got more important things to worry about. I'll have another handheld delivered to you with in a couple of hours. In the meantime, I need to pack up and be ready to move as soon as possible. Take only what you need because you can't stay here anymore. It's not safe."

She took his hands and slowly lowered them from her face. She wasn't Agent Saddon of the Mossad any longer. She was Tali. "But why?"

He looked at her television. "You'll see."

O N THE CAB ride back to Twenty-Third Street, Hicks' handheld buzzed. He could tell it wasn't a secure transmission by the pattern of the vibration. It was a Breaking News alert from one of the many civilian news apps he had installed on the device. He already knew what the alert would say. Scott had always been an artist with explosives.

He checked the alert anyway.

BREAKING NEWS

A private jet has exploded over the Atlantic Ocean shortly after takeoff from Floyd Bennett Air Field this evening. Details are still coming in, but we now know the jet was scheduled to arrive in London before going on to Tel Aviv for the second leg of its flight. NTSB officials say a joint rescue effort from the US Navy and the US Coast Guard is currently underway. There is currently no information on how many people were on board or if this was an act of terrorism. More details as they become available.

Hicks knew there wouldn't be more details. There may be a quick mention of the incident in the next day's paper, along with the unfortunate shooting at the CN Tower in Toronto. No suspects would be named and no motives would be given in either instance. With the exception of a few conspiracy bloggers, no one would attempt to link the shootings in London and the killing in Toronto or the private plane crash in the Atlantic.

The dead in all of those incidences would be forgotten by all but a select few people. People like Hicks.

In several months, the NTSB would quietly issue a final report that would include whatever the NSA and the Mossad agreed upon. There would be no mention of Schneider or the Mossad or of OMNI or of Jabbar. There would be inquires within the intelligence community, of course, but Hicks could manage the process from the shadows.

The Mossad wouldn't miss the unpopular Schneider. They'd be too busy enjoying the new notch on their belt—the execution of Israel's most wanted terrorist by a loyal Mossad agent. There was no reason to mar such a victory by emphasizing the death of a minor intelligence official. If anything, they'd turn him into a hero, not a reason for revenge.

Hicks put the phone back in his pocket and laid his head against the window of the cab. It was a chilly spring evening. The cool glass dulled his growing headache. For the first time since he could remember, the Carousel of Concern in his mind had begun to slow.

Jabbar was dead. A preliminary search of her computer showed it was a treasure trove of information. Stephens had been neutralized. Schneider had fulfilled his purpose by corroborating the leak on the Weehawken black site and had also paid the price for crossing the University. His Mossad technicians were dead. The OMNI technology they'd stolen was in charred bits at the bottom of the Atlantic. The Trustees still loomed. The University was safe for now.

He hoped he'd be able to fall asleep when he got back to Twenty-Third Street. He'd need plenty of rest.

A cold war was about to heat up.

CHAPTER 33

One Month Later

ICKS HAD PARKED his Buick around the corner from Mark Stephens' house. For the past half hour he had been watching the disgraced DIA operative via the OMNI satellite feed on his dashboard. Stephens had been working on the engine of a black Dodge Charger in the driveway of his garage.

The Stephens' family home was located in a nice neighborhood in Franklin Lakes, New Jersey. The house had five bedrooms, an attached garage, and a nice deck Stephens had built himself the previous summer. It even had a pool. The domicile was suburbia personified. The American Dream. It couldn't have been more Rockwell if Stephens had built a white picket fence around the place.

But Stephens didn't look like any of the happy people one might see in a Rockwell painting. He was wearing an old tracksuit and looked like he hadn't shaved in days. His head and face—both normally smooth—had stubble with flecks of gray. Hicks understood why. Nobody liked to be fired, especially spies.

Especially when evidence of the leak about the Weehawken facility pointed to an anonymous account that appeared to be controlled by him.

Hicks tried to work up a little sympathy for the man whose life he'd ruined as he watched him work on his car. But sympathy had never come easy for Hicks, and it didn't come easy now. Stephens had been warned, but had laughed at the thunder. Now he'd been burned by the lightning.

Hicks had hacked the calendar on Mrs. Stephens' phone. He knew she would be leaving soon to take the girls to doctors' appointments before picking up a present for her husband's upcoming birthday. Hicks decided to wait until they'd left before he made his move. No sense in making a scene with the family around.

From his dashboard screen, Hicks watched Stephens' five-year old twin girls run out of their house and hug their father's legs. Stephens was careful to wipe the motor grease from his hands before he pulled them closer to them.

Even from a satellite camera high above the earth, he could see the relief the little girls brought to their father's face. He heard their delighted squeals echo through the neighborhood. The image was beamed from thousands of miles away, but the sound was immediate.

Hicks decided to forget about Tali for the moment. He wasn't certain she was pregnant. He wasn't even sure if he hoped she had been lying.

He watched the dashboard screen as Mrs. Stephens give her husband a kiss on the cheek before shepherding the girls into the Honda minivan. Stephens gave them a final waive as they backed out the driveway, before he went back beneath the hood to working on his engine.

Hicks waited until the minivan was down the block and out of sight before he turned on the engine. The V-12 roared to life as he hit the gas. *Showtime.*

He knew Stephens wouldn't be glad to see him. He hoped he was smart enough to not do anything stupid. It would have been a shame to kill him. Those little girls seemed to love him so.

Hicks steered the Buick through the lazy tree lined streets of suburbia and slowly pulled into Stephens' driveway. A presumptive move on his part, but one he hoped would show Stephens he had nothing to fear.

Stephens looked out at him from beneath the hood when the Buick pulled in and parked. He looked up when Hicks killed the engine and stepped out of the vehicle.

Hicks kept his hands up and bumped the door closed with his hip. Stephens might not be with the DIA anymore, but he was still highly trained and most likely armed.

"Don't do anything stupid, Ace." Hicks kept his hands up as he slowly turned in a complete circle. "I'm not here to hurt you. I'm not armed, and I've got nothing to hide. I even wore shorts so you could see I've got nothing on my ankle. You obviously rate pretty high with me because I fucking hate shorts."

When he'd finished his circle, Hicks was glad to see Stephens hadn't moved, either. But he didn't look happy. "A man like you doesn't need a gun to kill someone."

"You need intent, too," Hicks said, "and I didn't come here to harm you, Ace. If I wanted you dead, I could've done it a whole lot quieter and from a lot farther away."

Stephens checked both ends of the street. "You come alone?"

"I'm always alone." He leaned against the hood of the Buick, as he had the last time they had seen each other. "I came here to talk. I'm going to lower my hands now if you don't mind."

Hicks lowered his hands as Stephens grabbed a rag and began to wipe at the motor oil on his arms. "I must be crazy for letting you stand there. The last time we talked didn't turn out to well for either of us."

"That was on you, Ace."

"Yeah, no shit." The shadow of the garage fell across Stephens' face, but Hicks was bathed in sunlight. The sun would peak over the garage soon and be in his eyes. Hicks would be blinded, which was what he wanted Stephens to see. The reason for his visit was too important to risk a violent confrontation.

Stephens folded his arms and leaned against the side of his Charger. "I guess you got us all, didn't you? Me, Avery, the joint task force. All of it shut down and boxed up and forgotten, especially the part about you and Bajjah. I don't know how you did it, but you did. Fucked me over real good, too."

Hicks saw no reason to deny or admit anything. "You flatter me, sir. Guys like you make a lot of enemies, especially in Washington. And last I heard, you didn't get fired. You've been placed on leave pending the outcome of the Senate investigation."

"Yeah, we all know how that's going to go. This morning, the House Intelligence Committee announced they're launching their own investigation this week. Avery and I will get blamed for overstepping our authority while the bastards who told us to go after you in the first place skate."

Hicks had known it, too. "Avery's a lot older than you. He's got his pension and he'll be allowed to retire. Fat fuck will be on his boat down in Boca this time next month."

"His boat isn't in Boca. It's in Key Biscayne."

Hicks knew Avery had bought a new boat in Boca last week in advance of his forced retirement. But he decided to let Stephens figure it out for himself. "You've been a good soldier in every sense of the word. And as bleak as it looks now, you still have a chance to come out way ahead of this thing."

"Look at you being hopeful. I don't know who you are, but I'd bet you know it doesn't work that way."

"Maybe in your world, Ace, but not in mine."

Stephens stood a little straighter, examining Hicks as though he'd seen him for the first time. "All the time I spent chasing you, I never figured out who you were. I spent hours looking at your picture, trying to follow your movements, running down the shit you pulled to get Bajjah out of Philly. You look like some bum who lost his last buck at the track, but you not only kept me at bay, but you outran a semi and a Valkyrie drone and threw the entire American intelligence community into turmoil. And you still managed to find enough time to ruin my career."

Hicks shrugged. "Maybe I did all of that and maybe I didn't. But I'll admit that I can do a lot of things, Mark. Things you could help with if you're smart enough to see a good thing when it pulls into your driveway."

Stephens laughed again. "You want to be my friend, man?"

"Why not? I'm not your enemy anymore. And if there's anyone who ever needed a friend, it's you."

"Well my friends don't get wrapped up in shootings at tourist spots in Toronto. And they sure as hell don't have planes carrying Mossad members blown out of the sky. And don't bother denying it. Just because I'm not in the game anymore doesn't mean I don't have my sources."

Hicks smiled. "Now why on earth would I have had anything to do with such a tragedy?"

"Because guys like you have something to do with those kinds of tragedies."

"You're a cynical man."

"No, but like you said, Stranger Man, I've been a good soldier for a long time. All I've got is a lot of random consequences that don't seem to fit together, but it's awfully strange when all the same kind of shit happens at once. I can't prove a damned thing against you, but I guess I'm not supposed to, am I?"

Hicks avoided the question. "You're not a soldier anymore. That part of your life is gone forever and it's never coming back. But spending your time fiddling with an engine is a waste of fine talent. You're out of the game now, but life doesn't always have to be difficult."

"Tell me how you'd make it different."

"I could guarantee you an honorable discharge from the Army, full benefits for the rest of your life and a chance to keep doing the only job you've ever been good at."

"Why?"

"Your record says you were one of the best Beekeepers in the DIA. I'm working on something where those skills would come in pretty handy."

"Working for you? For the son of a bitch who ruined my life in the first place?" Stephens shook his head. "Now you're talking a special kind of crazy. No thanks."

"We all have bosses, Ace. No one says we have to like each other to get the job done."

"No, but we have to be able to trust each other and I sure as hell don't trust you."

"You should. I haven't lied to you yet, including bringing you down. I put you in this mess. And I'm the only one who can get you out of it. Sign on with me and I'll have you discharged by the end of the week. You work for me the next day."

"That fast? Mister, you don't know the Army."

"Son, you don't know me."

Stephens eased himself off the Charger and began walking around the garage. Hicks had seen Targets act like this before, mill around like a tiger in a cage, looking for a way out until they finally accepted they were trapped and laid down.

"Would working for you have anything to do with why you grabbed Bajjah?"

"Not directly. We'd be going after the people who paid Bajjah."

"Jabbar?"

"Jabbar's dead. And believe it or not, he had nothing to do with Bajjah. I've got all the proof you need in my car. I'll let you see it, too, if you agree to work with me."

"If Bajjah wasn't working for Jabbar, who the hell was he working for?"

Hicks was glad Stephens was listening to reason. It would have been a shame to have to kill him. "How's your Russian these days?"

THE END

ACKNOWLEDGMENTS

Thanks to Dale Laszig, Debora Oliveira, Melissa Gardella, Esther Cohen Bezborodko, Phyllis Sambuco and Elite Rubin for providing invaluable insight on this book in its earliest stages.

Thanks to my resident gun experts Blackie Noir and Derek Viljoen for their advice on the various weapons that appear in this book, especially Blackie who first told me about the Ruger .454 Alaskan. They had me at 'it can core a charging bear'.

Thanks to Pam Stack, C.J. Carpenter, Eric Beetner, Maegan Beaumont, Leah Canzoneri, Joe Clifford, Andrew Borja, Dana andCorky King, Brian Madden and the lovely Todd Robinson for their constant support that keeps me going.

Thanks to the crew at The Nat Sherman Townhouse in New York City: The entire Sherman Family, their staff, and all the regulars: Buddha, Billy Judo, The Desert Rose, Mickey Two-Fingers, Joe-Joe, Hector, Mark and the Chairman of the Bored (that's not a typo) for all the great times and all the great cigars.

Thanks to my agent – The Mick Whisperer - Doug Grad of the Doug Grad Literary Agency for his wisdom, patience and hardwork. Thanks to Jason Pinter at Polis Books who was gracious enough to allow me to be part of the impressive, growing Polis family.

And thank you to Arcenia for always being there.

My love and gratitude to you all.

ABOUT THE AUTHOR

Terrence McCauley is an award-winning writer living in New York City. In 2014, he won the New Pulp Award for Best Author and Best Short Story for *A Bullet's All it Takes*. His short stories have been featured in *Thuglit, Shotgun Honey, Atomic Noir*, and *Matt Hilton's Action: Pulse Pounding Tales Vol. 1 & 2*. He recently published *The Dogs of Belleau Wood*, which benefits The Semper Fi Fund. He is the author of *Sympathy for the Devil*, as well as two acclaimed historical crime thrillers, *Prohibition* and *Slow Burn*, all of which are available from Polis Books. Visit him online at www.terrencepmccauley.com or on Twitter at @tmccauley_nyc.